leaving the canoe club
a novel

LEAVING THE CANOE CLUB

Copyright © 2006 by Mathew Lee Gill

10-Digit ISBN 1-59113-967-8
13-Digit ISBN 978-1-59113-967-6

All rights reserved. Except for use in any review, the reproduction or utilization of this work in whole or in part in any form by any electronic, mechanical or other means, now known or hereafter invented, including xerography, photocopying and recording, or in any information storage or retrieval system, is forbidden without the express written permission of the author.

This is a work of fiction and the characters and events are products of the author's imagination. Any similarity to real persons, living or dead, is coincidental and not intended by the author.

www.Booklocker.com

Printed in the United States of America.

First Printing: June 2006

leaving the canoe club
a novel

mathew lee gill

**For
Deb, my heart, my wife
and
Chelsea Kyal, my angel, my daughter**

**prelude
sunday, june 6**

Anderson Monk took a great deal of comfort in the mingled rhythms of his daily run; the persistent slapping of his dark gray and gold size fourteen Nikes on the asphalt, the ragged rasp of his breath, the pounding pulse in his veins. He lived for this daily ritual, a chance to exorcise the frustrations of the day and start the evening fresh. For about forty-five minutes a day this stretch of road was his best friend. Forty-five minutes with nothing to prove and no one to impress. Just him, the road and the trees.

The events of the last day and a half demanded the forced expulsion of energy and stress that welled up in his chest. The decision had been difficult to make, but his fear and desire for self-preservation, coupled with his anger at having been used for so long, finally drove him into action. He was going to cover his backside and he was going to do it as quietly as he possibly could. He'd even put in leave papers so that no one would expect him around the ship for the next couple of days. The Navy had a tendency to take notice when sailors unexpectedly missed a muster or a watch. He hoped the ploy worked; that it would give him the head start he knew he'd need. Although not an overly religious man, he prayed for success. There was no future in the alternative.

He smiled briefly and took a deep breath – his massive chest expanding and stretching the blue material of his t-shirt. The sun was still well above the horizon, the shadows had yet to begin their long run into night and the heat of the day lingered. Sweat ran freely from his always close-cropped blonde hair. He raised a hand to swipe the stinging sweat out of his eyes.

Anderson – Monk to everyone who knew him – was not a classically handsome man. He had some of the features: broad shoulders and a thick chest, massive arms and sweeping height. He cut a fairly impressive figure. His bright blue eyes reflected his emotions much the same way as the open ocean reflects clouds; crystal blue on the sunny days and murky gray on the stormy ones. His smile, though not overly joyful, could in fact be quite disarming.

But there was something in the way he looked at people that made them nervous, a casually predatory glint that sent chills. The way his granite jaw set when he was angry, the tendons standing out like cables with his thick eyebrows draw into a sharp V; it was intimidating. The thick white scar running down his tanned cheek and neck, a garish souvenir from a car accident at the age of seventeen, did nothing to soften his visage. All things being equal, which, more often than not, they weren't, people tended not to push their luck with the large, fierce-looking man; choosing instead, placation as a means of self-preservation.

It was that intimidation factor that got him noticed by Noah and his crew.

It was Noah's money that lured him into the morass through which he found himself struggling.

Monk's Navy salary paled in comparison to the cash he brought in bouncing at the club and it was nothing if not laughable, chump change, really, when put up against the money he pulled down running collections and enforcement. The jobs were simple really, requiring little thought or imagination. It was physical, sometimes brutal, work convincing people to pay their debts. He was good at it, though. Good at physical and better at brutal.

Not being the curious sort helped with that too. He never asked questions, never wondered about the debts he collected or the threats he fulfilled. They gave him a name and an address and reason to pay the visit; and he did it. Now he felt like kicking his own ass for being so stupid.

Down the block and around the corner he ran, willpower pushing his thick legs faster and faster as the gunshots echoed through his brain. He struggled with his mind for days after witnessing the triple homicide. Anderson Monk wanted no part of what he had seen, wanted no part of the world he knew he was already caught up in. He wanted nothing to do with drugs or smuggling or murder. He was a fighter, not a killer. And damn sure not some pusher. He dreamed of the days when he was just a sailor who bounced at a club on the side; the days before all of the craziness and duplicity he now wore like an uncomfortable second skin.

The gears of Monk's dim memory clicked almost audibly as he catalogued the events of the past three and a half years. Every beating he delivered, every person he escorted or intimidated, every package he handed off; they were all suspect now. He was pissed that he could be so stupid as to allow himself to wade so deeply into this mess. His anger was tempered by his fear and the knowledge that he was in over his head. Uncertainty stayed his hand and only thirty-six hours earlier he finally broke down and called the NCIS, arranged to give himself up and turn states' evidence.

Relief flowed through him as he thought of that and worry sloughed off of him like a tired skin. In thirteen hours he would be in protective custody. Less than a day and he could unload his conscience and get a little revenge on those who had used him. His worries about the choices he had made and the fears of what tomorrow would bring disappeared, all lost in the steady rhythm of his feet.

The asphalt turned, pushing away from the street and heading into the park. Monk sped along the broad, tree-lined path, knowing it was only a matter of time before he lost the light, which shone brightly through the leaves of the close branches.

It was such an incredible evening for a run.

Peaceful.

Pain exploded along the side and back of Monk's head, sending him reeling off the narrow running path and into the bushes. Starbursts filled his vision. He shook his head, trying to get his eyes to focus. Twigs snapped behind him and Monk spun around, off balance, to face his attacker only to catch the solid butt of an aluminum bat squarely between the eyes. The lights went out with thunderclap.

Monk woke with a start, acrid fumes working their way into his brain and forcing him from the comfortable darkness. He wondered, not for the first time, if it had all been a dream. But with the first shallow breath, the blinding pain rushed back in, crashing over him in overpowering waves. Fighting through the fiery haze clouding his mind, he tried to take a mental inventory of his injuries. His thick arms, bound over his head and bearing the majority of his body weight, had long ago gone numb, but every turn and jerk of his body brought new explosions of pain blazing down from his shoulders. He knew that at a minimum they were dislocated. His shallow gasps were raspy with blood. His stretched rib cage had taken a severe beating and the broken bones ground and clicked with each breath.

Monk lifted his excruciatingly heavy head and tried to look around. His left eye was swollen shut and his right was blurry with blood and sweat. He was not altogether sure where he was or how long he had been there. He was unconscious when they brought him in. He knew it had to be somewhere down by the water, probably in one of the industrial warehouses that lined the harbor – when he first woke up he could smell the salt in the air and he could hear the boat traffic, whistles and horns and wakes, echoing as though his captors were holding him in a large cavern. But that was before they smashed his nose, breaking and turning it into a hopeless mess smeared across his face; before the painful ringing in his ears drowned out everything but his ragged breathing. There were no real expectations of getting out of this predicament, but it was nice to know where you were going to die.

A blur of motion to his right and a wrecking ball collided with his skull.

Black spots danced around the edges of his vision as fire raced along his jaw line, through his tortured shoulders, settling in his chest. The thick muscles of his torso seized up with the rush of pain, cramping and squeezing his lungs until drawing breath was impossible. He could taste the copper sliding down the back of his throat as he gasped for air. Pain mounted on pain, and for the third time that night, the acid in his gullet betrayed him and he vomited bile and blood down over his chin and onto his chest. He shuddered through the spasms; the chains binding him upright jingling like wind chimes. Starved for oxygen, his field of vision turned murky and started to fade into darkness.

Monk's head snapped up painfully as the acrid salts passed under his nose. He dry heaved and gasped in pain, the muscles in his chest relaxing enough to let his lungs expand. He was so tired. He just wanted to fall to the cement floor and – well, he wasn't sure what the "and" was, but he would agree to just about anything at this point to end this sadistic game.

"Wakie, wakie, there Mr. Monk." The voice was taunting, ominous.

Monk could barely lift his head to look at the person talking to him. All he could make out was a pale shadow – blurred lines that were as familiar as the voice. He shuddered again and leaned away from the man in front of him, despite the agony that rolled throughout him at the movement.

"What did you and the agent talk about, Monk?"

Monk tried to reply, but his throat denied him, allowing only a muffled gurgle to escape his mouth.

"C'mon, Monk! Talk to me. It's the only way any of this is gonna get any better for you."

"Nuthin'!" Monk slurred through battered lips. "I didn't say nuthin' to nobody!"

Blood rolled freely down his chin, connecting the individual flecks of blood on his t-shirt and staining it a brilliant crimson.

"Nuthin', huh?" The voice was mocking. "I know you talked to him, Monk. I wanna know what the two of you talked about. What arrangements the two of you made. How long you've been feeding him information about us."

Monk wanted to respond, but his strength was tapped. It was all he could do to shake his head in a negative response. He thought about begging, but that had failed miserably some time ago. And the goons beating him had no real sense of mercy – no matter what he said they would just keep on going until he died. And giving up the ghost was rapidly overtaking this ass beating as the option of choice. His head hung heavy and low. He silently contemplated the designs his blood was making as it dripped and splattered on the floor around his feet.

Three meaty blows to his kidneys roused Monk from his grim reverie. Black stars and brilliant colors commingled in his vision.

"I can do this all night, Monk. I'll give you a fuckin' blood transfusion to keep your dumb ass alive if I have to. You're gonna tell me what I wanna know."

The bored tone of voice shook Monk to his core. He was dead already – it was just going to take a lot of time and pain to prove it. And though he thought he was past it, panic took a hold of him and he began to shake as he struggled to find the strength to loose himself from his bonds.

"No reply? After all this, you think I'm jokin'? Fine. Fuck you! Take a knee, Joey."

Monk shook his head crazily, finally finding his voice as the bat arced down and slammed into his kneecap with an audible crack. Shoulders and ribs and face forgotten, Monk screamed through blood and acid as his leg collapsed beneath him.

And everything went black.

Again, the acrid salts caused his head to jerk violently as they forced him back into consciousness. And the six foot three inch, two hundred sixty seven pound knuckle-breaker mechanic began to weep.

"I believe you, Monk. I don't think you talked to the NCIS."

A chance – Monk thought, nodding his head as vigorously as he could. Somewhere within him there was still some small glimmer of hope alive.

"But that's just because you didn't have a chance!"

A hand reached through the haze around his head and grabbed a hold of his face. It was like a vice, fingers pushing through the skin and grinding the bones underneath it. Monk's head was yanked so that he was looking up. Blood and sweat and tears stole what little vision he had left, leaving him only a smear of disjointed colors.

"You brought this on yourself, you sack of shit! And after everything that's been done for you – the money, the favors – you turned on us. Fuck you, Monk! What'd you think? We wouldn't find you out? That you'd fuck us and live to walk away?"

Monk tried to shake his head, but the disembodied hand wouldn't let him.

"You're through, Monk." The hand disappeared.

His head slumped down to his chest, Anderson Monk had time for one thought; a curse sworn of hot blood and sorrow for the day he met Noah Lawson.

"Make sure it has to be a closed casket service."

monday, june 7

chapter 1

The digital buzz cut through the comfortable darkness, preternaturally loud in the stillness of the room.
Special Agent James Storenn grunted and rolled over, not even close to being awake. The multicolored cotton sheets, a gray smear in the pre-morning half-light, were knotted about his tired body. Bleary eyed, he turned his head and looked over at the alarm clock next to his bed, trying to force the blurry red lines to resemble numbers. 4:05am.
"Who the hell...?" he started.
The phone screamed at him again, demanding to be answered. Whoever it was, they obviously weren't giving up.
Huffing unhappily, he reached over and fumbled with the receiver, knocking it from its cradle and onto the carpeted floor. Swearing under his breath, he groped around under the edge of the bed until he felt the smooth plastic of the handset. It belched out another uncomfortably loud ring. Eyes still closed, James pressed down on the talk button just to shut the thing up.
"Yeah?!" he asked, his tired voice gravelly and harsh.
The familiar voice was filled with worry that was thick enough to penetrate the haze filling his head. Jessica shouldn't be calling this early in the morning. Not with the clipped tones and tightness that wrapped themselves around the words pouring from the receiver. James tried to blink past the sleep in his eyes, find some focus.
"Slow down, Jess. What happened?"
For once, his imagination didn't even come close to how profane the reality actually was. At Jessica's first three words, James' face blanched and his knuckles turned white, his grip on the phone tightening to the point of pain. His stomach turned and his mouth began to sweat. James was wide awake. His hand began to shake as he listened the details being relayed to him. He was suddenly quite sure he was going to throw up.
"I'm on my way," he muttered, his mouth sweating profusely.
Slamming the receiver down, James Storenn jumped out of bed and headed for the bathroom. This was no way to start the day.

chapter 2

The scene was as bloody as it was populated with police officers. A small army of blue uniforms manned the doors to the warehouse and the crime scene barrier, keeping away members of the press and curious passers-by. James always wondered at the numbers of 'curious passers-by' that seemed to materialize at crime scenes, no matter the time of day or remoteness of location. That most base of human drives amazed him - the compulsion to see the train wreck, that seminal need to view the suffering of others - he simply didn't understand the attraction.

Blue-jacketed members of the San Diego City Police Crime Scene Unit walked the broad interior of the yellow-taped boundary, their white-booted feet stepping carefully as they marked and gathered evidence. A veritable forest of little yellow evidence flags and tape lay in their wake, marking their various findings. James studied the area with an experienced eye, needing no help to discern where the majority of the violence had taken place; a garish pool of black blood marked the dirty floor beneath a length of chain that hung from the ceiling.

"I didn't see you come in," Lieutenant Jessica Muir said from behind him.

He jumped at the sound of her voice cutting through the steady hum of procedure that surrounded them, cursing himself for it. He smiled a sheepish half grin as Jessica slipped past him, leading the way towards the dark stain. She stepped lightly, keeping to the path marked by the Crime Scene officers. James followed the bright yellow SDPD on her windbreaker, letting her gold detective's shield answer any questions of access.

"They're picking up blood spatter as far as thirty feet away." Her normally sweet voice was hard. "No murder weapon on the scene, but there was obvious blunt force trauma. I'm guessing it was a bat or a pipe, maybe a tire iron; something you could take a full swing with. They were thorough, whatever they used. I'd be surprised if the ME's office found something that hadn't been either broken or ruptured."

"That bad, huh?"

She nodded gravely.

"Verdin's boys already pick up the body?"

"Said he'd have some word later on today or tomorrow with more details. He ruled out accidental death, obviously, but for now all he's giving us is an approximate time of death. We'll have to wait on the exact cause of death."

James expected nothing more. If there was one thing you could say about the county Coroner's office, it was deliberate in the calls it made. There were no wild guesses or improvable hypotheses. If science couldn't prove it, it wasn't an answer.

"So what's our TOD?"

"Between three and four this morning."

James did the math in his head while he looked over the pool of congealing blood. Nine hours between the time Anderson Monk disappeared and the Coroner's estimation of time of death. Nine hours was a long time to stay alive when someone was working to change that. It was an eternity. James could feel the ball of anger and disgust growing in his stomach as he thought about it. He could only imagine the kind of animal it would take to do something like that. What was really pissing him off was the fact that it shouldn't have happened in the first place. The two police officers covering Petty Officer Monk should have been more than enough to ensure that he was able to hand himself over in one piece. He looked around, hoping to catch sight of either one of them lurking in the shadows.

"Where are Kamiski and Hafner?" he asked evenly. His face was hot with blood as he tried to maintain his temper.

Jessica stopped short. Her back was still to him and he watched her shoulders tense as she turned. "They were here earlier, two of the first to arrive. I sent them home about fifteen minutes ago."

James watched her brace for the eruption. He wanted to be angry at her for letting them go, use it as an excuse to vent his fury. But she was right to get her officers away from the scene. As much as he wanted to shove their noses in the shit they had left for him to clean up, castigating them in front of their fellow officers and the various media representatives would do nothing for the case and even less for the task force.

Jessica placed a hand on his arm. "They know, James. Believe me, they know."

James decided to take her word on it; Kamiski and Hafner were officers out of her department. He closed his eyes and inhaled deeply, trying to steel himself to the frustration so that he could look at the crime scene objectively. When he let the breath go and opened his eye, Jessica was still there in front of him, a curious look painted on her face. James just shrugged, biting back the frustration.

"Let's see what we have going on here."

Jessica shadowed him as he circled the central portion of the crime scene. His nose wrinkled in disgust. The closer he looked, the nastier the scene appeared. The blood beneath the chain was churned and frothy with smears running all directions. Monk had tried to escape – not that it did him any discernible good. There was waste and food mixed into the gore. The strong smell almost emptied James' stomach.

"What happened to Petty Officer Monk's shoes?"

Jessica shrugged. "Not sure."

James continued as though he hadn't heard her. "He was running when they lost him but there is a clear outline of a bare foot in there. Considering Belk and Johnson, any similarities?"

Jessica referred to her notes and shook her head. "I didn't write anything down. Near as I can tell, the feet were untouched. As for the shoes, I'll get a hold of the CSU and see what they have."

James nodded, satisfied, and leaned in closer. He swept his arm in a semi-circle, indicating the blood on the floor. "What's this pool – four feet across? Maybe four-and-a-half? Pattern in the middle is obviously from Monk. We've got three sets of prints going around the outside."

Jessica nodded. Only two distinct sets of shoe prints stood out, smearing the blood around the perimeter but three were visible marching, crimson, towards the door.

James stared at the markings in the blood for a few more seconds and then followed the footfalls across the floor. "Three guys walked out of here," he said softly. "Two big bastards that did all the work, at least at the end, and another there to watch. See how the shoe prints there in the blood are twisted, kind of like a ball player taking a swing. The prints are big, both of them. Judging by the shoe sizes and the length of the stride for each set, I'd put the both of them at about six foot four." He leaned over the pool, pointing at a swirl pattern. "See how this one runs clockwise? That guy's a lefty."

James could hear the scratching as Jessica scribbled in her notebook, trying to capture every word he said. James knew that no matter what was on the tape recorder in his pocket, they'd be using Jessica's notes when they sat down to reconstruct the scene. Most cops used recorders, but Jessica didn't trust them completely – they always ate the tape or had dead batteries. And so she continued with her notes as he talked.

"The other guy, the watcher; his shoes are different. They're not athletic shoes, they're more like loafers, maybe boat shoes. There's no mark in the pool of blood where he would have stepped in, but he left bloody footprints here in front of the chains and part of the way out. He got in close at some point. Don't know what for but I don't think he was doing any of the attacking. He was the controller. See how long the other strides are heading out of here? Those guys were in a hurry. This guy's stride was short; he strolled out of here. No hurry at all. That's the guy I want to get my hands on: the one that strolled outta here."

James' cell phone interrupted him. He unhooked it from his belt and checked the number. He groaned audibly, letting it ring twice more before finally answering it.

"Storenn."

He could feel Jessica's eyes on him as he listened to the familiar voice on the other end of the line. He turned his back so that she would not see the anger in his face; she already felt bad about this, no use in rubbing it in.

"I know, Vince. I'll be in as soon as I'm done here." His voice was not far from shaking. It was all he could do to not throw the phone across the broad room. He snapped it closed and reattached it to his belt. He paused for a moment before turning around.

"Bad news?" Jessica asked.

"No worse than this," James replied quietly, scanning the scene again. He knew that he was not going to be able to get his head back in the game until he went in and talked to the office. "Make sure the records are thorough. I want good sketches, photos and tape. You've got this, Jess."

She nodded. It was a statement, not a question.

"Give me a call when you finish up."

She looked at him evenly. "You do the same."

chapter 3

Cameron hung up the phone and rolled over. Kali sat there with a concerned look on her face; the sheets bundled loosely about her waist, the unhappy look of concentration on Cameron's face causing the ball of tension in her belly to grow sharp spines.

"Monk isn't gonna be making his shift at the club tonight."

Kali brushed the hair back from her face, her hand shaking ever so slightly. She knew what he meant, knew what it meant for the both of them. The demise of Anderson Monk, for reasons beyond her comprehension, was the blip on the radar that Cameron had been waiting for, the starting point for his exit strategy. Her eyes never wavered from his. She was worried, she was scared, but her eyes never wavered from his.

"It's time to play."

She nodded almost imperceptibly, not questioning his judgment. "And if Noah figures out what you're planning?"

"He won't."

"So sure of yourself?"

"He's smart, honey, but by no means a rocket scientist. Everything's either in place or heading that direction. I just need a few days to tie things up and everything will be all right." She sat there looking at him, her face expressionless. "We got into this knowing how it would end, Kali. It's time to play the card we've got and leave the game."

"It's not a game, Cam." Her voice wavered. "He takes this personally. Monk's proof enough of that."

Cameron stood up from the bed and turned around. He was large and muscular. The standard he held himself against would never allow him to be anything but stronger and faster and smarter than the next guy. It was a sense of discipline unlike anything Kalina had ever seen in her life. That discipline had served him well over the thirteen years he'd served in the Navy; as others got fatter and out of shape with age, he stayed strong and fit, pushing himself to excel. His abs weren't quite what they were at twenty-one, but at thirty-one you could still wash your clothes on them.

Heavily muscled shoulders and chest strained and rolled as he stretched. Kali liked watching him do that. She loved his body – his size made her feel small and vulnerable. Just as she liked his sense of calm and power, comforting to her when she felt things were getting out of control. He was always in control, even when everyone else was running around with their hair on fire. He was her unshakable rock; her Iron Dog, according to the Chinese astrological calendar her mother had studied so often when she was a little girl back in Hawaii.

He ran a hand through the messy brown tangle on top of his head and looked her in the face. It made her tingly when he got so serious with her. "Kali, that's not us. We're the ones with everything to lose and that makes me take this more seriously than any of them could even comprehend. And that's just what it is - a game. But we're not pieces, baby, we're players; and we're playing our game. They're our pieces and our rules. Hell, there wouldn't even be a game if I didn't know for a fact that we could walk when our time came." He paused for a moment. "It's not gonna be easy, but we will walk out of this."

She sat there, her large brown-black eyes pools of trust. She would follow him into the fire if he told her it wasn't going to burn. He was right; things with Noah were starting to get out of hand. They had been slipping for the last several months, the arguments and disagreements with him coming more frequently. Cameron tried to play it all off, tried to not let it touch her; but she had eyes and she knew how to listen. She knew her man, knew when things were bothering him and when he was upset. If Cameron was convinced that now was the best time to go, then that was how it would be. She might not like some of the details of his plan, but she trusted his judgment without question.

"Breathe deep, baby. It'll work itself out, one way or the other. Always does. We just gotta follow the plan." He half smiled as he turned away to get ready for work, pulling on the white polyester uniform shirt. She watched him pin on his ribbons and nametag and button the white buttons. Despite her strong feelings about the Navy, she liked how professional he looked in uniform; all perfectly pressed with the brilliant white cotton polyester material offsetting his evenly tanned skin. If only she could get past the circa nineteen fifties Good Humor man comparisons running through her head.

"You're leaving awfully early today," she said, noticing the time on the clock.

"Gotta pick up a medical record and start a fight with Noah."

She arched an eyebrow.

"Just taking care of business," he said reassuringly. He bent in to kiss her but only got her cheek as she turned her head. She hated kissing in the morning, at least until she brushed her teeth. That never seemed to stop him from trying, though.

"Don't forget to shave."

He kissed her on the cheek and stood up. "I'll get it on the way to work. I might be home a little early. Got a dentist appointment. Maybe we'll go out to dinner tonight, before heading to the club. Sound good?"

She smiled and nodded, suddenly sleepy. He smiled back and leaned in for another kiss. She gave in, offering her cheek once again. Freshly pecked, she lay back and snuggled deep into the covers. The garage door rumbled open and closed. She could, probably should, get up, but the bed was just too comfortable for words. Content to lie there, she let the mattress sap the strength from her limbs. Maybe she'd get a little more sleep before facing the day.

chapter 4

The Naval Criminal Investigative Service field office on Welles Street was a dark brown brick building filled with the professional offices of some two hundred agents and support staff. It was the largest of the field offices controlling operations at one hundred fifty locations around the world, rivaled in size and staffing only by the offices located in Norfolk, Virginia.

With only sixteen hundred personnel, the organization monitored and protected Navy and Marine Corps bases around the world, providing commanding officers general investigative services, counter-drug programs and resources to combat economic crimes. It was a massive undertaking, one that generally left many agents feeling overwhelmed and overworked, that emphasized the organizations reliance on outside agencies.

None of that bothered James. He liked the closeness of the organization, the camaraderie of working on a small, elite team of investigative specialists. They were independent and fast moving, with their own technical support, criminal intelligence and forensics facilities. They also had the full support of any of the other federal agencies out there, and the NCIS used them and their resources extensively. It really was the best of both worlds.

James stepped over the eagle and shield seal inlaid in the shiny gray marble of the foyer. The great seal of the Navy sat prominently in the center of the striped shield. He barely noticed any of it as he walked past the armed guards and through the metal detectors guarding the building's entrance, flashing a gold badge that matched the eagle and shield of the seal with exacting detail. The corridors of the headquarters building fell away under his steady pace, the news of the morning heavy on his mind. His black shoes clicked on the shiny tiles lining the floor. It was a nervous rhythm, slowing as he neared the door to his office.

Despite the speed with which he had left his apartment, James was dressed to impress. His gray suit pants were sharply creased, as was the blindingly white shirt under his nicely fitting gray suit coat. His light brown hair was gelled, solidly slicked back against his skull. He looked like he just stepped out of a magazine.

Except for the eyes. No Brooks Brother's model ever had eyes like James'; experienced eyes that had seen more than their fair share of misery and the worst that man had to offer. The smoothly shaved jaw line was the same though, as was the manicured and polished confidence that one would generally associate with a 'pretty boy'. He was anything but. Clothes and carriage aside, he was as solid and aggressive as he had been during high school, when he played football, making the all-state team as a linebacker his senior year.

He won a scholarship to junior college, playing ball both years. Unfortunately, the players at that level were just that much faster and that much stronger, and his previously stand out play was only run of the mill. He lost himself in his studies as it became all too apparent that the only professional football he would ever play was the virtual kind. At the end of his sophomore year he transferred to New Mexico State to chase his new passion.

Criminal law became all consuming, absorbing all of his time and energy and attention. The degree came two years later as he walked proudly down the aisle to receive his Cum Laude degree. Three years as a San Diego city police officer forced him to stay in decent shape, and since then working out had become his basic release for stress. Now as an NCIS agent, his athleticism and the ease with which he carried his size served him well as an intimidation factor.

The clicks of his shoes stopped outside his office door as he paused and took a breath. The events of the last twelve hours left little doubt as to what awaited him beyond that dark door. He might well be removed from the case. Reassigned. His stomach was nothing but slimy knots. He sighed deeply as he opened the door and stepped into the room.

chapter 5

Ian finished his breakfast, swallowing down the last of his orange juice as he checked his watch. He smiled broadly. He wasn't just going to make it to work on time; he was going to be early, despite this out of the way rendezvous. On a day like today, Ian didn't care if he was an hour late for work and got put on report by the charge nurse; breakfast was more than worth it. Steak and eggs over easy, hash browned potatoes, and buttery croissants sitting on plates in front of him and ten thousand dollars in twenties lying quite comfortably at the bottom of his green nylon knapsack. No meal ever tasted so good. All for a weekend's worth of work putting together a couple of medical records. What a chump. Ian would have put them together for free if he'd asked.

Since his host had been so kind as to pick up the check, Ian finished the last bite of croissant and stood up ready to go. He picked up his bag and slung it over his shoulder, smiling at a young Latina waitress as he headed out the door. Stopping on the sidewalk, he looked around at the people walking along around him, all of them looking sleepy and rushed as they started their day. He almost felt sorry for them.

This is going to be a good day - he thought.

He breathed deep, inhaling the salt in the air. Somewhere, a gull cried out. Perhaps he would just call in sick today and head out to La Jolla, spend the day on the beach relaxing. He had the sick days to do it. He turned and headed towards his beat up old Subaru, thinking on a good illness to give himself for the day. You had to be careful coming up with bogus illnesses when you worked at a hospital.

He made it as far as the alley alongside the restaurant, when an arm shot from the gap, grabbing his collar and dragging him forcefully into the shadow. He tried to struggle, but the disembodied hand slammed him face first into the brick wall. His head rang and a brilliant light flashed behind his eyes, blurring his vision.

Burning pain blossomed in the middle of his back. Again. And again. His legs weren't holding him up so well. He wobbled and fell to the hard concrete. For some odd reason he was having a difficult time catching his breath. The bag on his shoulder was gone, disappeared. He could see a distorted vision of himself reflected back at him from the shiny black surface of a pair of well cared for patent leather dress shoes. His face was stretched out, disturbingly twisted and barely recognizable.

Crap - he thought - *I forgot to call for help.*
But his lungs wouldn't fill with air now.

And suddenly he was cold. Not a 'hey-I-just-got-out-of-the-shower-and-my-nipples-are-hard' cold, but a bone-deep, aching kind of cold that spread out from his stomach; enveloping his limbs and sapping their strength. He couldn't feel the concrete beneath him. His vision swam in and out and he quit struggling, quit fighting to get up. Perhaps a little nap would be all right. So he closed his eyes and fell asleep forever.

chapter 6

Vincent Tameric sat behind James' desk, a look of concern and disappointment solid on his face. James could barely look him in the eyes.

Vincent shook his head, the disappointment etched in the tired lines of his face. "This is one for the books. You mind telling me what the hell happened last night?"

James exhaled and regarded his mentor seriously. "I don't know, Vince. Kamiski and Hafner said they had him running. He headed into the park by his house, ran into a stand of trees and didn't come out the other side…"

Vincent didn't let him finish. "I read their weak-assed report and that's not what I'm talking about. James, they didn't even call in to say they'd lost him until after midnight. Hell, you're the lead investigator on this case and you didn't even know he was gone until after the body was found this morning. How am I supposed to defend that? Your boys really screwed the pooch on this one."

"I don't know. How am I supposed to defend it? I can't. Communication broke down, for whatever reason, and the info didn't flow up the chain. So, yes, it's incompetence bordering on criminal negligence, but if we order them off the case, Jessica's intimating that City might not give us any replacements, so we'd be running two people short. Their reprimand is City's problem, so let's let City deal with it. I can't afford to lose the manpower at this point."

Vince just sat there. "I don't know about 'can't afford to lose the manpower.' That break down in communication cost you a witness. Anderson Monk is dead because those two officers didn't do their jobs. What you can't afford is a loss of witnesses. What you can't afford is to have this task force running around looking like a bunch of retarded monkeys trying to fuck a football. And if the complaint is about manpower, believe me, DEA would be all too happy to step in and take control of this case. The offices up the hall are demanding results. Yesterday if not sooner."

James felt the anger welling up inside of him. "The sidelines are an easy place to judge the game from. Comfy seats, instant replay – all the time in the world to Monday morning quarterback. It's my guys in the trenches, banging out thirty-six hour days wading around through this dead-end crap! I know how this looks, but it's not like we're just sitting around jerking each other off. If they've got some suggestions on how this investigation should be going, they're more than welcome to get off their asses and hop in the game!"

"This isn't about who's doing what, James. It's about what's not getting done. It's about control. DEA is arguing that this case is larger than what is going on here and that it fits better in their field of play. It's bullshit, but they're starting to gain an audience."

"Screw all that!" James spat back. "This is straight up NCIS jurisdiction! We set up this task force with the SDPD; we should be the one running it. Damn it, Vince, we're doing the best we can!"

"That's precisely their argument," came Vincent's quiet reply.

James was suddenly aware of how drawn Vincent looked. It showed in the tightness around his green eyes and the stiffness of his posture. He knew that his supervisor had taken a lot of flack this morning, trying to provide some measure of cover for the members of the task force. James wanted to argue that despite last night's idiotic mistakes, they were making headway, but the look on Vince's face froze the argument in his throat.

Vincent stood up and walked from behind the desk, clapping James on the shoulder as he headed for the door. "I've got you on this end," he stated sternly as he opened the door, "get back out there, get your team together, and put this thing to bed."

The door shut with a metallic click before James could respond.

chapter 7

Silence filled the space between the two men. It was an almost palpable thing. Noah sat looking at Cameron, staring intently as though he were trying to read the other man's mind. He hated the angry looks he got from Cameron lately, judging and disappointed. The accusing look he was getting right now, he liked that even less.

"Look, I don't know what to tell you, Cameron."

He wasn't lying. He was actually surprised by the news he was hearing.

"I don't know either, Noah. What I do know is that my name is apparently being bandied about NCIS headquarters. No one I've asked seems to know where it's coming from, but people are starting to listen. Someone's talking, Noah, and I want to know who it is."

"Or talked. Did it ever occur to you that maybe Monk might have said something to someone before his accident?"

Cameron winced at the euphemism.

"Maybe, but I don't think so. If he'd have so much as mentioned my name, the NCIS would've been tearing down my door last night. Besides, what could he have said? I was the one that tried to talk him out of working collections in the first place. No, someone else is feeding them."

A shrug was his answer.

Cameron leaned in close, his voice low and dangerous. "Don't shrug your fucking shoulders at me, Noah!" His eyes burned with intensity. "Pluggin' leaks and keeping this venture secure – that's your job one. I catch enough crap from you on how I handle my end of the business; I don't wanna hear 'boo' from you when I come back with legitimate concerns. I want answers."

Noah felt the heat bloom in his cheeks as he fought to keep his ire in check. "I'll look into it."

A brief smile played across Cameron's face otherwise tight features. He seemed to accept Noah's acquiescence. "Thanks, Noah."

Noah nodded, returning a brief smile that never reached his eyes. There was no feeling behind it; no humor or kindness. It was just muscle tissue reacting the way it was trained. It bothered Noah, that what had once been a tight relationship was now so strained. Sure, events in recent months had spread that trust pretty thin; it was damn near see through by now. Too many people talking and too much interest from the feds will have that effect. But the clean up was getting tedious and Noah had started wondering if maybe it was time to get out, kill them all and walk away on top of the game.

He had enough money in the bank to last him for a very long time, quite probably for the rest of his life.

Cameron stood to leave but Noah stopped him.

"Stay away for a while. Maintain some distance 'til we know who's doing what. If you need to get a hold of me, you know how, otherwise..." He left it hanging there.

"We'll be in touch when I get more information," Cameron answered. "I'm sure I'm just being paranoid."

Noah's look was serious. "That's why you get paid."

"Yeah, I guess it is," Cameron said, turning towards the door. "Just keep me posted."

Noah watched him make his way out of the lounge. "Yeah, I'll let you know," he muttered under his breath.

Noah couldn't believe that someone might be talking to the cops again, but if he figured out who was doing the talking, there would be a fresh supply of corpses for the morgue to sort out. But then again, with Cameron implicated in the deal, maybe this was not such a bad thing after all. Maybe this would give him the chance, the excuse, truth be told, he had been looking for to end it all. Just put a bullet in the back of Cameron's head and walk away. He shook his head knowing he wouldn't do it, not as long as the money kept coming in the way it was.

For now Noah had to figure out who was talking and plug the leak, permanently. He would let the Cameron thing develop for a few days, let it percolate a little and see what came of it. You just never knew. Opportunity had a tendency to knock at the most inopportune of times.

chapter 8

Jessica pulled up to the small private docks, the long wooden ramps running off into the water. Sailboats and powerboats of every size were moored there, a long row of shiny white hulls bobbing gently in the protected water. People in loose clothing milled about on the docks, puttering with their boats or jawing back in forth with one another. Jessica guessed that it was a community unto itself, life here at the harbor. Everyone knew everyone else's business and who was rocking the boat with whom. She wondered what they would be saying after she and James went for their 'three hour tour'. Unbidden, she also wondered what they could tell her about any other visitors James might be having. She pushed the thought from her brain.

Jealous wasn't her style, but you had to wonder if there was competition out there.

About half way down the dock she spotted James walking the deck of a brawny white boat, twenty-two feet along the beam with navy blue and gold striping running along the edge of the hull. In her mind, it resembled what a muscle car would look like if you dropped it in the water; strong lines that spoke of power and speed. 'SANITY' was the name painted in dark blue scroll just below the gold stripe on the bow of the boat. She smiled at that.

He looked up and saw her. Raising a hand, he waved her over.

She approached almost gingerly. In seven months he had never asked her out on his boat despite the fact he was out on it almost every day. She knew it was his escape – a safe place for him. It was a big step, asking her out here. She was happy he was finally taking it.

"Permission to come aboard?" she called out, smiling.

He returned her smile. "Permission granted."

He held out his hand, helping her down and in, and immediately started working on the lines to free the boat from its moorings. Jessica dipped and dodged trying to stay out of his way in the small open space in the middle of the boat. It was mostly unsuccessful. In a matter moments the lines were all loosed and the boat was floating freely in its berth. James stepped behind the wheel and smiled over at her again. Given the gravity of the day, Jessica couldn't believe how relaxed he looked.

"You ready?" he asked, turning the ignition and allowing the engine to rumble to life.

chapter 9

Noah clicked off the phone and tossed it into the passenger's seat. His insider was dispatched and any information that was floating around out there would be collected and delivered. He eased back into the drivers seat.

With everything else that had gone on recently, this complication was the last thing he needed. Cameron was seldom wrong and when he was, it was not so far off the mark as to be a complete miss.

If Cameron was under the spotlight, how did he get there? Monk hadn't spoken to anyone about what he knew; there was no doubt in Noah's mind as to that. And even if he had, there was no way he could have said anything about Cameron or his connections to the business because he simply hadn't known anything about them. He'd never been given access to that information. That meant it had to be someone else; a fact that bothered Noah a great deal. Too many leaks lately.

Well, time would tell if Cameron was on the money or if he was just on edge. Either way, Noah would try to distance himself for a while; apply some thought as to how much further he wanted to go with this venture. He'd entertained thoughts like the ones that had filled his head earlier that morning for sometime. Kill them all and walk away. Problem was, that was a lot of damn people to kill. He needed a better exit strategy. Unfortunately, planning was not one of his strong suits; he was all about execution, not details. Details were Cameron's bag of tricks.

Then again, wasn't that part of the overall problem? Noah had played his role well, expanding his control over various aspects of their shared enterprise. He had his fingers in all kinds of pies; gambling, drugs, collections. A hit now and again wasn't beyond reason. But for all of the ancillary pieces of the business he conducted, it was the core that he had no insight into. That was where the big money rolled in. Cameron kept those connections close to vest, simply informing Noah when actions with deliveries or collections might be needed.

If he truly wanted the money to keep rolling with Cameron out of the picture, he was going to have to crack that core. The question was how. Ten years had yielded little in the way of clues and with the way things were between them now ... well, the chances were slim to none that Cameron would be giving up the crown jewels. And slim just left the building.

He mulled over his options and the alternative futures they represented.

Strange days.

Noah shrugged; it would work itself out. He just had to be ready to act when the opportunity presented itself.

He glanced at the gunmetal watch on his wrist and frowned slightly. Where did the time go?

chapter 10

The sun beat down on the bay, golden light reflecting and refracting off the azure blue of the calm waters of the bay. James couldn't think of a better way to get his head back together than sitting on his boat out in the middle of nowhere. The company couldn't be better either. He stretched out on the white decking of the boat, his suit and tie traded in for a pair of sun bleached khaki shorts and an old faded surf t-shirt an ex-girlfriend had given him. He let the sun soak into his limbs, hot and comforting. Some three feet away from him, a woman he could probably fall in love with was soaking up the same sunshine, her long hair blowing carelessly in the breeze as she studied the distant horizon.

He loved the ocean. It was beautiful and powerful and mysterious, a seductive mistress, both haughty and unpredictable, revealing only those secrets she wanted known. It held sway over him from the first time he walked along the shore. He was in college at the time, getting his ass kicked all over the practice field and spending no time on the playing field. He was frustrated and struggling with some of his courses. A friend of his, a guy from one of his law enforcement classes named Owen, seeing that he was floundering, invited James out to San Diego to spend spring break on his father's forty foot sail boat. James had never seen the ocean and decided that he would get as much done there as he would cramped up in his tiny dorm room or working behind the bar at the Dulcet Lounge. He accepted the invitation, drove the twelve hours down and fell in love with the water. That week on the boat was the most relaxing time he had ever had. He came back to school tan and relaxed and determined to make his way to the coast.

For quite a while now the ocean had been the only consistent lady in his life. He ran to her whenever his burdens got too heavy and he let her rock him to sleep, the gentle whisper of her waves a soothing lullaby. He could drive by the beach and feel the knots in his neck and shoulders begin to work themselves out. And when things got real bad, when the world was raging at his door, he would sleep in the small cabin of his boat; yielding up his secrets and his pain to the deep. The ocean was peace. A peace he jealously guarded and rarely shared with anyone.

His fanaticism was a running joke with those who knew him. Everything in his house was either nautical or reminiscent of the sea. Every birthday card, every gift he got from friends, every vacation he took all had something to do with the ocean. It was actually ironic that he worked for the Department of the Navy since the massive gray ships of the fleet did nothing at all for him. As far as he was concerned, they were nothing more than floating buildings with as much to do with the sea as the massive condos that lined the shore downtown. The Sailors of the iron ships had nothing to do with sailing. They were mechanics and radio operators and cooks, not sailors. The majority couldn't navigate their way around a sailing ship if their life depended on it. Despite spending the majority of his adult life defending and working for the maritime services, James wasn't too big on the Navy as a whole.

He was big on the law. It was order from chaos, righteousness from injustice. It was his driving passion. A passion that had kept him single and ended every serious relationship he'd had since college. There was no line for him, he was a cop twenty-four hours a day, seven days a week; and that proved to be too much for the women he ended up involved with. They could not take the constantly shifting schedule and the fact that their needs and wants and plans were subject to his pager. In the end they would get angry and walk. It bothered him some, not having that special someone to talk to at the end of the day. But he had always been a solitary person, so he didn't dwell on the loneliness of his situation.

Today was the exception. He was out on 'SANITY' with a beautiful woman who shared his passion for the job. Someone he could talk to. The sun shone overhead and the waves lapped gently at the hull, rocking the boat with tender hands. He rolled off the deck and stepped over to the cooler sitting in front of the low bench that ran along the stern. Pulling out a beer and popping the top, he sipped at it and leaned back into the padded seat. The gulls cried to the east, circling the beach and looking for food. The sun baked his soul and his lids grew heavier and heavier.

He shook his head, trying to loosen the grip of sleepiness as it tried to snare him in its web. He looked over at Jessica, standing there next to the passengers seat. She was a golden goddess in the sunlight. He smiled and sighed.

"This is something else, James," she said, not looking back over her shoulder. She had been staring at the water and the distant coastline since they left the safety of the harbor. "It's so calm out here."

He hated to ruin it. "I brought the case files out." He left it hanging there, letting her decide what to do.

"Might as well dig them out," she said reluctantly.

Standing, he ducked down into the low cabin and picked up the small briefcase from the deck and laid it on the table. She followed his motion with her eyes, already aware that she didn't have to follow him around the small boat. The brass hasps clicked open and he dug through the mass of papers and files. Finding the ones he wanted, he headed back out to the warmth of the sun to sort through the information.

"You want a beer before we get started on this?"

She nodded and he leaned back over to the cooler and dug out another silver can. She took it from him and popped it open as he began to lay out the case files they were going over. Company aside, they both knew this was going to be a grim way to spend the afternoon.

The torture and murder of Anderson Monk was disturbing enough. That it was the third of three horrific murders made it all the worse. The pictures spilled out onto the white vinyl seat cover. Jessica winced. He looked the pictures over and felt the bile rising in his throat. Shots were taken from every angle, fully capturing the nature of the crime in graphic detail. The bloodied husk was barely even recognizable as having once been human. It was a mess. They would get the full forensic report tomorrow morning; the pictures would have to suffice for now.

They had the forensic reports for the other two murders. Kevin Johnson, a hapless young Boatswain's Mate Third Class, was found with nearly every bone in his body shattered. Someone tied him to a chair, took a ball peen hammer and, starting at his toes, worked their way up, crushing every bone along the way. The body sat tied to that chair for five days, the tight ropes biting into the rotting flesh, digging in until they became imbedded in the bloated meat. A teenage couple looking for an out-of-the-way place to make-out made the unfortunate discovery and reported it to the local police. More than one officer had lost his lunch while working that crime scene. James winced at the thought. Jessica had cleaned him up after he spewed his breakfast all over the asphalt.

The second murder of the three was that of Anwar Belk, another Boatswain's Mate who had also been beaten to death. He left the ship on a Tuesday afternoon and never made it home to his wife and young son. A dockworker showed up early to work on Wednesday morning, finding Belk's shattered body there on the wooden pier. Metal spikes were driven through his feet, pinning him into place on the pier and then he was beaten to a pulp. The weapon had yet to be disclosed, probably never would be. Not that it really mattered. Knowing what killed Petty Officer Belk didn't clean the mess left behind. James guessed that the weapon was a bat or a thick pipe. The bruising on the body and the break points of the various bones supported his theory.

James couldn't imagine any of those deaths, what that hopeless suffering would have been like. The pathologist who conducted each of the autopsies confirmed everyone's worst fears; the deaths had been long in coming. They were tortuous and cruel with the victim being conscious of the pain and brutality until the bitter end. Evidence from each of the scenes proved that theory; urine and feces and vomit on the victims and on the ground surrounding them. They died scared. James grunted in dismay, knowing that similar evidence had been gathered at this crime scene.

They finished poring over the records, comparing the physical evidence found at each scene and guessing at the possible connection between the men. Their individual service jackets yielded nothing of value. The sailors had never served together, never been stationed together. They didn't live in the same parts of town or go to school with one another. They had nothing in common except for the fact that each one had volunteered information to the NCIS and that each one had paid an unimaginable price as a result. The frustration was mounting.

"Well?" James asked, taking a long pull from a fresh beer.

"Well what?" Jessica asked incredulously, disgust painted on her face. "It took one incredibly sick bastard to come up with this and an even sicker one to execute it. I don't think there's a connection other than the fact that each one of these guys got into something he shouldn't have and got plugged before he could get out."

James nodded. He looked at the shattered men in the pictures and shuddered. The murders were a warning to anyone who decided to talk. Talk to the police and you will meet a death more unspeakable than anything you have ever imagined. It was an effective means for relaying a message. As his instructor in college had once told him before a final, "Fear, Mr. Storenn, is such a valuable teacher."

"I think that the same guy did them all," she continued. "There's no real marriage to style besides the sheer brutality with which each of them was beaten. That could qualify as a signature, I guess. We are dealing with one angry guy who has the brains enough to leave behind a very clean crime scene. And it's personal. Each of these guys was killed slow and nasty. He was right there, up close the entire time. I think he was out to do more than make a point, though. Popping some guy in the back of the head execution style makes a point, torturing him like these guys," she said with a wave of her hand, "man, that does something else to you. It's a promise that if you cross these guys, they can make your worst nightmares come to life. I think the info we get tomorrow's going to be interesting."

He looked at the brightly glistening water around him, shot through with golden sunlight, and breathed a tired sigh. Tomorrow was not going to be interesting; it was going to be sickening. He hated sitting through the ME's report. He hated the smell of death that clung to the examiners and their offices. He hated looking over a dead-too-soon corpse pieced together with rough stitching while listening to the detached, academic viewpoint of why the person died. James already knew how Anderson Monk died – he was beaten to a pulp. The rest was just details that he probably didn't really want.

"There's more tying it together than brutal," James said quietly. "This guy is patient, confident. These killings weren't quick. He took his time with them. The areas were all fairly accessible, all with unpredictable traffic patterns. And yet, look at the crime scene info – nothing. I'm talking goose egg. No random prints, discarded weapons. No witnesses. He wants us to think that he's some raging, out-of-control maniac; but he's worse than all that. He's smart and he's careful. The guy's not gonna stick out in a crowd. Though we don't have any profiles from the Behavioral Sciences Unit in Quantico, I would lay money that the guy is a highly functioning social psychopath, one of those guys who, when all of this is over, his neighbors will talk in surprised voices about how he was the perfect neighbor. Kept to himself, never bothered anybody."

Jessica nodded. "I'll call your 'social psycho' and raise you 'highly organized'. But I've gotta tell you, I think we're just trackin' a cog on the wheel. Bad ass, yes, but I have doubts that the guy who's been knocking off our witnesses is the one driving this thing."

James chewed on that for a moment, looking out over the water at a gull hanging on the breeze. She was right. The Dons were seldom, if ever, the triggermen once they were seated. They gave orders. This killer was probably just some lieutenant in the organization. Maybe less than that. If they could get their hands on him, they would finally be on a path to get some answers.

"I want to walk the scene with you tomorrow. Use your notes and the base report from CSU to reconstruct as best we can."

Jessica didn't answer.

James had started to gather up the scattered pictures and put them back into their respective files when he noticed the haunted look in Jessica's eyes. It occurred to him how appalling those pictures where to him, he had just taken her presence as a matter of course – another cop checking out the evidence. She was no wilting flower. She had a stronger stomach than he did when it came to the gore, but for some inexplicable reason he was embarrassed that he had put her through looking at them again.

"Hey, you ever see La Jolla from the sea?"

She looked at him, confused at the change of subject. "No. No, I don't believe I have."

James scooped up the files and stepped down into the shade of the cabin, dropping them back into the dark briefcase. Snapping it shut, he turned around. "It's definitely something to see. You get a good look at all those million dollar homes. What do you say?"

She shrugged, a slight smile playing across her lips. "I guess I have time."

"Excellent," he said, stepping up to the wheel. He turned the key to the ignition, letting the motor idle with a powerful, low rumble. Smiling at her, he levered down the accelerator, pushing the boat into motion.

chapter 11

Thomas Pinfield sat behind the heavy metal desk that marked his territory in the cramped quarters of the dental office. He looked up at Cameron Leasig, standing in front of him expectantly.

"I found most of the older documents in Doc's files. Everything is pretty much done. Should have it all together before I head out tonight."

A smile cracked Cameron's serious face and relief flooded through the scrawny Dental Tech. He was behind schedule on building out the record and had pushed Cameron's patience pretty close to the breaking point. Thomas was glad to have this coming to an end – it was much more stress than he was equipped to deal with.

"Thanks for your help, Doc. Is cash all right?"

It was Thomas's turn to smile. "Sounds good to me. The records will be in the system tomorrow morning."

Cameron's grin grew bigger, maturing into a genuine smile. "Good news all around then. See you around, Thomas."

"Yeah. See you around."

Thomas watched the door close behind the larger man and he breathed out audibly. He hoped that the reward was worth the risk.

chapter 12

James tooled around the boat, wiping at dirt and water spots. Jessica was headed home now; the day having faded in the wake of the boat. Despite their broad review, both gut wrenching and boring, the rest of the afternoon seemed to go swimmingly. Jessica laughed at his jokes and cooed appropriately at sights he showed her. All in all, it had been a successful trip. She left with a promise to return for another trip sometime soon. Ah, yes, murder investigation doubling as a dating service.

The musical ring of his cell phone interrupted his reverie. It took him a few seconds to locate the small phone. Recognizing the number, he flipped it open. "Storenn here."

A perplexed look filled his eyes. He listened to the voice on the other end of the line delivering its message. The last few days had thrown him some curves; it was almost becoming passé.

"Club 'Kittie' at ten o'clock? Right. She didn't leave any name or anything, just said she wanted to talk to me about Anderson Monk? All right. Yeah, thanks for the message. Bye."

He closed the phone and plunked down on the seat, mulling over the message. It had all the hallmarks of a set up – anonymous woman calls and requests a meeting about an unforeseen twist in a case that had frustrated his every effort, all at a very well known strip club. His instincts were tripping like a jackhammer in the back of his head. He'd be walking into a situation that was nothing but unknowns. Could be entertaining, could end up getting his brains spread all over the sidewalk. Nope, the decisions weren't getting any easier, but at least he had plans for the evening.

He looked down at the closed phone in his hand and thought that he should call Jessica and let her know about the meeting. She really should be there. The thought of hearing her voice again found him with the phone flipped back open and ready to dial, but the idea of asking her to accompany him to a high-end strip club was just a tad outside his normal frame of reference.

A sarcastic smile crossed his lips. Yeah, that couldn't possibly be taken the wrong way. 'Hey, baby, wanna go to a strip club with me – strictly professional of course. Whadaya say?' Nope. No way to misconstrue that.

He couldn't bring himself to dial the digits. For all he knew, it was just some of the guys on the task force trying to blow off steam after a particularly grueling day. If ever there was a 'damned if you do, damned if you don't' type situation, this was definitely it. He sported a wry grin as

flipped the phone closed again and slid it back onto his belt. Resigned to carry out the evening solo he glanced down at his watch and grimaced.
Six thirty.
And the hits just keep on coming.

chapter 13

The waiter walked away, the check and Cameron's credit card in his hand. Kalina watched him go and looked at Cameron over the small flame of the candle that rested between them. "So what was it you wanted to tell me over dinner?" she asked.

"Oh, yeah. I almost forgot," he said with a chuckle. "I talked to Noah today. Game on." He gave his head a little tilt to the side when he said it.

Kalina was speechless. He had talked about putting his plan in to motion this morning before he left for work, but she didn't think that he meant immediately. It was so dangerous.

"I didn't push it too much, but the seeds are definitely planted. It's just a matter of applying the right pressures now."

"Cameron, he'll kill you." She was worried.

"No, Kali. He's not gonna kill me; I'm worth too much to him alive. Of course, by the time this is over he will have given it the old college try. It won't matter though, by the time he figures out what's happening, it'll be too late. It'll be over."

The waiter returned with the bill and a pen, leaving the burgundy leather cover on the table with a smile. "Please, take your time," he said warmly.

Cameron waited for him to walk away. "Kali, you know this has to happen. We've talked about this, baby. I have too much time left on my contract and Noah's venturing out on his own more and more. It's gonna come to a head at some point, it has to. Too many bulls in the paddock. We have an opportunity to steer it now, call the shots."

He signed the bill and slid the credit card back into his wallet. He paused for a moment as if thinking about whether or not to continue.

"Oh, and that NCIS investigator, Storenn, is going to be at the club tonight."

She didn't reply, she didn't know how. She was nervous and scared for the both of them. He was confidence personified, unaffected by the risk inherent to the game he was playing with both their lives. It bothered her that he could be so unaffected, that he could walk without worries.

"Tonight? Why?" she asked finally, her voice low. "Why can't we walk, Cam? Just disappear? We have enough money between the two of us that we could disappear forever."

One more try. She knew it wouldn't work, the conversation was old, but she felt she had to at least make the attempt before things went too far.

He shook his head. "Everyone would be looking for us. We've covered this, Kali. Noah would put a contract on my head faster than I even want to think about. The DEA and the NCIS would be looking for us; the Navy would be hunting me as a deserter. The only way out is to make everyone happy, win-win across the board. That means making it so no one has a reason to come after us. It has to be this way Kali. It has to."

"But you're throwing down the glove and challenging the Feds to figure it out. They're not going to take that lying down."

"We can't crank up one side without spinning up the other. Storenn and his NCIS buddies have to play." When she did not respond, he continued on. "They're part of it too, babe, just as important as Noah to make it work. I just have to figure how I want to play it with Storenn tonight; hard or soft."

Kalina regarded him solemnly. "Just be yourself, that'll be more than enough to piss him off."

A smile played across his lips. "That's probably true," he said with a chuckle.

Silence was Kalina's reply. She tried to project anger instead of fear; righteous indignation over discomfort. They were both there, protesting Cameron's cavalier attitude towards their security. She knew, though, that despite her best efforts, all she was showing was worry.

"Don't worry about it right now," he said gently. "It's gonna be alright."

She shrugged. He stood up and walked around the table, pulling out her chair so she could stand. She looked in his eyes and saw her concerns reflected back at her. He was worried about her worrying. That almost struck her as humorous. He wasn't wringing his hands over the idea of a homicidal maniac coming after him. He wasn't sweating over facing down a Federal Agent and his team of investigators. Cameron was worried about his girlfriend being upset. A snigger of disbelief escaped her and the corners of her mouth curled upwards in an exasperated grim. He returned her smile encouragingly, stepping aside to follow her out of the restaurant.

Cameron Leasig was unbelievable.

chapter 14

Jessica sat in her car looking up at James' apartment windows. She'd been there a couple of times in passing, picking something up or dropping it off, but never staying for any real period of time. She could feel the knots in her stomach tightening and loosening, only to cinch back up again. She wasn't quite sure why she felt so nervous. Everything had gone so well that afternoon. He had finally relaxed around her, more than a bit, allowing her to see another side of him, one she was sure not many women had. The timing for this was perfect, she should have nothing to worry about.

So James was attractive, handsome even; Jessica had been with her fair share of good-looking men. Maybe it was the restraint he showed towards her, always looking like there was something else he wanted to say. Maybe it was something in the lingering looks that passed between them. Fire danced along those glances, smoky and hypnotic. If forced, she would describe them as hungry, on her part as well as his.

She looked through the glass of the windshield, trying to guess what his reaction might be to this late night visit. She hoped that he would be pleasantly surprised, fumbling around trying to pick up quickly before she noticed something out of place. She figured that she could use the case and the events of the last several days to get through the door and that she could use the bottle of wine lying on the passenger seat to stick around for a while. Perhaps things would relax between them.

The what-ifs of the situation ran though her brain, a flood of uncertainty and self doubt; uncharacteristic of her in the worst of cases. She took a deep breath, holding it for a second and then letting it out slowly. She was not misreading the situation. It was beyond professional courtesy. This was not going to screw everything up.

She checked her make-up one last time in the rear view mirror. It was as flawlessly applied as it had been the last time she checked, some two minutes ago. She was impatient sitting down in the parking lot, a nervous schoolgirl trying to build up her courage to ask the cute quarterback to the dance.

Screw it - she thought, grabbing the bottle of wine from the passenger seat and shoving open the driver's side door. No better time than the present, especially if he wasn't going to get off his butt and ask her out. The car door shut loudly behind her, startling her a little. She looked around as she smoothed the silky material of her pink flowered dress. Not a soul to be seen.

She ran through her excuse as she walked up to the apartment building.

chapter 15

The silver Honda Accord sped along the damp road, street lamps and stoplights shining like gems in the beads of moisture on the windshield. The brief summer shower did its best to dull the edge of the days heat, leaving behind swirls of fog as the water evaporated off the still warm asphalt. James looked at the clock glowing in the dash and gave the gas a little more pressure. His night wasn't getting any better. Ten minutes to get through downtown and out to Hawthorne Street. He'd make it, he was sure. He just hated being late.

Not that he was overly sure what it was he was rushing toward.

Oh, yeah, a strip club. An image of Jessica, sun-kissed and smiling, long hair flipping in a light breeze sprang to mind. Thoughts of her were popping up more often, generally at inopportune times. What troubled him was that as his musings became more commonplace, they were becoming more daring, and not just in the base terms of commingled passion. Longevity, thoughts of an actual relationship were creeping into his consciousness. She was the only woman he'd felt comfortable with to invite out on the boat in he didn't know how long.

He wondered what she was doing tonight, where she was. He silently wished that he was on his way to her apartment instead of heading who knew where to do whatever it was he was going to do.

He yawned broadly, shaking his head like a roaring lion. The emotional roller-coaster ride was taking a toll on him. He was exhausted. He squeezed his eyes shut for a minute and then blinked to focus on the road.

Towering warehouses and darkened car rental lots slipped by in the night. A jet roared in the darkness, reminding James how close he was to the airport. He thought that it was odd that this club could be so successful out on the fringes of the city in an area that was more industrial than not, while so many of the clubs that littered the four blocks of San Diego's meager red light district struggled. Perhaps it was the lack of accessible competition. He shrugged. It was a business he didn't understand.

He pulled into the parking lot with three minutes to spare.

The lot was crowded with cars, from clunkers to high-end sedans to flat out expensive sports cars. Club Kittie was definitely open for business. The pink neon cartoon cat - obviously female - glowed welcomingly over the broad double doors, also pink, that made up the entrance. James had heard much about the club, especially over the last three hours. It was apparently 'the shit', a statement that was nothing if not contradictory, in local live adult entertainment, at least according to one of the college interns working at the headquarters building.

It had been years since James had been to a strip club, college, as near as he could remember. Quite suddenly he became self-conscious and ran a nervous hand through his thick brown hair and tried to smooth out the non-existent wrinkles from his freshly pressed sports jacket. He was more relieved than ever that he had not told Jessica about this little venture. She was going to kick his ass all over the headquarters building when she found out about it in the morning, but for now he knew that he would just be immensely uncomfortable and unable to concentrate.

A monstrously large man in black slacks and a black t-shirt that was straining to hold itself together met him at the door. His jaw was a cinder block and his voice sounded like gravel in a mixing machine.

"ID."

James pulled out his driver's license and handed it over to the man. It had been a long while since he'd been carded. The giant looked at the license and spoke softly into the microphone strapped to his head.

"Thank you, Mr. Storenn," the man rumbled, handing the card back.

James took it and nodded. After so many years of police work, it was second nature to size up possible opponents. James hoped he never had to find out about this guy. He was fairly convinced that outside of hitting him with a bat or a Chevy, the best he could hope for was pissing the big fella off. And pissing him off was probably not a real bright idea.

A stunning brunette materialized at the bouncer's side, her well-proportioned body wrapped in skin-tight lycra. The electric blue mini-skirt accentuated more than hid the rounded lines of her tight hips. Her legs were long and muscular. He guessed her age at twenty-one, twenty-two tops.

"Good evening, Mr. Storenn. Mr. Leasig is expecting you. I'll escort you back to the office. Would you care for something to drink?"

James was fairly certain that this woman got her way an awful lot. He shook his head. "No thanks."

She smiled, brilliant liquid ruby lips parting slightly to reveal even white teeth. "Just follow me then," she said turning and walking trough the large double doors and into the crowded room on the other side. James followed her through the doors, unable to tear his eyes from her gyrating hips and the gravity-defying buttocks they framed. He felt like a dirty old man.

The club was jumping. The scattered tables were full; men and women of all shapes and sizes spending their hard earned dollars from the relative anonymity afforded by the purposely dim lighting. They clamored around the two stages, the small one positioned by the door and the larger platform running along the back wall. A long wooden bar lined the far wall beyond the smaller stage, its bottles shimmering like so many precious gems under the purple and pink fluorescent lighting that hung around the bar.

    A tall, light skinned black girl danced on the smaller stage by the door, her lean, well shaped body grinding seductively to the beat. She danced for the dollars laid out on the edge of the stage, giving each patron a personal show for their 'donation'. She hovered over a young blonde woman sitting ringside, three one-dollar bills folded neatly on the wooden rail in front of her. The dancer looked down at the girl, smiling broadly at the eager expression that painted her face, she grabbed the girls face and pulled her close, teasing. She buried the girls face between her ample bosoms, smothering her in the soft flesh before releasing her with a coy smile and walking on to her next admirer.

    James followed his nymphet guide through the maze of tables, past dancers wandering the floor looking for the next patron to buy them a drink or buy a 'personal' dance. They were all gaudily and skimpily clothed, skin-tight miniskirts over florescent thongs, bright bras under see-through shirts. The girls were young and beautiful and hustling for a buck. And from the looks of it, they were doing very well.

    They approached the back stage. A compact blonde wearing nothing more than pale blue g-string and a smile graced it with her presence, swaying rhythmically to the beat. She charged the shining pole imbedded in the stage, grasping it with her small hands and flipping her lithe body upside down, muscular legs akimbo as she slid down the smooth shaft. It was an impressive feat that brought a multitude of dollar bills up to the railing.

    James could feel the blood rushing to his face, embarrassed by his inability to look away. Everywhere he looked was another nubile young body wandering about in some painted on outfit. He was uncomfortable in those surroundings, knowing that he was old enough to be any one of these young girls' father. Well, maybe a young uncle. Either way, he felt every inch the lecher. Not for lack of appreciation, an inaudible sigh of relief escaped him as they rounded the stage and headed up the stairs.

chapter 16

"I think the price is more than fair, Kalina." Tony La Paola was trying to sell her.

Cameron nodded slightly. Taking his cue, Kalina smiled broadly and stood up. It was work to do it – she didn't like the idea of doing business with La Paola. He was greasy, the stereotypical strip club owner with the gold chains and slicked back hair, and she felt dirty just being in his presence. She wouldn't have let him in her club at all if Cameron hadn't insisted on it.

"I can't argue on that point, Tony. I'll have my lawyers put the documents together. They'll be in touch with you to tomorrow to finalize the deal. My only stipulation is that no one know about the deal until after the contract is executed. I'm serious, Tony, nothing before Friday night."

Cameron picked La Paola because he was an extremely successful club owner with a chain of six popular clubs in the San Diego area and could easily come up with financing short notice. Kali knew those clubs though, and wasn't so keen on how they were run. The buildings were dark and not in the best condition. The women who danced were highly suspect; a couple of the clubs were notorious for prostitution and strung-out dancers. Kali forbade both in Kittie and she did not like the idea of all of her hard work going to waste. But Cameron was right about one thing, Kittie was major competition for La Paola's organization and he was more than happy to attempt a deal now, even if it meant paying a premium. The negotiating strength was all theirs.

Tony smiled an oily smile. She could see the dollar bills dancing in front of his eyes as he stood up to meet her. Kali, shuddering in her mind, returned his smile as best she could and shook his hand.

She needed a shower.

"Always a pleasure, Kalina, always a pleasure. Cameron," he said turning his head toward the couch.

"Take 'er easy, Tony," Cameron replied, standing up.

chapter 17

No one answered the buzzer. The seconds limped by, a painfully slow procession traveling around the face of her watch. Twenty-nine seconds, thirty seconds. Impatient for an answer, she pressed the intercom button again. The buzzer sounded shrill in the otherwise silent foyer.

Jessica could feel the heat bloom in her cheeks as the time stretched out; several seconds turning into several minutes. No answer came. She checked to make sure she pushed the right apartment number on the security panel. STORENN, Apt three-oh-one. No mistaking that. She glanced down at her watch, grimacing. It was already after ten o'clock. And then it hit her. James wasn't home. It was after ten o'clock and here she was standing outside his door like some groupie and he wasn't even home. Her face felt like it was on fire. She looked around, hoping that nobody was around to see her; hoping desperately that she did not run into James coming home.

She made her way back to the car and all but dove inside.

"Well, that wasn't embarrassing," she said to herself.

Jessica started the engine, kicking herself for being so stupid. Better to just get back home and drink the bottle of wine herself.

chapter 18

James stood at the doorway alone, his exquisite guide having already headed back down the bouncer-guarded stairway. It was a shame to see her go, but following her up the stairs had made it worth the trip. The office in which he now stood was sparsely, if not tastefully, decorated. The carpeting was light, as were the walls. A large, heavy executive desk with computer perched on it sat near the middle of the room, its dark wood standing out against the lighter surroundings. To the far side of the room was a sitting area with a large, comfortable-looking tan and green couch and two over-stuffed easy chairs. A wall length window of mirrored glass lent a complete view of the club below.

A tall woman stood with her back to him, seeming to address the two men seated before her. Even from across the room, the air about her was one of confidence, self-reliance. She stood with poise, addressing equals, whatever her dress. Although - it was a very clingy, shape hugging, body enhancing dress that complimented her long legs and broad shoulders.

Obviously, this wasn't going to be some off-the-hook male bonding session; he was in an office guarded by a pair of behemoth steroid freaks that would, like as not, tear his head off if that slip of a woman standing with her back to him so much as thought it. Sure, he had to navigate temptation island to end up here, but now the question was blaring in his highly efficient mind: Why am I here?

He strained his ears to over hear what they were speaking about, an unfortunately rude habit was eavesdropping, but it came with the job. The muffled bass from the club below covered any conversation.

The man on the sofa, dark with slicked back hair and a dark suit, stood up and held out his hand. The woman shook it lightly and turned towards the door. The dark man nodded to the man in the easy chair to the right of the couch and followed the woman towards the door.

The woman smiled as she approached him, even more attractive from the front than she was from behind. Her skin was smooth and tan. Her face was lean and pleasant with high cheekbones and slightly tilted almond eyes. Midnight hair piled on her head, exposing a long delicate neck. The bare shoulders and arms were evenly muscled and nicely toned. She reminded him of a painting he'd seen some years ago in college of Athena-Nike gracing a battlefield in ancient Greece. He could picture her in his head, wrapped in white linen, golden sword shining in golden sunlight as she inspired her troops to victory.

"I'll be with you in a moment, Mr. Storenn." Her voice was lilting, sweet.

James stepped aside and let the both of them pass by. The woman stopped at the door, opening it for the darkly dressed man. "Until the signing, Tony."

"You won't regret this, Kalina."

She smiled wanly and nodded as he walked through the door. "That remains to be seen," she muttered, shutting the door behind him.

Her smile brightened again as she turned to regard him. "Sorry about that, Mr. Storenn. Didn't mean to keep you waiting. Please, follow me."

She sashayed past, leading James to his mysterious host.

"Mr. Storenn, I'd like to introduce you to Mr. Cameron Leasig, the reason you are here this evening." She sounded nervous, but she produced a beautiful smile for him.

"And you are…"

"Ms. Kalina Morris. I own 'Club Kittie'."

He offered his hand and she took it, shaking it much more daintily than he expected. He couldn't help but wonder what a woman like this was doing in a place like this. She had the looks but didn't seem the type. Not that he was real sure what type of woman would own a strip club, but he had to imagine that she didn't fit the stereotype.

James inspected the man lounging in the easy chair. Cameron Leasig was broad and solid with neatly trimmed hair and a strong jaw line. He had the relaxed air of an overgrown surfer, dressed in a brightly printed Hawaiian shirt, a pair of khaki shorts and some rubber slippers. He leaned comfortably into the couch, at home with his surroundings. Underneath the relaxed façade, James saw the tensed muscles of a jungle cat ready to pounce on its prey; the dark brown eyes were serious and observant. James knew that he was being inspected as well, that the man opposite him was taking his measure.

Cameron stood. "Offer you a drink Mr. Storenn? Rum and Coke? Or are you on the clock?"

James hid his surprise at the fact Leasig knew his favorite drink. "Minus the rum, thanks."

Kalina looked at Cameron, "You want anything, Cam?"

"Diet Coke."

Without a word, Kalina turned and headed towards the office door.

Cameron smiled and offered his hand, "Figured we might have one to break the ice, especially since we're going to be working together."

The surprise registered on James' face as he took Cameron's hand. "We are?"

Cameron waved at the seat to his right, offering it up, as he sat down. Perplexed, James took the proffered seat.

"Yes, Mr. Storenn, we are."

"Perhaps I missed something somewhere, but I came here for information about the murder of Anderson Monk. What are you talking about?"

Cameron fixed him with a level gaze. "You are the lead investigator on this big NCIS – DEA drug smuggling, murder, racketeering thing, right?"

James wasn't sure how to respond so he sat there studying his opponent.

"Of course you are. And me? I'm the guy with the information you need to shut it all down. I can tell you who and where and when and how."

James was dumbfounded. Perhaps it was the perfectly calm, off-hand way he said it, or maybe it was the fact that he was saying it at all.

"Back up there a minute. What the hell are you talking about?"

"You heard me." Cameron's voice was perfectly even. "I have the information you need to put some very bad gentlemen out of business. God only knows you could use the help."

James shifted in his seat, uncomfortable with the sudden wash of defensiveness that slid over him. They needed help, sure, but that shouldn't be public knowledge. Vince's tired face popped into his brain for a moment and guilt slid into place along side the defensiveness. His voice revealed more than he hoped it would, clipped and irritated. "We've had a few setbacks, but we're making headway."

His host all but guffawed. "Setbacks? You've been working this case, what, eighteen months? Eighteen months and only two arrests; both of them small timers who couldn't or wouldn't give up the guy in the organization ahead of them. How many witnesses have you buried in that time frame? Setbacks, please! Your case is in the shitter Special Agent Storenn. You need my help."

James felt the blood rush to his face as anger swelled up in him. It had been a very long day and the last thing he was in the mood for was getting his nose rubbed in it. He leaned forward so that he was only a few feet from were Cameron sat smugly.

"I'll play your game, Mr. Leasig. Let me take you in …"

"I don't think so, Special Agent Storenn," Cameron interrupted, his voice still calm, almost gentle. "I've waited almost three years watching various police organizations stumble around and fumble fuck this thing until it doesn't even resemble what's actually going on! I'm getting tired of waiting for you to pull your heads out of your collective ass holes and start doing the math on this so that I can get on with my life."

James couldn't tell if he was being baited or Leasig was just that cocky. He regarded his feisty host evenly. There was a lot going on here, more than he could have counted on walking through the door. That intuition was thumping at the back of his skull, reminding him that something that looked too good to be true on the surface generally was. This, undoubtedly, was not the exception to that rule.

Cameron leaned forward and looked sternly at James, regarding him as one would a small child. "Let me put it this in a way you might understand. Don't worry; I'll use small words so you can keep up. I've been working on this for the last three years, gathering information and putting together files. I've watched the entire thing grow and now it's time to put an end to it. For me, it's all or nothing. You'll get it all at once or you don't get anything at all. You do it my way or we don't play. I don't feel like watching you piss away information I've risked so much to compile because you can't figure out how to make sense of it. So, do we have a deal?"

James let the feigned hostility wash over him, refusing to rise to the bait. Leasig was really working to sell his side of the story. It was a good story, convincing on several levels. As to how much of it was pure fabrication, no way of telling, but James played along to see where it led.

"'Do we have a deal?' What deal are you looking for, Mr. Leasig? States' evidence, witness protection? I need something concrete to make that work. To be frank, I don't know who you are, much less how reliable your information is. I'm still sitting here, still listening. I have yet to hear anything solid about who killed Anderson Monk or how his death is connected to the flow of drugs through Coronado. I think we're some ways away from making demands."

Cameron sat back at that. Thoughtfulness played across his face, followed quickly by a sly smirk. "Fair enough. You're an investigator, so I'll let you investigate. I'm not ready to start dropping names; I'm not going to go out of my way to bury myself. You have my name and all the resources you'll need to get the basics and that'll have to be enough for now. Other than that, time is running out on this side. I know what they did to Monk and I'm not hanging around to let them do the same to me. What I need from you is time; time to get my affairs in order. And I want an extra set of eyes on my back while I'm doing it. It's crunch time and I don't want to get taken out right before the ol' coup de grace."

"I understand that. But if you have all of this potent information, why are you waiting 'til now to bring it up?" It was hard for James to keep the cynicism out of his voice.

"Because I didn't like the thought of waking up dead. Still don't. I got in over my head a long time ago and figured that at some time, if the timing was right, I'd need an out. This is it. I paid attention, put stuff together as I came across it. But why come forward – you guys are on the case right? Why put my head on the chopping block if I can just let you guys solve it all. And if something falls my direction, I've got the leverage to bargain my way out of it. But you guys didn't come through."

Frustration nagged. James heard the words and they made sense. There was nothing unique or unusual about someone getting in over their head. It happened every day in every walk of life. But the bearing was all wrong. Cameron Leasig's placid face contrasted with his intensely studious eyes. There was no nervousness in his actions or his voice; no telltale bead of sweat beading on his worried brow. It was all matter-of-fact and that bothered James a great deal.

He nodded toward the door through which Kalina had yet to return. "What about her?"

"What about her? She's got nothing to do with this."

"You made her a part of this when you brought me into her club."

Cameron paused and took a shallow breath. He leaned back into the couch as he exhaled.

"Think before you act, Special Agent Storenn. Anything comes back on Kalina and I will walk. You try to turn her or use her against me in any way; I will walk. Remember, I approached you on this. I'm not going anywhere; not that you'd let me even if I wanted to. Besides, I've got business to attend to. You just watch my back 'til Friday and I'll give you everything you'll need to close it all down."

James watched the relative ease with which Cameron Leasig delivered his little diatribe. It was obvious to James that Cameron was confident that he could deliver on his claims, that he had the information to shut it all down. Current events being what they were, James wasn't all that comfortable with another potential witness running around loose on the streets.

"If what you say is true, come in and let us protect you."

"This isn't a negotiation. The information I'm offering you is on my terms and my terms alone. I don't see that you have much of an option. It's basically no risk to you. If what I have doesn't play out, the only thing you've lost is time. But if what I say is true, it breaks your case wide open. Really, from a risk management perspective, I think you'd be jumping at the offer. It's all up side for you. You want to know more about me, you've got a couple of days to get all the information you want. You don't trust me, that's not my problem. You want the evidence you need, then you've gotta work with me."

It was James who sat back now. There wasn't a whole lot to say. He had the terms, the choice was to accept them or force his hosts hand. Force didn't seem like the road to travel at this point. You had to prove obstruction, and with the nothing he had on this guy, proving anything of the sort would be a challenge. A few days might change that.

He didn't get the chance to come back with a clever retort. The door opened and Kalina walked in carrying three glasses filled with dark liquid. With the practiced sway in her hips, James was surprised that liquid managed to stay in the cups at all. But that was supposed to be how it looked, wasn't it? He took the cup when offered and drank deeply. He needed something to get the moisture back into his mouth.

Kalina walked around the table and sat down on the arm of the easy chair next to Cameron, careful not to walk between the two men.

"Thanks."

She smiled warmly at him. "Not a problem."

An uncomfortable silence filled the room than as James sat there looking at his cup. Cameron took a sip from his drink, just as comfortable as could be, and watched James carefully.

"Tell you what, Special Agent Storenn. The USS MILIUS pulls back in Wednesday at about ten o'clock in the morning. You run those serial numbers against the master list in supply and you'll know how they're getting the product into the states."

He nodded to a small piece of paper sitting on the end table next to Storenn. James picked it up and saw it was a list of ten fifteen-digit numbers. They looked arbitrary. He looked at Cameron who just shrugged his shoulders.

"Just working on my credibility."

James nodded noncommittally.

"You let me know what you decide, Mr. Storenn. My requirements are rigid and will not change. I need to know if you can live with them and if we will indeed be working together."

James took another sip of his drink and stood up. "I'll be in touch, Mr. Leasig."

He looked down at Kalina and gave her a feeble smile. "Thank you for the drink and all your hospitality, Ms. Morris."

"You are more than welcome to stay for a while and enjoy the club as my personal guest, Mr. Storenn."

It was a very tempting offer; sitting back, downing a few beers, and letting the debauchery surround him. Out of character, but tempting none the less. The room was suddenly quite warm and the bass from the massive speakers downstairs was pounding it arcane rhythm through his veins and up into the back of his head. James needed fresh air, needed to clear his head and try to think through everything that was swimming through his brain. But that bass just kept on thumping.

"Thank you, but I'm afraid I have other plans for this evening."

With that, he turned and walked towards the door leading down into the club.

"Perhaps another time," she called after him.

Yeah, right - he thought as he headed down the stairs and into the flow of bodies below.

chapter 19

Kali watched Special Agent Storenn wend his way back through the crowded floor of the club. She frowned at the fact that his head didn't swivel once as he walked. Obviously deep in thought – a little too deep for Kali's liking - he was oblivious to the crowd and the dancers all around him.

Working in a world of fantasy and distraction, Kali had a real appreciation for people who could maintain focus. It was a true discipline. She was also of the firm belief that you could tell a lot about a man by the way he reacted to a woman, no matter what she looked like. Though his glances had been appreciative enough at the onset, they had quickly turned surgical, dissecting her every gesture and move. He wasn't looking at her; he was studying her.

The NCIS agent was not the way she originally pictured him. He was much more than the tired expression he was wearing around. He was serious and smart and paid attention to the details, his meticulously manicured nails and still smooth jaw line at this hour spoke towards that conclusion. That made Kali nervous. She questioned again the wisdom of trying this deal. Maybe it would be better to just walk.

Turning from the window, she looked with worried eyes on Cameron. He was lost in thought, never having moved from the comfortable depths of the overstuffed chair. The fingers of his right hand unconsciously tugged at his thick eyebrows. It was one of his little quirks, a tell that he had much on his mind. She watched him for a few moments and took a step in his direction. He looked up at her as she started towards him. His glower of concentration disappeared into a brilliant smile.

"Baby..." he said reassuringly, holding his arms out wide to her. She quickly moved into them, plopping down on his lap and letting him wrap her up in his warmth and strength. "Don't worry, beautiful. Everything will work out - one way or the other. It always does."

Kali pulled her head up off his thick shoulder and fixed him with a withering gaze. "I hate it when you say that."

Cameron smiled broadly. "I know. But it's true."

Kali pushed away and sat looking him in the face. She lost herself in the depths of his dark brown eyes for a moment. Blinking, she came back to herself. "Cameron, this guy is no slouch. He's gonna come after us."

"I know, baby. But he's only gonna find what I leave out for him. Have some faith. He can look around work all day long – there's nothing there for him. And we already expect taps and surveillance. Lots of questions. It's part of a game we're ready for. Just a few more days and all of this will be behind us."

His confidence lent her calm. It didn't silence her doubts, but it did sooth them, taking the edge off of the worry. She loved him for how safe he made her feel – safe even in the face of so much violence and uncertainty. She smiled a bit, knowing that however disciplined and determined Storenn was, the man holding her was even more so. That stupid grin and those big brown eyes. They gave away everything or nothing at all. Right now they were just making her tingly.

"There you go," he said in response to her smile. "Just breath deep. This'll be over before you know it."

She flashed him a broader smile, trying to ignore the warning itching at the back of her mind. Storenn wasn't going to give up and disappear. Overconfidence here would be a mistake.

"Don't worry. This is our party. He was only vaguely aware it even existed until we invited him. We've talked about this. It's planned to the nth degree. This is the time to go."

She nodded slightly. "I know," she said softly. "It's just that a lot has happened around here lately. I don't want to overlook something or play it wrong and lose everything we've worked so hard for."

Cameron nodded reassuringly. "Baby..." he started.

Kali silenced him with a hand laid gently across his mouth.

"You don't have to 'baby' me, Cameron."

Her smile was gone and her voice was all but a whisper.

"I trust you. I always have. If you say now is the time to act, then now is the time to act. I don't question that. I just worry. For us."

Cameron looked at her, his brown eyes burning with intensity. "We're gonna do this, Kali. I won't let you down."

Kali took some relief in that answer, sighing to hear the promise in his tone. It was going to be all right.

"In the meantime, I have to go make my rounds and make sure the house is doing all right."

Cameron looked at her as she stood up.

She looked back over her shoulder at him. "You comin' with me or are you gonna sit up here all night and brood?"

He smiled. "I'll roll with you. Wouldn't want the business to suffer."

"You just wanna look at all the nekkid girlies dancin' around," she said accusingly, her voice suddenly girlish and coy.

"Naw, baby," he retorted smoothly, "that's just one of the perks."

She tried to look cross but he grabbed a hold of her and pulled her down into his strong embrace, smothering her feeble protests with a smoldering kiss. After a few lusty moments she pushed herself away. Gasping for breath, flustered and flushed, she shot him a nasty look.

"Down, boy," she said, her voice mockingly stern, as she stood up and tried to adjust her hair and outfit. "We've got work to do; play will have to wait."

Smiling, Cameron stood up and took her hand. Together they headed out the door and down into the club.

chapter 20

James walked back to his car with the definite feeling he had just made a deal with the devil himself. And he was fairly certain that he had gotten the proverbial business end of the poker for his troubles. The fact that he had brought no bargaining power to the table had not helped things at all. The whole evening produced more questions than it did answers.

Hopping into his car and strapping on his seat belt, he looked up at the pink neon cartoon cat glowing over the club and shook his head.

"That was bullshit," he muttered under his breath. James hated being taken by surprise. And he had expected nothing that had happened in that meeting. Hell, most of it didn't even make sense.

Where was the motive? Sure, vengeance was a reasonable motivator for this kind of thing, but Leasig did not have that angry fire in his eyes when he delivered the line. His bearing was too relaxed, too controlled – like he was auditioning for a part in a play and was afraid of overdoing it. And with all of the violence and murder that had occurred over the past two years, Cameron Leasig's calm demeanor was more than a little unsettling. He was all confidence – like he had the inside track on a race, so there were no worries about laying it all on the line in one bet.

And why the wait? He had to know that he would have a tail on him and his woman every minute of the day until they were both in custody. What was he trying to do?

The questions nagged at the back of James Storenn's head, little idiosyncrasies rubbing his instincts the wrong way.

Definitely more going on here than meets the eye - he thought.

So now the game began. He shrugged - at least he had a couple of days to find out everything he could about the mysterious Mr. Cameron Leasig and his beautiful counterpart, Ms. Kalina Morris. Roughly thirty-six hours before the USS MILIUS pulled into port and he could check Leasig's story. A lot of work to be done in that short period of time, but James wouldn't be taken by surprise next time. Maybe he could even turn the play.

James silently hoped that Cameron's confidence was more than bravado because, though he hated to admit it, he needed Cameron Leasig. He needed his testimony and the evidence he promised to provide. He needed him to stay alive. Lose this one and another would probably never step forward. Every instinct told him to scoop Cameron Leasig up and hold him in protective custody, but that wasn't going to happen. It was an easy guess that any premature jump by him would result in Leasig clamming up and taking his game elsewhere. Leasig had been point blank with regards to that.

Six of one, half dozen of the other; James lost out either way.

He frowned at his own desperate thoughts. Then, with a sigh, he shrugged again. "Screw it. I need him," he said to the empty passenger seat.

Completely lost in thought, James unconsciously guided his car through the sparse late-night traffic. It was only when he rolled to a stop that he realized he had steered his car to the NCIS Headquarters building and not his condo. He sat there for a few minutes, the Honda's engine idling quietly as he stared at the twin globes of light on the buildings brick wall.

Oh, well - he thought - *probably wouldn't have slept anyway.*

Sighing, he shut off the car and stepped out into the cool night air.

chapter 21

She lay there watching him sleep, the moon hovering outside the window marking one half of his face with eerie yellowish light. He slept soundly, a soft snore following the rhythm of his relaxed breathing. She loved him so much, relied on him so much for his strength and calm. This plan of his made her nervous. It risked too much; it risked everything. She didn't care about the money or the house or the cars. That was just a bunch of stuff, things that could be replaced. Cameron was irreplaceable. Losing him meant losing everything she valued in her life.

She closed her dark eyes remembering the horrors of her youth. The beatings by her drunken father still haunted her dreams, bringing back the sting of shame and the mental anguish of self-blame, an unwelcome by-product of the abuse. She could see his wild eyes, crimson with drink, flashing in anger as his hand struck out at anything with the temerity to move. She had defended her mother, despite the fact that her mother never defended her; throwing herself into the fray to save her from the old man's vicious blows. She had been rewarded with a week long hospital stay for her efforts and her mother never once spoke of the incident, never thanked her or offered to leave the brute who tortured her and her young daughter. It was a week of relaxation and peace, rare commodities in her short life.

And for some reason, after having fled the torment and terror of one abusive household, she found herself marrying into another. Randy beat her relentlessly, swearing at her, telling her how worthless and ugly she was. He tortured her and he raped her and he told her that she deserved it. She wondered why, if she were so horrid he stayed with her. The only answer she came up with was the fact that he enjoyed her pain, enjoyed the fear in her eyes and the flinches at his unhappiness. He was an ogre out of a fairy tale, brutish and cruel. And he was her husband.

She began to live his lie, to accept his truths. She was stupid and ugly and useless. Perhaps she truly did deserve the beatings and mistreatment she had continually received since her earliest memories. Perhaps that was what love was. It had suited her mother. Maybe that was all that was meant for her, a life of fear and torment.

Cameron stirred in his sleep, pulling her wet-eyed from her reverie. She watched him breath, she watched him dream. He was beautiful to her. She reached out and stroked his hair softly, almost wishing he would wake up and take her in his arms and hold her in that warm embrace until she found sleep. Instead he laid there, a half smile on his placid face.

It was that beautiful face that changed her world. She could still remember the night he started bouncing at the club, the way he stood quietly watching the room. He was polite to the girls, charming. She didn't think then that he belonged there, that he was too sweet to sully himself with the likes of her and the others. But he came back night after night, sweet and polite. And then one night he talked to her. Not just in passing or simply to be polite, but an actual conversation. He asked her questions and asked her opinion and he listened when she replied, his gaze never leaving hers.

That startled her at first, the confidence and power of that gaze. She had never seen that before. Even during the worst of her days and the worst of her beatings all she had ever seen projected was anger and savagery; never power, never control.

That conversation was the first of many, and the first of many beatings she took for talking with him. On top of it all, Randy was a jealous man. But Cameron's calm soon invaded her spirit. He spoke soothingly to her, telling her that it would all work out in the end, that it always did. One way or another. She was flattered by his attention and appreciative of his friendship. He was the only man, the only person really, in all her life that truly listened to her and cared what she thought. He spoke of her worth, not in terms of money or service, but as a human, as a woman. It was overwhelming.

The night came, as had to eventually happen, when Randy, in a fit of drunken rage, challenged Cameron. Verbally at first, but when Cameron refused his baiting and insults, physically. The fight was over before it really even started; Cameron blocked Randy's clumsy swing and laid the drunk out cold with a single shot. Kalina was beside herself.

The beating she took the next day left her hospitalized for yet another week. He had beaten her with his fists, screaming in rage. And when his hands began to swell and hurt, he took off his belt and beat her until bloody welts raised on her back and legs and arms, brutal gashes opened and blood flowed freely. Cameron came and visited her in the hospital that day, vowing that her days of suffering were over, that Randy would never lay a hand on her again.

And he never did. His ship deployed ten days later for a routine two-week drug interdiction operation off the coast of Baja and when the ship returned to port, Randy wasn't onboard. Somewhere along the way, under the cover of darkness and the stealth of night, he fell overboard. No alarms were sounded until the next morning when Randy missed muster, but by then it was too late. The body was never recovered and the Navy dutifully informed the grieving widow that her husband, one Machinist Mate First Class Randall Godfrey, was indeed dead. Kalina was free.

Cameron was there for her, as he was now, lending her strength and security, two feelings she had never in her life experienced. He confided things to her, telling her of his hopes and dreams and begging of her her hopes and dreams. Until that point, she had none, but with his prodding and encouragement, she found that she could dream. She could dream big, colorful dreams.

And he touched her. That was difficult at first, the touch of his hand, gentle and kind. She had not known that for some time. It made her tremble. But it was enough for him to simply hold her. He did not pry or force or threaten. He held her and kept her safe and warm. Their familiarity grew, as did her longing to be with him as a woman, to share that last bit of herself with him. He had all else that was her; he had her heart and her smile and her laughter – all things she discovered with his help. But she wanted to give him this last bit. It took months for her courage to build, but he was patient and attentive.

And finally the night came. She went to him hungry for his sex and instead it was he who devoured her, pleasuring her as she had never known. She wept and called his name. And throughout the night he pleasured her over and over, as she begged for him and pleaded of him. She sought to give him that last bit of herself and was surprised to find that it was he that gave it to her.

She blushed as she remembered the passion of that night. The heat of his breath, the throbbing of her sex as they made love time and again. She looked over at his slumbering figure, longing for his touch. She wanted him wrapped around her, embracing her. He didn't move. He was so peaceful.

And she was so thankful. He brought peace to her life. He taught her things about herself that she'd never known, he taught her she could grow. He made her feel important and necessary. He was fiercely devoted to her and loved her unwaveringly, never questioning her past or present, just accepting her for who she was. And that trust and openness showed her the woman she could be, the woman she wanted to be. The strong, beautiful woman she was with him by her side, believing in her and challenging her to be more.

She did not know where she would be without him; she was terrified to think of the alternative paths her life might have taken had she not met him, had he not involved himself with her. Had he not drawn her to him.

She frowned. That was all at risk now. The game was on, he had said. She looked at him sadly, knowing the part she had to play in his plan and not liking it one bit. It was dangerous for the both of them, but most of the risk was his. She would give anything to keep him safe, do anything to protect him. And it still might not be enough to keep him from harm. Tears again crept into her eyes. She could not lose him. She shuddered, fear gripping her heart. He stirred at her movement, his eyes opening to small slits.

"You ok, baby?" he questioned, his voice thick with sleep.

"Just a bad dream," she replied through her silent tears. She rolled over so her back was to him, not wanting him to see her crying.

He reached out one of his thick arms and wrapped it around her waist, pulling her nude body into his. He kissed her neck gently, his light beard scratching softly against her skin. "It's all right, baby. I'm right here. It's gonna be all right." His tired voice was soothing. He held her tightly; his chest and thighs warm against the skin of her back. His fingers aimlessly caressed her throat. "It's gonna be all right."

She snuggled into him, wrapped herself tightly in his embrace. Kissing his hand, she closed her eyes.

I hope so - she thought as slumber approached.

tuesday, june 8

chapter 22

Marilyn Peters walked along the long main hallway of the NCIS Headquarters building, her dark shoes clicking on the freshly waxed tiles. She hummed tunelessly under her breath, some annoying eighties song she'd heard on the radio right before she killed the ignition to come in. Now it was stuck in her head and would remain there until she piped some other song in to replace it. Her stride bounced in time to the tune, speaking as strongly of her good mood as the sparkle in her light blue eyes. Razor sharp creases marked her dark gray pants suit and she smelled delicately of gardenias, a perfume she wore on days she woke up feeling full of energy and life.

Pushing through the door to room 1A351, the small but comfortable office she called home for some fifty hours a week, she noticed the small sheaf of papers laying on her otherwise clean wooden desk. She doffed her sport coat, hanging it on a bronze hook on the back of the door. Walking around the table, she sat down in the cloth covered chair, reached over to the small refrigerator her father had given her as a graduation gift from college and, opening it, grabbed out a can of Diet Coke. She popped the top and stretched across the table to retrieve the stack of forms.

Might as well get the day going - she thought, picking them up and settling back to see what the day had in store for her. Flipping through the papers, she got the basic gist, wiretaps and surveillance authorizations. Six of them to be exact, with immediate priority checked on each of them, of course.

She took a long pull off the soda in her hand, enjoying the icy tartness as it slid over her tongue and down her throat. She hated coffee, but loved her caffeine addiction. All the way through freshman year of college she had tried to gain an appreciation for the bitter black, but never quite managed it. Her roommate at the time, a slip of a girl with aspirations of being a lawyer had turned her on to her now daily ritual, ice-cold soda in the morning. It had gotten her through cram sessions and early mornings. Her mother would never approve, but it got her started.

Marilyn looked down at the gunmetal gray face of her watch again. 7:05. Less than two hours to go before the courthouse opened for business. She looked through the requests again, taking her time to read through the details of what was being requested and why. It was going to be a tough haul trying to push a couple of these through, the justification was thin at best. She might be able to get one or two of them to fly though.

Glad I came in early - she thought as she took another long drink from the can and pulled her PDA out of the purse on her desk, she was going to have to rearrange her entire day to meet this deadline. Slipping the thin gray stylus from its sheath, she turned on the small computer and began surfing around, making the changes she required to get the job done. Lost in her work, the music slipped unnoticed back into her brain and she unconsciously picked up the song right where she'd left it at the door, tuneless and soft; background music for the start of her day.

chapter 23

Evan was rumpled and felt like crap. No amount of coffee was going to fix that and the breakfast sandwich he'd picked up in the cafeteria on the way in to his office was, more likely than not, going to cause him to throw up. It sat there mocking him, the yellow eggs and the greasy sausage sandwiched between slices of croissant. A shudder ran through him and he wrapped the paper around the would-be breakfast and tossed it into the trashcan near his chair.

He looked down at his cup of coffee; it was blonde and sweet.

Just like I like my women - he thought with a chuckle.

Three sugars, four creamers. Mike always asked him why he didn't just order a milkshake. He chuckled again, shaking his head. The slight movement brought a grimace to his young face. His head was throbbing and his dark brown eyes were ringed with dark brownish purple circles, speaking of the extent of his celebration last night.

Evan grabbed the two assignment folders from his in-box and sat back into his gray speckled chair. He closed his sore eyes, wishing that the world would just stop turning, spinning away. There was no way he should be in the office today. The two hours of alcohol-induced sleep he had gotten were far from restorative in nature and he was dragging. That and the fact he was still probably above the legal blood alcohol limit. If he had even one day of sick leave left, he would be home in bed right now.

Yeah, hard goddamn work making it look this easy - he thought with a tired smile. Will's bachelor party had been insane. He couldn't even begin to remember how many rounds they downed, but the thousand dollars he brought out for the night was gone and he was not really sure, but he thought he might have dropped some on the plastic as well. And as far as Evan was concerned it was money well spent on a night his best friend would never forget. That was assuming Will remembered anything at all.

He'd been completely smashed when they poured him into the limousine, all the dancers blowing him kisses and wishing him luck. They shut the place down, went back to the hotel and continued to drink. He didn't remember lying down on the floor to sleep. All he remembered was the alarm screaming bloody murder in his ears and stumbling around the dark living room trying to find his clothes to come in to work.

Oh, his head hurt.

Evan opened his desk and took a bottle of aspirin out of the drawer. He counted out five of the white tablets, threw them into his mouth and washed them down with a swig of coffee. Grimacing, he swallowed.

"Shoulda called in sick. This sucks ass."

Opening the folders, he read the brief synopses. The request forms were brief, giving only rough information on the people. Not that it was overly uncommon. It was, after all, his job to fill in the blanks with details. The forms appeared to be in order, nothing out of the ordinary. Nothing, except for the required by dates highlighted at the bottom of each request. He almost choked on the mouthful of coffee. Twenty-four hours? How in the hell was he supposed to do any kind of a bio in twenty-four hours, let alone two of them?

He hated it when they did that. Every agent thought that his or her case was the most important thing going and that everyone else should drop everything they were doing to make sure they got what they needed. It took days, sometimes weeks to get together good information. He had to subpoena bank records and get tax records and go through the Office of Public Records everywhere the person had ever lived. There were police and military records to go through. It wasn't like he could just snap his fingers and information just appeared.

Twenty-four hours? Freakin' ridiculous.

He picked up the phone and called Tameric's office. It was time people understood that deadlines had to be realistic and that obscenely short notice requests simply weren't feasible. The conversation was brief and Evan slipped the handset back into its cradle, his head throbbing worse than before. Tameric had been brief and to the point.

Twenty-four hours it was.

Sipping at the coffee and hoping that the caffeine would soon react with the aspirin to alleviate the throbbing in his head, Evan picked back up the two request forms.

So much for a slow day to let his head heal.

chapter 24

Comparing the two dental records on the table in front of him, Dental Technician Second Class Thomas Pinfield allowed himself a satisfied smile. Allowing for the different names, they were identical. No one would be able to tell which was which without the actual teeth there to determine who was who. He closed the records nervously as someone walked by the door of his office.

He hated all this real life cloak and dagger shit. He much preferred the make believe digital world of his video games and the anonymity of the web world he traveled so often. The real world, with it real possibilities for danger and pain, wasn't nearly so glamorous. There wasn't a soundtrack. His stomach was so ate up with nerves he had half a mind to just drop the records into a shredder and say that he'd changed his mind. He grimaced. He wouldn't have even made the damn things if it hadn't been a personal favor. Well, that and the ten thousand dollars in twenties sitting in a manila envelope at the bottom of the green knapsack he'd stuffed into his gym bag.

It was enough money to make things better for he and Sarah, and now that he had it in his hands, he wasn't about to let it go. This was going to go a long way.

Oh, well. No use sweating it now. The work was done, the record fixed. All he had to do was file it at the base clinic and start thinking on how he was going to spend his windfall. He slid the new record into the appropriate file cabinet and dropped the old record into the shredder standing next to his desk. After a momentary thought, he slid his gym bag, cash filled backpack and all, further under his desk with the ball of his foot.

That done, he stood up and stretched his back and walked to the front of the office to inspect the appointment book. He checked the clock on the wall to see how long he had before his next appointment. Petty Officer Cianci was already five minutes late for his cleaning. Much later and it would start pushing back the day's schedule.

chapter 25

James lifted his head from his desk as Vincent Tameric stepped into his office. He was bleary eyed, unshaven and had a headache the size of Texas. Lines criss-crossed his left cheek, impressions from the wrinkles of his shirtsleeve.

"You look like crap."

"Thanks, it took me all night to put this together." He yawned wide. "You wouldn't happen to have any coffee on you?"

Vincent shook his head in the negative. "You get any sleep last night?"

"Some," James replied, patting his desk with one hand and trying to cover another yawn with the other. "Crashed here for a few hours – had work to do."

Vincent nodded, a concerned look clouding his face. "I'll buy that. So what exactly was it that I missed yesterday?"

"What do you mean?" James sounded puzzled.

"Let's see, yesterday morning you reported to the chain of command and the DEA that you lost your only witness in this case and were pretty much left empty handed. I left you here in this office with orders to get your team together and that's the last I saw of you. This morning, I came in to find out that you have half of the department jumping through hoops to meet twenty four and thirty six hour deadlines – all concerning individuals I've never even heard of. Matter of fact, I just got off the phone with a very agitated Evan Pinsone from the bio's division. You're not making any friends there, you know. You've also made arrangements to run a search and seizure on the USS MILIUS when it pulls in tomorrow morning." Vincent sat down in the chair across the desk. "So, what did I miss?"

Big yawn. "You wouldn't believe it if I told you."

It was a stern gaze that met his seeming indifference. "Dazzle me, James."

Vincent's eyes went wide as he listened to the story James spun about his previous evening's activities.

"…so in a nutshell, he says he'll deal and that he's got enough to bury everyone involved."

"So bring him in." Vince sounded excited.

"Can't," James said shaking his head. "Won't come in except on his terms. He says he needs 'til Friday to get his stuff together and then he'll play."

"Bullshit! Screw Friday - you bring his ass in! These guys have killed anyone who's even thought of talking and you can't afford to lose this one. I want his ass locked up in a safe house."

"Vince, I feel the pressure to make this work more than anyone, even you. I know what losing this guy means. But I've got nothing to pin on him, at least nothing I know of. I have less than nothing on him. He wasn't even on the radar."

James fought to keep the strain out of his voice; this was the break he'd been looking for. He didn't know how he knew it, but he did. All of his misgivings aside, Cameron Leasig was their man. Then again, maybe it was just the exhaustion playing with emotions.

"And there's something else going on here, Vince. The guy's way too cool about it. It's one of those too-good-to-be-true type situations. With everything else going on, and then this just drops out of the sky? I don't like it. But like he said last night, I don't have to. I've got no choice in it. I'm telling you, Vince, the guy's like ice. And I believe him when he says he'll walk if we push him."

The thick vein running down the middle of Vincent Tameric's head was throbbing near the point of explosion. It was the barometer of Vince's temper. James wondered morbidly how much more stress would need to be applied to make that thing pop. Probably not much at all.

"If we give this guy the time he wants, it gives us time to do our homework on him, time to figure him out. We'll get backgrounds and surveillance wires, fill in some of the gaps and see where this guy falls out in the bigger scheme. Maybe we can get something and beat him to the punch. I just don't want to force it. Desperation isn't going to help us."

Vincent nodded his head slightly, chewing silently on James' plea. That was definitely what it was – a plea.

"And what about his safety? We're oh for three on that one."

James winced at that. "I don't think this guys gonna have any real problems with that. Can't give you any concrete reasons why, but I think this guy's got teeth. Anyone who steps up on him is probably gonna end up worse for the wear because of it."

"And the woman?"

James shrugged. "Don't know where she fits in, if she fits in at all. That's where the research comes in."

"Watch your step with her," Vincent warned. "I don't want some expensive assed lawyer pelting me with harassment claims. We'll end up in paperwork 'til Judgment Day."

"I'll be careful," James said reassuringly. "Sarah Rollins is handling her initial interviews this morning."

"Good, keep me posted." Vincent stated as he stood and turned for the door. He looked down at his watch. "Don't you have a meeting with the coroner this morning? Get a shower. Shave. Eat. You look like shit."

"Yeah, I'll get right on that," James said to Vince's retreating back. He pushed himself away from the desk, joints creaking and popping with every movement. Every muscle from his ears on down was sore.

Yeah - he thought - *a hot shower would feel good.*

chapter 26

Kalina stretched out her hamstrings and her calves. Rolling her ankles, she tried to loosen them up, preparing for a long run. The doubts and worries of the previous night still clouded her thoughts and her eyes. She didn't notice the cloudless sky overhead or the light, cool breeze coming in off of the water, lost in her dark thoughts.

She hated the Navy, hated it with everything she had in her. She hated the hold it had on her life, the thoughtless control it wielded. It was dispassionate and relentless, enforcing its decisions with phrases like 'needs of the Navy'. Screw her needs or Cameron's needs. It was the Navy's needs that mattered most. It was their needs that were served by him going away for months at a time to patrol some other country's coastline. She hated the social referendums that reduced the military to nothing more than a giant social experiment for politicians ignorant of the consequences their actions had on the members serving their country. It was crappy pay for long hours of work and contracts that bound too tightly for years at a time. They would have fled the area and the Navy years ago had Cameron not still been under contract to those ghouls. And if he just left, it would be considered a federal offense. Desertion, they called it.

Of the many criticisms she had of the Navy, probably the greatest was the forced separations from Cameron when he was on deployment. She understood that she was being selfish, but she didn't care. Throughout her life, others had been ordering her around, making asinine rules for her to obey. Now that she had something good, she hated them taking that away, seemingly on whim. She hated that time apart and how it dragged. Having to go on with her life like nothing was wrong, being expected to smile and carry on like business as usual when she couldn't talk to him. She knew she relied on his confidence and love to get through the day, but the small things cut to the bone as time wore on. She missed his voice and his touch and his curiosity about her day. He hadn't deployed in almost two years but the misery of those days still haunted her.

Her anger and frustration drove her legs on, pumping as she made her way down towards the beach. Sweat beaded on her forehead and ran in tiny rivulets down her cheeks. Her face was flushed and her breathing was heavy. Her long stride ate up the distance, with miles of concrete and asphalt falling away beneath her.

She had derided Cameron during his last re-enlistment, telling him it was a mistake. Facing another eighteen months of sea duty, Cameron protested that the only way for him to be around was to extend so that he could finish out at a shore station instead of being stuck on a ship. She'd reluctantly agreed, but now, with almost a year left on his contract, she began to question whether it had been worth it. Time and circumstance were working against them; events were spiraling now and there was not an out other than the dangerous game Cameron was playing. He jokingly called the Navy 'the Canoe Club'. She swore whenever she made reference to it, softening her curses in his presence, knowing that he was powerless to change the system. Either way, she couldn't wait until their membership expired and the demands of the Navy weren't hanging over their heads, a nameless, faceless entity controlling their lives.

Which of course was in direct contrast to the pride she felt whenever she saw him in his uniform. He looked good in uniform, pressed and polished, his rows of ribbons marking the milestones of his career. Her dislike of the Navy never stopped her from slipping into a ball gown and running off to the Navy Day Ball with him to spend an evening steeped in naval tradition and dancing. She settled on the fact that it was a love-hate relationship. She loved him and the job that he did and she hated the organization he worked for and the job he did. There was no use trying to make sense of it, it would all be over soon and she was glad of the fact.

She was almost surprised to see the house appearing up the street; the circuit was run. She couldn't remember a single section of the route, her feet guiding her unconsciously around her memorized tract. Her lungs burned and her legs ached, the strong muscles pushed hard. Slowing to a walk, she pushed the hair back from her forehead and stretched her rib cage, allowing sweet oxygen to fill her lungs.

chapter 27

James regretted his decision to keep Jessica out of the loop all over again the second he walked back through the door to his office. The shower in the locker room was boiling hot and the water pressure was high. The spray and heat had done wonders for the knotted muscles in his back. He was distracted by that moment of relaxation. Jessica froze mid-pace as he opened the door and stepped into the room. She turned to face him and James wanted to run. Jessica was livid, her pretty face colored with emotion. One hand was balled into a tight fist; the other gripped a handful of forms. She looked like a lioness eyeing a gazelle, preparing herself for the pounce and the kill. Anticipation and bloodlust commingled with the heat of anger. James gritted his teeth for the assault.

"What the hell is this?" she demanded, flinging the papers in his face. The pages separated in the air, flying in all directions and scattering across the floor. James made no move to block them and a few hit their mark, slapping against his cheek and falling to join their partners on the carpeted ground. "Did I miss the memo?"

The lack of surprise on James' tired face only infuriated her more.

"Why the hell didn't you call me, James? I'm supposed to be your partner on this and you're off playing cowboy or pirate or whatever the hell game you think this is! Gonna save the world on your own? That's bullshit!"

James didn't know how to begin. He knew that any claims of embarrassment would be taken the wrong way and only piss her off all the more. He tried to think quickly but she was closing on him, glowering as she came. All of his excuses escaped him. Not wanting to be backed up against the door, he pushed by her and moved behind his desk in hopes of opening the distance between them. Jessica moved with him and was right there as he plopped down into his chair. He held up his hand, preventing her from getting right up into his face.

"I know you're pissed, Jess, and I don't have a good answer for not calling you in on the meeting. I knew it was wrong the second I showed up, but it was too late to do anything about it."

"Too late? How was it too late? All it would have been was a phone call letting someone know what the hell you were up to so that if you disappeared there was a starting point to look for you. A way to trace your steps. That was as stupid as the crap those guys pulled on Sunday. You had no idea what you were walking in to and you didn't even think to give me a heads up – even afterwards? You think I'm pissed? Pissed doesn't even begin to describe it!"

There was no way to argue with the logic. He knew that what he'd done was first class stupidity and that it brought his evaluation of her and her contributions into a very critical light. It looked bad.

"Jess…"

She didn't let him get started. "Don't 'Jess' me! I want an answer. No double talk or 'what's done is done' bullshit; but an answer. Why the hell did you leave me out of this?"

He was tired, exhausted really. The highs and lows were wearing on him. The long hours behind the desk made his bones hurt. He felt like a guitar strung too tightly to play correctly; an instrument whose strings would snap if handled roughly. He felt vibration in his chest and instead of fighting he just gave in. He'd fought for everything over the past several months and was tired of the uphill battles. The last thing he wanted was to fight with Jessica. He did not want it to be her small hands that broke him. He sighed an enervated sigh and pushed back into his chair. She was going to be insulted; there was no way around it.

"I was embarrassed."

Jessica was dumbfounded. "Of what?"

James could see the worst possible scenarios flashing behind her eyes. He jumped in before she could lose her temper again. "The strip club. The meeting was at Club Kittie and I was embarrassed about it. It shouldn't matter because you're a cop on the case, but it did matter because you're you and asking you to go to a strip club with me – regardless of the reason – was embarrassing."

His cheeks were warm and he had to force himself to maintain eye contact with the diminutive woman standing two feet away from him. The barrage he expected didn't come. Instead, Jessica looked flustered, as if she were ready for any answer other than the one he gave. She started to speak, but stopped short.

"It was still stupid," she finally managed.

James sat there for several seconds looking at her, giving her a chance to rail at him and get it out of her system if that was what she really needed to do. He could see the fire was still in her eyes, she just didn't know what to do with it. She finally leveled a withering gaze on him, obviously meant to carry the seriousness of what she was about to say. She leaned in close, looking for all the world as though she wanted to bite him.

"Don't ever do that to me again, James. Embarrassment or no, we're partners on this. When you negate my presence, it allows everyone else to do the same; and I can't have that. Are we on the same page?"

James held her gaze, not challenging but accepting her decree. He nodded slightly. "We're there."

She blinked and the flames were gone. The problem was solved and it was time to move on. "You look like hell."

He shrugged. "Yeah, I've heard that somewhere. Thought the shower would've helped on that front."

Her nose wrinkled. "Didn't say you stank, though now that you mention it..."

James grimaced.

"Don't think that you're getting off that easy. We've got forty five minutes to get over to Verdin's office for the ME's report, you can fill me in on the way."

James looked down at his watch. The morning was getting away from him. Jessica spun away from his desk and headed for the door. Grace of a dancer, even in the most basic of movements. He pushed himself up to follow her out.

"Mind if we stop to get something to eat?" he asked. "I'm starving."

She looked at him incredulously.

"We're on our way to look at a butchered body and discuss the gruesome details of how it happened and you want to stop and get something to eat?"

James didn't answer for a moment, thinking on it. He nodded on their way out the door. "Yeah, I'm gonna need something to tide me over until lunch. Maybe a bagel or something."

"Well, no sympathy from me if you puke all over the place. You get any of it on my shoes, and Verdin will have two bodies on his table."

"Duly noted. Food. Now. Please."

The 'please' was an afterthought, no reason to push his luck.

chapter 28

The lounge was an efficient room, squeezed in between the restrooms and a storage closet. An ancient soda machine hummed in the far corner of the room, bridging the distance between an even older candy machine and a worn out microwave that smelled permanently of burnt popcorn. A talking head from one of the generic cable news channels droned on about the non-news story of the day on a relatively new television set anchored on the wall in front of a stained blue couch.

Noah hated talking business here but Cameron insisted that it was safer than pretty much anyplace else they could meet. It was hiding out in the open, two sailors having a conversation at work. Noah wasn't so sure he was gonna buy that particular bridge. This was his building and his work mates they were tempting fate with. If Cameron though that it was such a smooth idea, why weren't they getting together in the lounge next to his office?

"So dropping by my office is your idea of creating some distance?" Noah demanded.

Cameron brushed off the questions without even blinking. "Special Agent Storenn of the NCIS paid me a little visit at Kali's place last night."

"What? Why didn't you call me and let me know?"

"What would've been the point of calling you at one in the morning?"

Noah let out an exasperated sigh. "Well, for one thing, you wouldn't have had to drag your ass out here to talk to me about it. What did he want?"

Noah was all ears. His guy in the NCIS hadn't been able to dig anything up. As far as he knew, Cameron's name had never so much as been uttered in the building on Welles Street.

"Started with questions about Monk, turned into questions about money and the club. Dropped some so subtle references to the fact that this was more than a run-of-the-mill canvas, that I was considered a 'person of interest' and that he would be looking more closely into my finances and such."

Noah noticed the color change in Cameron's face and swallowed a smile before it had a chance to form. Cameron looked irritated, as though speaking about the incident pricked at him physically, ruffling his normally smooth exterior. It took a lot to ruffle Cameron, and the fact that he was sitting here now looking so perturbed soured Noah's initial feelings of triumph.

"You blaming me, Mr. I-drive-around-in-a-brand-new-BMW? I'm surprised you haven't attracted more attention than this; flashing all that cash, handing out loans like you were the Navy fucking Federal Credit Union."

What the hell did you think was going to happen? Sooner or later someone was bound to start asking questions."

Cameron leaned back in the metal and faux leather chair. "Hello, green eyed monster. Don't go gettin' all pissy 'cause I can roll. My cash is doing the exact same thing yours is – sitting in some off shore account collecting dust and interest. Everything I'm spending is club money!"

"So what? That money sets you apart, the car sets you apart. How many times have you warned me about the virtues of being invisible? I warned you when you hooked up with that bitch and started all of this private sector crap that it was going to come back to haunt you. But you didn't listen. You went ahead with your grand plans and trying to play the Don. Now you're surprised when the feds show up on your doorstep playing twenty questions about the money you're throwing around? C'mon, Cameron, don't insult me by playing stupid. We both know better."

A razor sharp glare held him and Noah knew he'd scored a hit. Anything having to do with Kalina was pretty much a sore point between them, especially when it came to the club and the lifestyle the two of them led. Noah remembered easier times between he and Cameron. But those were before Kalina and all of the drama and responsibility that came with her. He respected Cameron's dedication to the woman, but he'd never let some bitch run his life like that, no matter how fine she was. Noah probably would have tried to burn Kalina down years ago except for the fact he knew that any attempt to do so would result in an immediate, probably deadly, reaction from Cameron. Besides, she kept him happy and working, and that's what counted in the end. Except that now, those excesses in their living might well be jeopardizing his continued affluence and he couldn't have that. He thought back to Monday and the misgivings he'd had. What his first gut reaction had been. He tried to return Cameron's gaze without provoking him any more.

"Look, if there's an explanation for the money, give it to them and get them off your back. I don't know where they got your name, but I wouldn't look too far from home on it. You brought this spotlight down on yourself, make them turn it off."

The glare was still there. "I'll do what explaining I can, but I'm telling you, there's more to this than basic math. Someone's trying to burn me and I'm going to find out who it is, with or without your help."

The statement was pointed and Noah knew where.

"You do what you've gotta do. I told you I would look into it and I am. Nothings comin' up. You want to go off the reservation and start tearin' shit up – go crazy. But I'd wait 'til your friends in the NCIS turn their attentions elsewhere before you start dropping bombs."

He didn't get a reply, just more silence. Cameron stood up. "I don't know what the game is, Noah, but I don't like it. I'm tired of getting played."

Noah watched him turn his back and walk away for the second time that week. The only thing going through his mind this time was complete agreement with Cameron's statement. Noah was tired of getting played too.

chapter 29

Special Agents Sarah Rollins and Robert Keleman stepped out of Sarah's midnight blue Volkswagen Jetta. Sarah loved coming out to Coronado; the big houses, the Hotel del Coronado. She had come out so many times as a little girl, looking at the houses and walking through the shops. She'd always wanted to live out here, but the cost made it completely impractical. Maybe in a few years when she picked up some seniority and the pay that came with it she would be able to afford the move.

She looked over at Keleman and grinned an exasperated grin. He was like a big puppy dog, all fidgety and full of nervous energy. He was baby faced, smooth skin that required a razor every other day. At best. His diminutive height only added to the feeling that she was working with a teenager. But behind those electric blue eyes and that easy smile lurked a photographic memory and enough curiosity to ruin just about any bad guys day. She'd never dealt with the rookie before, but by all accounts very little escaped his notice.

Sarah adjusted her perfectly pressed blue suit, picked up her Italian leather briefcase, nodded towards Keleman and headed towards the massive house in front of them. To anyone watching, the pair was a study in contrast; his exuberance was offset by her control, his eyes sparkled with excitement while her gray green eyes were serious and studious, his hair was flipped carelessly to the side while hers was pulled straight back and perfectly done. She lacked his freshness and he lacked her seasoned expertise.

Up the carefully manicured walk, they wended their way past pruned bushes and professionally arranged and maintained flowers. Sarah couldn't help but admire the tightly controlled beauty of the landscaping, the attention to detail in the placement of the shrubs and selection of blooms.

Stepping up onto the porch, Robert reached out and thudded the antique doorknocker against its plate.

Knock, knock; it echoed through the house.

No answer.

Knock, knock.

"Who's there?" came a woman's voice from a cleverly concealed intercom system.

Robert and Sarah both looked around trying to identify a speaker. Not seeing one, Robert simply answered. "Special Agents Keleman and Rollins, ma'am."

"Special Agents Keleman and Rollins, ma'am, who?" came the erstwhile reply. Sarah rolled her eyes and Robert looked perplexed. "Pardon me, ma'am?"

The massive wooden door swung open silently and the two agents were met by a long - legged woman wearing only a sports bra, spandex shorts and a pair of beat up sneakers. Sweat rolled down out of her midnight hair, matting it to her forehead. Her high cheekbones were flushed pink. "You've really gotta come up with a better punch line," she said leaning against the edge of the door, a small white towel in her free hand.

Sarah looked at her partner and rolled her eyes in disgust. Keleman was standing there with a vacuous grin on his face, looking very much like he'd never seen a woman before. Sarah half expected his tongue to loll out of his mouth, the cartoon wolf in the Droopy cartoons, and start dripping saliva on his shoes.

"Yeah, we'll get on that," she said, embarrassed for her sophomoric partner. "Are you Ms. Kalina Morris?"

The woman smiled broadly, her eyes flashing brightly. It was a brilliant smile, Sarah had to admit.

"Yes, I am. And you would be…" she left the question hanging.

"Agents Keleman and Rollins, Naval Criminal Investigative Service," Sarah repeated indicating her partner and herself accordingly. Both of them flipped open and presented their credentials.

"Lovely. And what would the Naval Criminal Investigative Service like this morning?"

"We'd just like to ask you a few questions."

Kalina looked at the two of them, curiosity wrinkling her smooth face. "Regarding?"

Sarah regarded her evenly. "Regarding your relationship with a Mr. Cameron Leasig."

"Is he in some kind of trouble?"

Sarah tried to be reassuring, "No ma'am. This is just a routine follow up. A few questions to help us establish some background information."

Kalina stepped back into the house and held the door open. "Please come on in."

They walked through the broad foyer, following their hostess into the living room. Sarah gave Keleman another dirty look to which he smiled sheepishly and shrugged. She looked around the room appreciatively. It was well appointed with light carpets and high ceilings. A tan couch and matching love seat sat in the middle of the room perpendicular to one another, the corners framing a blonde wood coffee table covered with various magazines; Surfer Magazine, Kiplinger's Personal Finance, and Writer's

Digest among them. A large bookcase lined the far wall. It was loaded with an eclectic collection of hardbound books, both old and new. The entire back of the room was glass with a set of French doors leading out to a beautifully manicured back yard. A large painting hung on the near wall, a tasteful piece of modern art by an artist unknown to her.

"I like what you've done with the place," Sarah said.

"Thanks," Kalina replied. "We redid the room last fall. The lighter colors just seem to make it feel more open." She waved her hand at the large couch, offering them a seat. She remained standing.

Both agents sank into the depths of the couch, Sarah smiling slightly. It was important to put people at ease, keep it light and they had a tendency to ramble, giving up information without even thinking about it.

"So you want to know about my relationship with Cameron Leasig. Why don't you just ask him?" Kalina said facing the both of them.

Sarah returned her intent gaze. "We will Ms. Morris. Right now we'd just like to ask you a few questions."

"Please, call me Kalina."

Sarah pulled a blue, wire bound notebook from the depths of her briefcase. She would have preferred to use her digital recorder, but knew the general reaction of people who knew they were being recorded. For some reason, the display of that little recorder made everything official and they clammed up, afraid they would say something stupid or that the recording would be used against them later.

"All right, Kalina, can you describe your relationship with Mr. Leasig?"

"Yes, I can."

The room was silent. The two agents sat there looking at her expectantly. She simply smiled back at them as if waiting for the next question. Sarah glanced over at Keleman.

"Kalina, your relationship with Mr. Leasig?"

Kalina shook her head. "Actually, no. Not without embarrassing the both of you or sounding like some mushy Hallmark card. For the record, let's just say that we're together."

"We can do that. How long have the two of you been together?"

"I'd say seven, maybe eight years." Kalina squinted, apparently counting back. "Yeah, I'd go with eight years."

"And how did you come to know Mr. Leasig?"

"He was bouncing at the club. He was really nice and we used to talk all of the time. He was gentle and he listened. It was a nice change of pace. Then after Randy died, well we just sorta happened, you know? We've been together ever since."

A distant, reminiscing look came over her as she said it, remembering a happy time, a time of comfort and relative ease. She wasn't looking at the two agents sitting in her living room; she was looking at Cameron Leasig and the goodness he brought to her life.

Sarah scribbled in her notebook, a short hand she would have to transcribe later. She looked up when she was done and saw Kalina looking at her curiously.

"Sorry, I don't mean to be rude, writing while you speak. I'm listening to you, but I want to make sure that I am capturing your answers accurately," Sarah said apologetically.

"Why don't you just use a tape recorder? It'd be much easier."

Sarah smiled through clenched teeth. "Yes, I'm sure you're right about that."

An uncomfortable silence filled the space between them. Nice and easy, Sarah reminded herself. Just push on through the quiet.

"You were married to Randall Godfrey for three years."

Kalina held up her hand, stopping her from going on. "I would really prefer it if we didn't talk about that."

"Really, Ms. Morris, it would be very helpful," Keleman interjected.

Kalina fixed him with an icy glare. "How?"

Sarah heard the change in their subject's voice, the hard edge that slid along the word. A nerve had been struck. She tried to warn Keleman off with a look but he just plowed on ahead.

"Well, as we said earlier, we're trying to establish a baseline here, gather anything germane to the case we're working." He finished with a smile on his youthful face.

Sarah braced herself. So much for nice and easy.

Kalina was a statue at the end of the couch, clearly struggling with how to respond. "Agent Keleman?" she started, her voice tight.

He nodded, the smile still planted on his grill.

Sarah wanted to smack him. How stupid are you, Bob?

"How does it help your case to know that Randy hospitalized me six different times? That I used to change in the bathroom so that I could put make-up over all the bruises on my back and arms and legs? That I spent three years in hell, praying for either relief or release? You have the police reports - the complaints, the arrest reports, the hospital records. It didn't really seem to matter much to you while it was happening, why would it possibly interest you now? How could knowing any of that be helpful to your investigation?"

Keleman was having a hard time holding her gaze. Sarah was inspecting her notebook, embarrassed for him and the massively untenable situation he was in. She scanned the list of pre-written questions, looking for something to salvage the interview and bring Kalina back down into her comfort zone.

"How did you come to own Club Kittie?" she interjected.

Kalina scratched her eyebrow, turning her attention to Sarah.

"Bought it, though I'm not sure what my ownership of Kittie has to do with anything."

Sarah put on her most attentive face, trying to look as harmless and eager as possible. "Just trying to establish background info, Ms. Morris. You know what they say – the devil's in the details."

It was starting to sound passé, even to her ears. Of course what she could have added, if she wanted to spice things up, was that they could get pretty much all of the information they were looking for from the public record, which was exactly what they were going to do anyway to validate her story. Of course subpoenas could help fill in any remaining gaps, but this was supposed to be nice and easy. Subpoena talk probably wouldn't do much to help that. She gave a reassuring smile, dropping the hint in a not so subtle way, waiting for the rest the story.

"So how did you come to own Club Kittie?"

"The owner was into someone for a lot of cash. Cameron talked to him and struck a deal, and next thing I know I own forty nine percent of the club. Saving every cent I made from the club and my dancing and living on Cameron's pay, we bought him out about a year later."

"So Cameron's part owner of 'Club Kittie'?" Sarah asked.

"No, it's mine. One hundred percent. I couldn't have done it without him, but my name is the only one on the title. He does help me manage the place. Helps keep the peace is more like it."

Sarah scribbled away, thinking of questions as quickly as she was writing down answers.

Kalina jumped up from the couch, a look of dismay on her face. "Oh, God. Where are my manners? Can I offer either of you a drink, some soda or juice?"

Sarah looked up. "Uh, sure. Coke would be fine, if you have it. Thanks."

Keleman nodded in affirmation and Kalina hurried off through the door towards what could only be the kitchen. Sarah watched her go and turned to her partner.

"Excellent push on the whole dead husband thing," she said sarcastically. "Do they still teach interrogation at the academy?"

"Hey, I was just trying to back you up."

"Well, take it easy there, Torquemada. She's not under subpoena; she's got no obligation to speak with us. As long as we keep her relaxed and talking, we get free information. No lawyers, no paperwork, just answers to questions. Now isn't the time to push with the hard questions."

Keleman winced. Sarah hated feeling like some overbearing school marm, but she wasn't about to let Keleman's inexperience screw things up. Especially not with a peripheral line of questioning. The point was to keep it friendly. Confrontational could come later, if necessary.

Keleman looked around the room. "Sure is a nice place," he said, obviously trying to change the subject.

Sarah let him go. She glanced around the understated room. 'A place for everything and everything in its place', she recited silently, recalling her grandmother's favorite saying.

"Yeah, it is a beautiful piece of property."

Keleman chuckled, looking at her. "Bet it took one hell of a lot of lap dances to pay for this place."

Sarah whipped her head around to shoot him an angry look and thought she was going to die. Idiot boy's timing could not have been worse. Kalina stood some ten feet behind him, two glasses of soda gripped in white knuckled hands. Watching the muscles of her forearms strain, Sarah wondered if the glasses might shatter. Fire burned in Kalina's eyes and her beautiful face was already darkening to an angry red. She stomped over towards them, soda splashing out of the glasses and running down her hands and dripping on the light carpet. Rolling around the padded arm of the couch, she confronted Keleman, insulted and outraged.

"Who the hell do you think you are? Coming in to my house…" she couldn't find the words to express her anger. Her hands shook, splashing Keleman with soda from the now half empty glasses.

He tried to stand but she towered over him, refusing to move. If possible, his face was even more crimson than hers, embarrassment marking his face with heat and color. There was no possible response, he'd said what he'd said and there was no way to un-ring that bell.

Kalina poured the remnants of the soda over Keleman's head and slammed the empty vessels on the table. Sarah was afraid she might throw them, not that her partner didn't deserve it. The insult was blatant and obscene and Sarah refused to step forward and help this time. He would get what he got.

Empty handed, Kalina stepped back. Her voice was calm and ice cold. "You want to know about Cameron and I, I'll tell you. The man means more to me than you will ever know. Everything I am today, *everything*, is thanks to him. I would die for him. Gladly. And the last thing I will ever do is provide the two of you information to go after him. If you want to speak to me, contact my lawyer. You come back here again and I will file a harassment complaint you wouldn't believe. Now get out of my house."

Her eyes never left Keleman's face. Without saying a word, he got up off of the wet couch and headed for the door. Sarah followed just as silently, fuming at Keleman's stupidity.

"Oh, and, Agent Keleman," Kalina called out.

He stopped and turned around.

"I'll have one of my girls stop by with a bill for the cleaning of the couch and the carpet."

He turned back around and the both of them walked outside, Sarah shutting the door quietly behind them. She could barely contain the fury that was percolating. Her pulse pounded in her head as they walked down the drive to her car.

Five questions!

Five whole questions. That had to be some kind of record. In her entire time with the Service, she had never seen an interview go down that miserably or that quickly. It was the Titanic of interviews.

The car beeped as they drew near, the doors unlocking. Sarah opened her door and sat down, sliding the key into the ignition. She started the car and slipped it into gear while Keleman was still getting in. He sat quickly, shutting the door and grabbing at his seat belt as she gunned the engine and the car shot backwards.

"Sarah," he started.

"Shut up! I don't want to hear it." It was acid.

"But I ..."

She slammed on the brakes, cutting him off with a brief squeal of rubber. She stared out the windshield, regarding the world moving around them. Such a beautiful summer day beyond that glass, peaceful and calm. She tried to let that calm soak into her, damp her anger. It wasn't working.

"One more word, Bob. Just one more and your ass will be walking back to headquarters."

She didn't look to see the expression of shock and acceptance that painted his face. She waited a few seconds for the message to sink in, let the silence settle over them before stomping on the gas and sending the car speeding forward with a burp of burnt rubber.

chapter 30

James stepped out of the autopsy room, sweat glistening on his brow and the chorizo and egg breakfast burrito he'd wolfed down earlier churning violently in his stomach. Virden had eyed him angrily when the phone went off, the ringing interrupting his graphic dissertation on the various physical violations of Anderson Monk's person. James took the ringing cell phone as a God-send, far preferring to be embarrassed by an intruding phone call forcing him from the room than by spewing half digested chunks of egg and sausage and tortilla all over the floor. Him puking up his breakfast would've given Jessica far too much satisfaction.

He gulped fresh air; glad to be away from the smells of decay and blood. With his stomach slowly untying itself, he held the phone up to his ear. "Hey, Marilyn. What do you have for me?"

"In a word - notadamnthing. I knew that a couple of the requests wouldn't fly, but Judge Connors said no to all of them - not enough evidence. Well, that and the abbreviated time frame. We're only asking for a couple of days worth of coverage. He said it was desperate and that he wasn't going to get drawn into the harassment suit we were building against ourselves."

She sounded depressed and exhausted. Marilyn Peters was a pit bull and James knew it had to be tough for her to strike out like that. It wasn't all sympathy for her delicate nature though; not getting those taps was a real kick in the crotch for his case.

"Hey, don't beat yourself up. It was a long shot at best. I was the one who put in requests for everything under the sun. I mistakenly figured that the cards would have to fall our way at some point. Thanks for the effort."

James was sorely disappointed. He hadn't really expected all of the requests to fly, but there was a very real expectation that he would get at least one. Just one to get his ears in there on something, get some inside information that might shed some light on Cameron Leasig and his intentions.

"Not a problem, James. I just wish I could have gotten at least one of those things to walk for you."

He tried to smile at her over the phone, put some pep in his voice. "Don't worry about it. We don't need a writ to put a tail on them or work the background info. We'll just have to make do with what we have for now."

"Well, just wanted you to know where we ended up on it. I'll look the requests over again this afternoon and see if I can't think of another way to approach this, maybe change the wording and get one of these through Connors yet. Keep me posted on how things go, maybe something will come up that I can use for fodder."

"Sounds good, Marilyn. I'll make sure to keep you in the loop."
"I'll let you know if there's any progress on this end."
"Thanks. I'll talk to you then."

James pressed the hook button and closed the small phone. Not the news he'd been hoping for, but at least he could move forward solidly from here. He looked up and down the empty hallway, stalling his return to the autopsy room. He got the point; Anderson Monk died a horrible death. The level of detail as to how it happened and viewing the damage to the body in such an intimate way was a little overwhelming. His stomach was still roiling. He wasn't sure how much longer he was going to be able to last in there. Of course, there couldn't possibly be that much more to show. Sighing, James breathed in and headed back into the fray.

chapter 31

Kalina was furious. It was the stereotype she hated and the one that made her never mention what it was she did. She didn't really care that she'd danced or that she owned a strip club. She'd never been overly proud of it, but she was far from ashamed. People in 'polite' society could think what they would about her, but she'd earned her way through this world, fighting every step of the way. And now, now that she'd come so far, she refused to apologize for surviving circumstances they could never comprehend from the safety and comfort of their bought and paid for sideline seats.

She grew up lean and hard, and when she had needed money to eat, dancing put food on the table. She wasn't a drug addict and she wasn't a whore, she was a dancer - though few, including the male patrons, ever recognized the difference. Her body didn't embarrass her; she loved it, both in form and function. She wouldn't apologize for that either and she couldn't stand the way that people looked down their noses at her like she was human trash because of it.

Those two-faced guys that snubbed her and talked smack about her for their girlfriends' sakes were the same ones that had spent their evenings dumping dollar bills on the stage and twenties and fifties into her garter belt just for a chance to be closer and feel her touch. They were the same guys that, now that she owned the club, had made her a millionaire several times over and ensured that her girls would stay employed for as long as the stages were there to dance on.

Kalina hadn't danced in years and she didn't miss it. Cameron showered her with adoration, enough to satisfy any needs for attention she could have. And not just in a sexual way. He made her feel special, necessary. Like he couldn't survive without her by his side.

But for some reason others could never get past the fact that she had danced; like she could never grow or evolve into something more. She hated to admit it; it had taken Cameron a while to convince her of that very same thing. That she could be more. That she could go to college, own a business, be involved with things she believed in. Too many years of being looked at like a piece of meat, a product to be passed around.

But she refused to be seen that way now; she drew the line at that. It was not who she was. Yet, the insults and comments had found their way into her home. The cops asking her questions about Cameron and looking at her like she was back up on the stage again. That rude-assed NCIS agent, coming into their house and insulting her, it chaffed.

She hoped that she hadn't screwed Cam with her reaction, but there was no way she was going to let it slide. Besides, that female agent, Sarah Rollins, looked ready to spit nails when they walked out. She expected that the glass of soda and her tirade were going to seem pleasant compared to what he was going to get when he got in that car to go back to the office. Fuck him, he deserved it. It would get a lot worse if he tried to use any of it against Cameron. Much worse.

Dabbing at the soda on the couch with a wet paper towel, she tried to calm herself, but cleaning up after the jerk wasn't quite doing it. She knew something that would, though. Sitting down on the far side of the couch, making sure to avoid the surprisingly large mess she'd made of the cushions, Kalina picked up the phone and began dialing.

"Hello. Edmund Howeth, please."

chapter 32

It was a good day for the market. Stocks soared and Noah watched the clock as well as the television on the far wall, he was waiting for lunchtime so he could head home, get on-line and check out some of his accounts. Not only did he want to see what his portfolio was doing, he wanted to check on whether or not the deposit had been made in his account for a delivery that was supposed to have taken place yesterday. He loved getting paid. It made the game worth it, all the intrigue and the headaches.

Speaking of headaches, he also had to check to see if there was any news from his 'friend' out at NCIS headquarters. He'd written an e-mail from one of his ghost accounts requesting information and was expecting an answer soon.

The small box in the lower corner of the screen flipped from the NASDAQ to the S&P. The market was up another five points.

Screw it - he thought.

"Hey, Chris, I'm gonna get some chow. I'll be back in a little bit." He didn't stick around to hear the murmured 'yeah' that followed him out the door.

chapter 33

Vincent Tameric sat behind his thick computer desk and looked around the walls of his office. Certificates and diplomas and pictures of himself with various important figures, a twenty-year old collection spanning an entire generation in law enforcement. It was amazing how much things had changed without really changing at all. Maybe it was just the faces that changed. Hell, it certainly wasn't the politics. That was still alive and well.

Kevin Ambert was living proof of that. The DEA Senior Agent was really becoming a pain in the ass with all of his political posturing. He was getting tired of being a support Agent on the case and was once again beginning to grumble about the fact that neither the NCIS or San Diego Police Department were equipped to handle this case and that their incompetence was jeopardizing any chances of success. The difference between past complaints and those presently being bandied about was that people in the management levels were starting to listen and a more active DEA role was being considered.

Vince shuddered at the thought of Ambert or any of his DEA ilk having a say in this case. He almost wished that they had never come on board at all. But that was just wishful thinking. The drug game was their game; their participation was a burden that would have to be bourn through to the end.

Vince spent the last two days fighting to retain NCIS control of the case. His conversation with James earlier in the day had helped that fight; showing that despite the horrible setback of the previous day, progress was still happening. He just hoped that James could put this thing to bed soon. Another mistake, any more bad press and the NCIS was going to become an also ran on their own case.

The phone rang loudly, breaking Vince's dark thoughts. He leaned forward and picked up the receiver. "Hello?"

"I'm looking for Senior Agent in Charge Vincent Tameric's office."

"This is Vincent Tameric. How may I help you?"

The voice on the other end of the line was deep and smooth, a resonant bass that spoke of calm and control. "This is Edmund Howeth, how are you doing today?"

Vince frowned deeply. Edmund Howeth was no joke. He was a high-powered attorney with ungodly connections and an unparalleled reputation as an unstoppable force in the courtroom. He didn't just win, he won big. The fact that he was calling could only mean that bad things were afoot. Great.

"I'm doing all right. How can we help you this afternoon, Mr. Howeth?"

"As you may or may not know, I represent Ms. Kalina Morris and her interests."

Vince's stomach turned as Edmund Howeth repeated the events of the morning. His jaw stood out as he clenched and unclenched and re-clenched the muscles, grinding his teeth unconsciously. He had warned James about this very thing only hours before.

"If you have something to say to my client, Mr. Tameric, I recommend that you coordinate it through my office. Anything else, any contact from your office or agents without myself being present, and we will be entering a harassment complaint against your office. I am speaking to you on this out of professional courtesy, Mr. Tameric, as I wish to avoid entering into a litigious relationship with your Agency. But take me at my word on this, leave Kalina Morris alone."

Vince sat there for a moment, a ball of anger sitting hot in his stomach. He wasn't sure how to answer without sounding weak. "We'll be in touch then, Mr. Howeth."

A deep chuckle answered him. "I'm sure we will, Mr. Tameric. I'm sure we will. You have a good day now."

"Thanks. You too."

Vince hung up the phone. God, this case sucked.

chapter 34

James followed Jessica through the deserted club; it was still too early for the traffic that would fill the scattered tables standing attentively around the empty stage. He was impressed that they were even there. His description of the previous nights events had intrigued her. She soaked up every detail, including his description of a slimy guy named Tony who was meeting with Kalina Morris when he first showed up at the club. Jessica had immediately named him as a major player in San Diego's adult playground arena. She'd been involved with several cases involving various employees of Tony La Paola, never successfully being able to tie any of the prostitution, drugs, or blackmail back to the man himself. She was more than happy to have another shot at him. On her word, they bee-lined it here to this musty, broken down excuse for a club just so Jessica could run a round of 'bad cop, worse cop' on her least favorite scum bag.

A thin, bleach-blonde behind the bar greeted them as they walked in. As they approached, James noticed that she wasn't thin, she was damn near anorexic; her tan skin stretched shiny over her high cheekbones giving her the look of dirty death's head. Her striped top was tight on her bony frame.

"Help you?" she asked with a voice raspy from years of cigarettes and hard drinking.

"Yeah," Jessica told her, "We're looking for Tony La Paola."

"Business or …," she stopped at the sight of Jessica's badge flashing the half-light. She motioned over to the far side of the club. "Office behind the DJ booth."

Jessica didn't slow her gait, skirting the tables and chairs and making her way past the empty DJ booth. She made it to the black painted door steps ahead James, rapping sharply and pushing her way in without waiting for an answer.

"Afternoon, Tony," Jessica shot out.

James made it through the door as La Paola jumped up from his chair, clearly surprised by the two strangers barging into his office. "What the fuck?"

"Oh, don't feel like you have to stand up for us, Tony," Jessica said as she plopped down into the chair across the alarmed club owner.

James looked around the office. It was a shitty little room with off-white walls decorated with signed eight-by-tens of porn stars, all hung in neat little rows. On the wall directly across from the desk, three adult movie posters were mixed in with the racy décor. James didn't have to look hard to find Tony La Paola's name among the credits.

"Didn't know you were into the porn game, Tony."

La Paola stared him down. "I'm a man of many parts," he said casually, easing himself back into his chair. "Now, what can I do for you officers?"

James looked over to Jessica, but La Paola didn't take his eyes off of the Agent.

"C'mon, you guys stink of it," he spat out with disdain. "Whadaya want? I got a business to run here."

James reached past Jessica and laid his credentials on the cluttered desk. "Just want to ask you a few questions, Mr. La Paola."

La Paola scoffed at the badge. "I ain't in the fucking Navy, pal."

Jessica slapped her city badge down on the desktop next to James'. "Just answer the questions."

Tony leaned back into the black leather of his chair and considered the two momentarily. His eyes narrowed as he studied James' face again. "I know you. You were at Club Kittie last night. Look if you guys came in here to shake me down, I got bad news for you; the competition's got you beat. I'm already paying for more insurance than I'll ever need and…"

"We're not here to jerk you around, Mr. La Paola; we're here to ask you some questions." James didn't want to get off on a tangent.

Tony settled himself, still glancing back and forth between the two of them suspiciously.

"What were you doing at Club Kittie last night, Tony?"

"Minding my fuckin business, what were you doing there?"

James saw Jessica's back go rigid and her posture straighten. He decided that it was time to play 'bad cop' for Tony La Paola's sake.

"Answer the …," Jessica started, but cut off abruptly as James' fist slammed down against the edge of the desk with a booming thud. The cheap plastic hula girl standing under the lamp danced crazily at the jolt.

La Paola jumped in his seat caught off guard and Jessica stared up at the large, seemingly angry man now beside her.

"Answer the question! You were at Club Kittie last night talking with Kalina Morris and Cameron Leasig. I want to know what you were talking about."

The club owner chewed on his lip for a moment, weighing his options and how forthcoming he really wanted to be. Shrugging he maintained his eye contact with James. "We were talking business; nothing more, nothing less."

James wanted to look back over his shoulder at Jessica, get a read from her, but he wasn't about to break eye contact with his subject. He had Tony LaPaola's undivided attention. "I'm waiting for an answer."

"Well, you might just have to wait for my attorney to get here. I'm not sure where you two are going with this, but I'm not going to let you corral me into something. I know my rights."

James clenched his jaw, readying himself to verbally pounce on the smaller man across from him. Jessica's hand on his back stopped him. Her gaze was ice as she looked over Tony La Paola, measuring him in the sudden silence of the room. He returned her look expectantly, waiting for her to speak.

"You know, Billy Forrester knew his rights too. Backwards and forwards as I remember it." La Paola paled visibly and a small line of sweat peppered his upper lip. "It's just a couple of questions, Tony. Nothing to get your panties in a knot over. What were you doing at Club Kittie?" Her voice was calm and cordial. She may as well have been speaking with an old acquaintance, asking them how they'd spent an evening.

Tony was visibly shaken by the shift in gears. James had absolutely no idea what the hell was going on or how the balance of power had shifted. Who was Billy Forrester and what did he have to do with anything? James stepped back from the desk, trying to assume Jessica's calm demeanor. He was pretty sure he was screwing it up.

"Look it's like I said, I was there on business." La Paola sounded defeated.

"There are all kinds of business, Tony. Which one were you there for?"

He tried to look defiant once more, but he couldn't pull it off. He sighed and shrugged, resigned to his failure. "If I tell the two of you, it can't go outside this office 'til Friday. You guys say anything and I'm screwed."

"Oh, so dramatic, Tony." Her voice was still bored but an interested glimmer sparked in her eyes and she leaned slightly forward.

"Seriously. Nothing before Friday."

Jessica looked over at James who only shrugged slightly. She was driving this train; he was just along for the ride.

"Thursday night then," she agreed. "What do you have for us?"

"Come Saturday morning, I own Club Kittie."

chapter 35

Noah sat at the computer in the small study across from his bedroom. The glow from the computer screen lit his face evilly, painting it the pale green of a "B-movie" horror flick. He punched in his trading account and smiled broadly, the numbers were way up. He watched the real time ticker roll along the bottom of the screen, the prices of his stocks rising and falling as he ate his sandwich. It was hypnotic really, that little scrolling line of letters and numbers. Constantly changing, begging for attention. Cameron turned him on to investing, got him addicted to the ticker.

Tearing his eyes away to look at the clock, he swore, seeing that the time was getting away from him and he had to get back to work. Signing off the account, he opened the desk drawer and pulled out a small sheet of paper. It held his important account numbers, the ones that belonged to the offshore accounts holding his untouchable millions. He punched in the account number and the access code and waited for the account to come up. His grin grew even broader, splitting his face. The monies from the SARATOGA shipment had made it to his account, a cool five hundred and eighty thousand dollars.

He was going to have to send the Hoyle brothers a fruit basket, do the whole customer appreciation thing. His account was bulging at the seams. He loved it. Only two more years until his contract was up. Civilian life was calling from just around the corner and Noah had every intention of answering that call. Only two more years and he would have the freedom to tap into his nest egg and live out the rest of his days in luxury. A life of travel and leisure awaited.

It was amazing that he'd come as far as he had. He looked back at the meager beginnings of his life and he couldn't believe how far he'd come. Things started well enough for him, his younger years blurred by life in a happy family with loving parents. It was every fifties family sitcom ever made.

Right up until Noah's eleventh birthday.

chapter 36

The animal sounds coming from the guest room were to alluring too be ignored, a siren's call drawing the newly eleven-year-old Noah into the shadow darkened room to discover its source. What he found, much to his horror, was his idol, the man he wanted to be, his father, pounding away, sexing the neighbor's seventeen-year-old daughter. Eleven-year-old Noah didn't know what to do or how to respond. He just stood there, feeling embarrassed and scared and sad. His father lay on top of the girl grunting and sweating, her small breasts, so ivory white, bouncing up and down in time to his thrusts.

His world narrowed and slowed, bogged down by the overload of his mental circuitry. He didn't understand what was happening, and yet he knew all too well. He had to be dreaming. But he wasn't. This was his birthday party. Happy birthday, Big Boy!

The neighbor's daughter looked over in slow motion, her pale hair glimmering white in the half light, and saw Noah standing there watching and she screamed. His dad leapt off of her, grabbing at the loose bed sheets for cover. His normally kind eyes blazed with anger and embarrassment, terrifying the birthday boy to his quick. He yelled at Noah to get the hell out.

And when eleven-year-old Noah, too frozen with shock and fear to move, simply stood there, his father charged across the room and backhanded him across the face.

Noah unconsciously raised his hand to his mouth and cheek, his brow furrowed angrily as he remembered the stroke that had bloodied his face and sent him flying across the room.

Things changed drastically in the Marion home that day. The innocence was shattered and the laugh track was conspicuously missing. The harshness of the outside world became all too real as Noah's parents did their proverbial laundry out in the open for the world to see.

Teenage Noah became withdrawn and angry as his father flaunted his infidelities and his mother self medicated with various narcotics and her ever-present bottle of Jack. It was a never-ending carnival of crazy with the both of them so self-involved, he may well have not even existed. Self-preservation, along with a great deal of trial and error, taught cooking and laundry. He fought the marital impulses of his battling parents, choosing self-reliance and slackerdom over addiction.

And suddenly the Marion household was no more. A handful of pills and a fifth of Jack helped his mother wash away her misery forever, leaving teenage Noah under the non-existent care of his absentee father. Noah chose the streets over living with the abusive stranger his father had become. With his newly earned high school diploma in hand and nowhere else to go, he joined the Navy. He could use the paycheck and the meals and the bed. The four hundred dollars every two weeks was a fortune to him then.

chapter 37

And now here he was, millions of dollars in the bank and a life of leisure and luxury just around the corner. It was amazing. That of course depended on things remaining as they were, nothing major going wrong. The whole 'nothing major' definition had changed for him over the last several years, much like the definition of the word 'fortune'. When he started with this enterprise, anything that happened and wasn't planned was a major event. He sweated it, over-reacted, made mistakes. Sometimes serious ones.

Cameron was the exact opposite, remained calm and cool – never lost his temper or train of thought. Everything was exacting and precisely managed. It was one of the things about the man that impressed Noah, one of the things that had prolonged their working relationship. Noah respected Cameron's temperament and advice. Times had changed both of them. While Cameron allowed the distraction that was Kalina to dominate his life, Noah had grown much colder, more methodical and capable. A guy talked to the cops and needs to be made an example of, not a problem. Catch a guy stealing and he's got to be killed, not a problem. Have to hide fifteen million dollars from the IRS, the NCIS, and the DEA, not a problem. Anything was manageable.

Well, almost anything.

Cameron Leasig getting nabbed by the NCIS; that wasn't manageable, that was a problem. A big hairy, scary problem with teeth and claws.

Closing his account, he logged on to one of his e-mail accounts and checked the new messages. The reply he was looking for sat unopened in the in-box. He clicked on it and read the brief note. It delivered the information he had expected. He pulled a small green notebook from his pocket and made several notes to himself and then reached over and deleted the message.

Another unread message in his in-box begged his attention with the glowing red exclamation point marking it as urgent. The coded reference line told him that he had another clean-up job to do. He sighed irritably and clicked on the message to open it. Not really believing his eyes, he read and re-read the message to be sure that there was nothing he missed or misunderstood, not that there was much open to interpretation in the short message. Things were happening quickly now and Noah didn't really like that. Liking it wasn't a part of the deal, though; he was who he was and there were some requests that required action, even if he didn't fully understand the reasons behind them. Loose ends couldn't just be allowed to flap in the breeze after all.

At least it wasn't anything major, something he could handle personally and quickly. He scribbled more notes in the green book. The clock in the corner of the screen warned him that he had to be on his way, so he deleted the message and signed off the system. Turning off the computer, he picked up his dishes and headed down to the kitchen. It was time to get back to work.

chapter 38

James stalked the perimeter of the warehouse, his mind actively chewing on the visit to La Paola's dumpy club. So many things about this bothered him, not the least of which was ensuring that his new witness stayed alive long enough to testify. Two experienced detectives from the San Diego Police Department, cops Jessica knew and trusted, were covering Leasig right now. It was twenty-four – seven coverage until Leasig was safely locked away.

James closed his eyes and exhaled deeply. It was a cleansing breath, meant to clear his mind and allow him to focus on the task at hand. Working a crime scene demanded concentration, focus. He drew another deep breath, held it for a second, and released.

The crime scene awaited.

He opened his eyes and scanned the area in its entirety, giving his eyes an opportunity to adjust to the dim half-light of the cement and steel building. The bright sun shining outside provided little illumination beyond the blinding rectangle lying before the massive double doors. The forest of tape and flags signifying physical evidence remained in place, marking the passage of the San Diego Crime Scene Unit.

The air was heavy and cool, damp; an odd mixture of salt air and heavy machinery. James grimaced. He couldn't smell the blood, at least not yet.

The scrape of a sole on the concrete floor had James peering over his shoulder, his hand sliding unconsciously to the hilt of his service weapon. Jessica was right there behind him, an expectant look on her face.

At their team meeting, prior to the autopsy, James and Jessica had gone through the crime scene photos and drawings. They reviewed the initial reports from the CSU, comparing them with Jessica's extensive notes. The scene was clean. No prints, no discarded weapons. Even if there was some DNA evidence left behind, there was no suspect to judge it against.

Just blood and violence and a broken, lifeless body, that's apparently all that was left behind.

Now they were here to take another run at the processed scene. James gave Jessica a small nod, donning a pair of latex gloves.

"Where do you want to start?" he asked.

"Front to back I guess. We can sweep the entry, track to place of death, spiral out from there and then track back out."

James nodded, looking towards the hoist hanging from the track system on the ceiling. Underneath that rusty hook was a pool of congealed blood. The aftermath of destruction. Ahh, joy.

"We'll use your notes, combined with the info from CSU to reconstruct." His voice was brusque, much harsher than he intended.

Pulling a small flashlight out of his jacket pocket, he gave Jessica a slight nod. "Let's do this."

chapter 39

The dark blue Toyota Corolla rolled along the street, staying within sight of the green Rav moving ahead of it in traffic. Music rolled and the bass line thumped and Noah bobbed his head in time with the beat. The angry lyrics slid through his brain, someone else's lethal dreams preparing him mentally for the task at hand. He liked gangsta rap. The rawness of the genre, the whole me against the world feel, it got his adrenaline flowing.

He gripped the steering wheel tightly in his hands, the anticipation welling up inside of him. The anticipation was new. Early kills involved nerves and the unpredictable energy that came with them; a sense of unease that darkened his dreams. He had evolved over the years, become colder, more capable. Lately, he began to look forward to the work, looked forward to pulling the trigger or pushing the blade. As much as he bitched about cleaning up other people's messes, he thrilled in the hunt.

Noah couldn't count the numbers he'd put to rest, their faces were a long blur in his mind. Only one face stood out. It was distinctive, familiar in every way. It was the only face that still haunted his dreams. Noah wondered for years why he couldn't shake the apparition. Maybe because it was his first kill, filled with rage and bloodlust and sloppy beyond belief. Maybe because it was his father.

Whatever.

Every kill was personal. His business and his financial welfare were personal; his credibility within the dark communities he traveled was personal. He could and would kill now to protect what he considered his without giving it a second thought. No one was going to stop the money from flowing. No one was going to ruin his street credibility. No one.

Especially not Thomas Pinfield. His time had come and his usefulness had apparently run out.

Noah liked doing jobs during the busier parts of the day. The increased confusion on the street made witnesses less reliable. Thirty different descriptions of the event and the suspect and the getaway car did nothing for the cops. Regardless of the time of day, he would protect what was his and he'd do it personally. That, and he was smart enough to know that the fewer people involved, the less talk there was. The last thing he wanted at this point was more people talking.

He could get through this and get some dinner.

The busy street crept past his tinted windows, traffic moving to his booming sound track. The Rav turned at the light. Noah grinned. Just like clockwork, straight to the computer store. He leaned over and opened the glove box. The nine-millimeter pistol sat on the registration paperwork. He pulled it out and turned into the parking lot.

chapter 40

Rebecca Weingert was a pretty young thing. Long, dirty blonde hair framing a lean angular face, the clear blue eyes almost stereotypical of the surfer girl lifestyle she grew up with. Her short, athletic build served her well on her board and got her noticed just about everywhere else. It also made people underestimate her on a regular basis.

She'd heard more than her fair share of 'dumb blonde' jokes and she tried not to react to them, regardless of how demeaning they were. She would just smile wanly and nod her head, trying to look vacuous while she memorized every fact she could about the person. Then, when she had time, she would sit down at her computer, get on-line and do everything within her very considerable powers to hack into that person's electronic life and make an utter shambles of it. It was amazing how many aspects of a persons life were on-line now days.

Now she was working at the "Computer Warehouser". The manager didn't think much of her; didn't seem to think much of anything at all. Becca was working register. Not the phones or in the programming / servicing center. No. She was just a girl and 'her pretty face should be out where the customers could appreciate it.' So she was working register.

That comment cost the fat bastard several credit cards and would probably keep him from getting a loan anywhere in the country. Becca gave his credit report a makeover that would make any potential creditor run away in abject fear. She smiled, thinking of the hassles those changes would create and the headaches he would have trying to make them go away.

Her smile faded as her eyes drifted to the clock hanging over the shop entrance - three more hours to go. "Shit!" she muttered, nudging at the register with her elbow.

chapter 41

Thomas smiled broadly as he strolled across the parking lot towards the computer store. The fat envelope had spent the entire afternoon burning a hole in his pocket, and now he was going to extinguish it. Reaching down, he patted the thick lump of bills stowed in the inner pocket of his leather jacket, reassuring himself that they were still there.

Ten thousand dollars. In his very young life, Thomas had never seen, let alone been in possession of, so much money. The size of the number was simply numbing. A new car, new clothes, pay off some bills, get something nice for Gena, his girlfriend since junior year of high school. He knew that he had to be careful with this windfall. He really didn't want anyone to question his sudden affluence. But hey, a new laptop and some games would definitely be explainable.

Thomas was a geek. A skater turned hacker in his formative years, and his skills with regards to both creative mediums had increased considerably over the last few years. He and Gena argued from time to time about the amount of time he spent on-line, but she was more than happy to watch the movies and play the games he ripped and burned. And his 'slacker' friends had been hers as well for years.

He smiled as her face floated in his head. It was longish and linear, with a sharp chin and pronounced jaw-line. But her gray eyes were large and soft, filled with kindness when she looked at him and lit by the smile that almost always graced her face. Thomas knew that there were prettier women out there, but Gena was his angel. She was home to him.

Perhaps he would get her that tennis bracelet she had been drooling over for as long as he'd known her. He'd never had the money before and she'd put up with him buying so much computer crap that he didn't *really* need. She deserved something nice. He nodded, the decision made. He would go to the jewelry store from here, get the bracelet, go home, take her to dinner and give it to her. He couldn't wait to see the surprised smile light up her angel's face.

Lost in thought and the fluorescent glow of the computer stores large sign, Thomas didn't notice the car slide up next to him. The passenger window slid down with a mechanical murmur.

"Thomas!"

Thomas whipped his head around, caught totally by surprise. "What? Oh, dude, what's up? You scared the piss outta me."

"Sorry, man."

Thomas stepped up to the car, leaning on the passenger door. "What's up?"

"Nothing. I guessed you would swing out here after work and there was something I needed to give you. Hold on a second, let me grab it."

Thomas watched him bend down to reach under the seat. When it looked like he found what he was looking for, he turned and looked into Thomas's blue eyes.

"This might sting a bit."

A perplexed look passed over Thomas' face. "What are you talking about?"

The barrel of the gun swung around. As it leveled with his eyes, Thomas was struck by how ridiculously large that barrel was. It was like looking down a well.

"What the ...?"

chapter 42

A flash of light filled the glass opening of the door followed by a thunderclap and the squeal of tires. Without thinking, Rebecca ran to the door and threw it open just in time to see the taillights of a dark car turning from the parking lot. A rumpled body lay motionless in the street. She ran across the sidewalk and out into the lot, dread softening her stomach. Still no movement. She slowed as she drew near, no need to guess at the sickeningly dark pool that was spreading rapidly around the blatantly ruined head. Chunks of bone and gray matter shone wetly in the matted hair. This guy was dead.

Rebecca lost her dinner onto the cooling asphalt at her feet as people from the surrounding stores rushed out into the parking lot to investigate the noise and movement.

chapter 43

James stared at the mounds of paperwork covering his dining room table. Reports on different activities, reports concerning various failings or findings, reports about reports that referred to evidence already reported on. The Agency's chain of paperwork was the modern-day embodiment of the mythical hydra – complete one set of forms and two others sprang up to take its place. The involvement of other agencies only served to complicate matters further. It was a grueling, seemingly never ending cycle. The only chore more exasperating was finding a means of filing the myriad documents that actually made some form of sense. Failing miserably at that task, James settled for the random pile approach that now decorated the room.

Jessica eyed the piles skeptically. They had yet to complete reporting on the events of either Monday morning or evening, let alone discuss those of the day. The mostly empty paper containers of Chinese food littered the few bare spots that weren't covered by documents; congealing buckets of General Tso's chicken and Lo Mien with steamed rice hardening on the side as it cooled. Her belly was full and that comfortable warmth was spreading over her, making it difficult to get motivated enough to dive into paperwork.

She eyed James just as skeptically. He'd been in a funk all day, growing worse since the interview with La Paola and carrying through his walk of the crime scene. She wasn't sure what to make of it. The day definitely hadn't been wine and roses, but it had gone a hell of a lot better than Monday. She smiled at him half-heartedly.

"You ready to start shuffling forms?"

James shot her an annoyed glance.

Jessica recoiled from the unexpected glare. "What the hell blew up your skirt? You've been grumping around all afternoon."

James didn't look at her but sat there regarding the stacks of papers on the table.

"Seriously, James. What is it?"

"Bad math."

"That's your answer? 'Bad math'?"

"Nothing adds up. C'mon, Jess. What about this makes any sense to you what so ever? I was really starting to believe that whole thing about third time being the charm; right up until Monk showed up dead. Immediately after, in walks prince fucking charming? I don't think so! There's nothing about Leasig in any of the paperwork. No mention of Club Kittie or Kalina Morris. Until now, this guy didn't even exist to us. There's absolutely no reason for this guy to work with us. And yet, here he is. Pushing all the right buttons and saying all the right things. I've had that itch at the back of my neck from the moment this guy walked into the picture. He's playing us. I mean, why bring us in on anything? What good does it do to have us running around asking questions and digging through his business? If he's sat it out for the last three years collecting information, why call on us early? Why not wait a few days and come in when everything is together."

He took a step towards her, looming over her small frame. He threw his left hand in the air, shaking it wildly about. Jessica stood her ground, frozen by the sudden movement.

"Know what this is?" he asked, nodding towards the waving hand.

Jessica shook her head, not comprehending.

"It's a distraction for this."

James held up his right hand. Jessica's slim gold watch hung delicately from his fingers. She looked down at her wrist in surprise and was amazed to find it bare. She hadn't felt a thing.

"He's distracting us, Jess. We're caught up in the sound and the fury, but we're missing the main event. That meeting with La Paola did nothing but confirm it. He's got us reacting. The question is, what is the main event? What are we missing? I've been wracking my brains all afternoon and can't figure it."

Jessica shrugged. "I don't have the answers either."

"Jess, we're walking onto the MILIUS tomorrow morning and holding the entire crew on board while we run our search. We put a lot of face into this, all on the word of a guy we can't trust. We have absolutely no idea what we're going to find on that ship, if we find anything at all."

Jessica felt the same uncertainty and asked herself the same questions. With everything else that had gone wrong, it would be absolutely disastrous if they tore that ship apart and came away empty handed. She knew that the DEA was doing nothing but complaining about how the case was being handled. She hated the idea of giving those suits any more fuel for their arguments.

"By the way, I've been meaning to ask you about something."

Jessica looked at him.

"Who is Billy Forrester?"

Jessica chuckled to herself, a broad smile coming to her face. "A mutual acquaintance of mine and your friend Tony La Paola's. About three years ago I brought in Billy for carrying distribution weight. I ran the interrogation on him. We're half way through it and he comes over the table at me. I don't remember the blow by blow on it, but long story short is that ol' Billy ended up in the hospital with a dislocated shoulder and two ruptured testicles."

James winced in mock pain. "You ruptured his nuts?"

Jessica nodded. "Both of them. No one on the outside ever got the details on it, but word spread around his little buddies about the little woman cop that crushed Billy's balls. I bring it up every now and again just to see the expression on their faces when they think about it."

"Effective."

"I thought so at the time."

James sat back in his chair and rubbed his eyes wearily. "I don't know, Jess."

"Don't sweat it." Her words carried far more conviction than she felt. She worried for him as she worried for the case. The weight on his strong shoulders was great. She knew that he could carry it, but at what cost she did not know. "Everyone is ready for tomorrow. The message is out to the ship, the team is ready to go. There's no better time to get this out of the way, find out whether or not Leasig is on his game. Either way, we'll know about him by the end of the day tomorrow."

"Just a crappy way to test the theory."

"No other way to do it, though."

James shrugged simply. "To the paperwork then?"

chapter 44

Cameron clicked off the small, prepaid cell phone and distractedly clipped it the pocket of his khakis. Kalina caught his attention, waving her hand in front his face and bringing out of his thoughts.

"Who was that?"

He shrugged. "Just someone letting me know that I'm gonna need to find myself another dentist."

Kalina knew that she had to look as confused as she felt by the comment.

Cameron answered by smiling his 'I-will-distract-you-with-my-charming-smile' smile and Kalina simply decided not to push it. If he wanted her to know, he would have told her, and besides, she had a lot of work to get done and not a whole lot of time to do it.

"Well, you promised that you would help me out here tonight. No distractions, just club business. We've got a lot to do here over the next few days."

He held up a hand in mock defense. "I know, I know. No more phone calls."

Kalina walked over and put her arm around his shoulders. "How much longer do I have you for?"

He leaned in and kissed her. "As long as you want," he replied coyly, trying to make his voice deep and sexy.

She giggled and pushed him away. "Eww. I'm talking about tonight. How much longer until you have to go home?"

"Oh. That. I have a couple more hours and I gotta bug out."

Kalina grimaced and chewed on her lip thoughtfully. "Can you go over the liquor inventory? Just the stuff in the storeroom. Brenda will get the bar at the end of the night."

"For you, I guess so. Just need an inventory to get started."

Reaching across her desk, Kalina grabbed a folder and pulled out a fist full of papers. "Viola! Now if you'll excuse me, I have customers to attend to. "

Cameron chuckled as she headed out of the office. He dug around in her desk, finding a pen and took off behind her.

wednesday, june 9

chapter 45

Captain Jeffrey Archer looked around his stateroom, taking in the Navy memorabilia he'd gathered over his twenty-three year career. There were patches and hats, plaques and pictures of him with various military and political figures hanging on all of the walls. On the small desk sat pictures of his wife and his three children, a boy and two daughters. He smiled slightly as he glanced at the pictures. It'd been one hundred and five days since they'd left port. He was anxious to get home. More and more, that was the way he felt - anxious to be home.

Keith, the spitting image of his old man, was heading into his senior year of high school. Kayla had apparently started dating one of the boys on the football team and Kimberly was a shoo-in for captain of the school's soccer team. He'd missed enough things in their lives already.

He wondered, and not for the first time, whether or not they would be waiting at the pier when the ship pulled in. It was becoming more and more of a battle for Pam to get them to come out. Wouldn't matter today though. No one was getting off the ship for a while.

He looked at the off-line encrypted message that sat on the desk and he felt his blood heat up once more. The orders came directly from Admiral Petite. The NCIS would be boarding his ship and conducting a search. No one was allowed off and no one excepting the team of Agents was allowed on. The pier would be secured, most probably sending every one of the spouses and girlfriends into apoplectic seizure. The order had also been passed to lock down all of the storerooms on board. Someone had used his ship to break the law. He wasn't sure who or how as of yet, but no one ruined the reputation of his ship.

He struggled, as of late, with his position as Captain. It was his job to maintain good order and discipline, to keep his vessel and crew in fighting shape at all times. His enthusiasm for the task was diminishing. The navy had changed so much during his career, more than he ever thought possible. Not all of the changes were bad. There were more opportunities for women to serve and progress, race was less and less of an issue across the board. Those things were good in his book.

What he struggled with was the slacker attitudes of this lazy-assed, self-centered generation coming up. They needed to be coddled and cared for. They demanded respect at the same time they showed blatant disrespect for everything and everyone around them. Nothing escaped their contempt. The institution, the traditions, the chain-of-command; nothing was immune.

And heaven forbid, you hold them accountable for their actions. The lawyers would be lining up around the block.

Things were changing, changing in ways that Captain Jeffrey Archer knew he could not. Would not. It would soon be time for him to go.

But not before he found out who had used his ship to traffic drugs. He would wait around for that. He would find out and rain down such misery on them that they would beg to be taken into custody.

The growler next to the desk whined out. He reached over and picked it up. He listened for a few seconds, his already clouded visage darkening further.

"I'm on my way. Have the XO meet me on the bridge."

chapter 46

James inspected the small team that stood around him. Sarah Rollins waited expectantly, as perfectly pressed and attentive as ever. Standing behind her, Bob Keleman looked as though he was trying to hide, which was probably the smart thing to do considering his exploits from the previous day. Special Agent Simeonson, a chemist from the NCIS crime lab was there; two massive briefcases full of equipment laying on the ground in front of him. Chief Kalvert, one of the K-9 officers from the base's military police canine unit sat in his white Explorer keeping his dark brown and black German Shepard, Runner, company.

It was a small team, designed to move in quickly and get the job done. James was sure that it would be effective, assuming Cameron's information was accurate. The military police were doing a bang up job of keeping the pier free of traffic. They had all of the sailors who would be tying the ship off to the pier and placing the brow and the heavy metal gangplank off to one side, waiting for the ship to come in. James could see her approaching, guided by the harbormaster's powerful red and white tugboat.

The USS MILIUS crept towards her berth. She was a large ship, thousands of tons of floating steel and firepower. James picked out her SPY-ID radar and the fat bulb that housed her AEGIS close defense weapons system. He knew that somewhere up there on the deck were the hatch doors for the Tomahawks. He shook his head. They built the Arleigh Burkes to fight; that was for sure.

Time was drawing near. His stomach fluttered as the thought crossed his mind again that the tip could be bogus. He shrugged it off. No reason to worry about it now. The team was assembled and ready to work. They would all know soon enough whether or not James had made a mistake.

chapter 47

Noah flipped through the newspaper, looking through the previous days stories. He came to the one he was looking for and read through it intently. He wasn't worried that anyone could place him at the scene. There were no details about his car, just the mention of a dark, late model sedan. He read on. There was mention of Thomas' naval service. Satisfied that there was nothing there, he was about to put the paper down when a set of numbers caught his curious eye. Pinfield had ten thousand dollars on his person when he was gunned down. A bloodstained knapsack found in his car. The police didn't make any claims as to why Thomas Pinfield was killed, but they did state that they were investigating the backpack as a part of another case. Noah was suddenly involved with more than he had expected.

What did Cameron have to do with it? More likely than not, everything. He'd ordered the hit; he had to have a reason for it.

Noah was curious about the money. Did Thomas collect it or was he paid? He didn't have the muscle or presence to be running collections. That could only mean a payday. But from who? Had he sold Cameron out and that was why he had to be put down or was he working for Cameron and just became a burden? The questions multiplied, each one more intriguing than the last.

What was up with the bloody backpack?
Did it have anything to do with the money?
Who did the blood belong to?

Not being a fan of puzzles, Noah read through the article again, picking points that he would ask questions about later. He knew his role and he was comfortable with it, but he liked to have a better idea of what he was caught up in.

chapter 48

Within thirty minutes of the USS MILIUS being tied off to the pier, James and his team of agents were wending their way through the labyrinth of freshly waxed and buffed, linoleum-covered passageways that made up the insides of the destroyer. Captain Jeffrey Archer, the MILIUS' Commanding Officer led the way. Commander Connor Franklin, the ship's Executive Officer, and Lieutenant Commander Miles Farmer, the Supply Officer, followed close behind with several of the ship's well-armed Masters-at-Arms in tow.

By James' estimation, Archer stood about six foot four inches, handily filling out his broad frame. James guessed that he was probably a nightmare for the crew around Physical Readiness Testing time. He was probably one of those CO's that challenged the crew to top his score, a feat only achieved by a spare handful of the crew. His thinning gray hair was the only thing that betrayed his age. In a few years that weak excuse for a comb-over wasn't going to work any more. James had no doubts as to the effectiveness of the man, though. The three Battle E's painted on superstructure of the bridge spoke to his competence and his aura of command left no doubt as to who was in charge. Captain Archer cut an intimidating figure, a man who gave orders and expected that those orders would be carried out to the letter; no mistakes, no excuses.

Sailors in dark blue jump suits and dungaree uniforms practically dove out of the way as the cluster of bad news sped along the passageway. Something important was going down and not a one of them wanted any part of it. There could be no joy when the Captain looked that pissed. No one was sure who the suits were, but it didn't take a genius to guess NCIS. The whispers traveled the ship fore to aft, with the reasons for liberty not being called down changing from telling to telling.

James actually felt sorry for the young Ensign, a slight, pale young man who looked like he couldn't be any older than about eighteen, who was standing behind the duty desk down in supply. He visibly blanched when Captain Archer stormed in, demanding the keys to the supply lockers and the inventories and copies of receipts and bills of lading.

The scramble was on, with blue shirted sailors running about, trying to get together the paperwork the Captain wanted while their Division Officer stood there trying not to sweat through his uniform.

Minutes later the paint locker was opened and the ten buckets listed on the sheet of paper Cameron had given to James, which James then checked against the Ensign's inventory and bill of lading, were pulled out. The buckets were transported under the guard of the Masters-at-Arms to the small flight deck of the destroyer where several empty fifty-gallon drums had been set up.

James watched as each of the buckets was emptied out. He watched ten large, heavily wrapped packages splat against the metal grating lying over the top of the drum. Special Agent Simeonson, his hands wrapped in thin rubber gloves, gingerly picked up each tightly wrapped package, carefully wiping away the gray paint and douching the plastic wrapping with saline solution. With all ten lined up on the blue plastic sheet, Simeonson turned to his portable chemistry lab.

Captain Archer's face was crimson with tightly wound rage. Those around him stepped back slightly, his anger a palpable mass that pushed them all away. His eyes never left Simeonson's steadily moving hands. James watched him, mentally crossing him off the list of suspects. Archer was flat out pissed that someone had used his ship to move drugs. He quickly scanned the faces of those officers standing around their Commanding Officer. They appeared more concerned with Captain Archer's reaction than what Simeonson was doing some fifteen feet away.

As Special Agent Simeonson finished with each package, he rebagged it in an evidence bag and slapped on the colorful tamper proof seal. Stripping off his gloves, he scribbled notes in a small evidence book, slipped on a new pair of gloves and moved on to processing the next package.

James could feel the tension building as the sun climbed into the clear summer sky. Minutes slid by and a small trickle of sweat ran down James' back. It was going to be a warm one.

chapter 49

With sweat beading thickly on his forehead, Adam Simeonson wiped his brow for a final time and closed the small notebook. Ten kilograms of uncut heroin was lying on the deck at his feet. Cut properly, it would turn into more than ten times that amount on the street and sell for well over a million dollars.

He looked up at James. "I want to get this back to the lab to certify the results, but initial testing puts this at better than ninety-nine percent pure, weight is right at ten kilograms. You're looking at well over a million dollars of uncut heroin."

James absorbed the information. After having watched the packages drop from the paint buckets, he really expected nothing less. It was paradoxically both comforting and disturbing to know that Leasig's information was right on the money. Distracted by his own thoughts, he turned and addressed Captain Archer. "Captain Archer, your ship is under quarantine until such time as the Supply Department can be gathered and questioned. Have your Master-at-Arms secure the scene until CSU can process it. Lieutenant Commander Farmer, I expect that you will have all of the lading bills and inventory paperwork together and that you will make personnel available as required."

He looked around at the group. "Adam, go ahead and get the evidence back to the lab for further testing. Shore Patrol will provide you an escort. Sarah, you and Keleman have the interviews. I'll get a hold of Vince and get some support out for you."

Special Agent Rollins regarded him curiously. "You taking off, James?"

He nodded in response. "I've got an appointment." His thoughts were obviously elsewhere. "You've got this. Give me a call if you come across anything unexpected."

Sarah nodded and dug into her bag for a tape recorder and a notepad.

Captain Archer stepped forward, his face red as he looked at the small team. "You have full use of the my wardroom. The Master-at-Arms will also be at your disposal. XO, ensure that every effort is made to accommodate the agents in their investigation." He turned and stalked angrily away.

The entire search and seizure had taken just over three hours. A million dollars of smack off the streets; James knew that heads would roll. He was pretty sure that heads were going to roll here on the USS MILIUS as well. Archer wasn't going to let this abuse of his ship slide. Archer's actions would be nothing compared to the fallout that would take place on the street.

Leasig's information was good, but how much more did he know? It was time for another meeting. It was time for more answers.

chapter 50

"What the fuck are you telling me? They got it all?" Noah paused listening to the answer, his face turning bright red and the knuckles on his hand holding the phone turning white. "You've got to be fucking kidding me! And where the hell were you while all of this was going down? What were you doing, hiding in the head?"

The interior of his car seemed to shrink around him. A million dollars plus gone in the blink of an eye. He was having a hard time catching his breath.

"Shut up, I don't want to hear any of your lame-assed excuses, Denny. I want answers and I want names. Do you understand me? Answers and names."

He squeezed the off button on the small cellular phone like it was the root of his problems and threw it down on the seat next to him. What the hell was going on here? First Cameron blows up at him, raging about how this Storenn guy barged in to Kalina's place two nights ago and gave him the third degree and now Denny's telling him that an entire shipment got boosted by the same agent the second the MILIUS pulled in to port. Now he was going to have to face Cameron this afternoon and explain the whole thing to him. Someone was playing a very dangerous game.

Frustration welling up inside of him, he punched the steering wheel full force, honking the horn loudly and twisting his wrist. He sat there for a second shaking out his hand. And suddenly it occurred to him the order in which he placed the bad events of the morning. Cameron talked to the NCIS agent and a load of product got confiscated.

Noah was not big on coincidence, not big at all. And here he saw a very probable cause and effect. Over the eight years he'd known Cameron Leasig, Noah had seen their friendship slip into a business relationship and, lately, even that was an optimistic view. There was a gap there. Cameron had his secrets and worked in his own circles, Noah did the same; each hiding their motives and reasons. It'd started back several years ago after a major fight over ownership of the club and it'd grown steadily ever since. Now the gap was roughly the size of the Grand Canyon. It was wearing on Noah; he was getting tired of the constant battle of wits. Making matters worse, they'd had some words over some of the decisions Noah had made recently, with Cameron leaving angry and silent in the end. Threats had been made on both sides.

He couldn't believe that it could come to this, though. There had to be another answer. Whatever their differences, Cameron wouldn't toss away a million and a quarter out of spite. He was a businessman first and foremost.

Noah had been nursing a mean-on for Cameron since they'd talked on Monday morning, thinking in the back of his mind that it would probably be easier to kill the bastard than clean up the mess that would result from him getting busted. But there were never any real feelings that he might actually have to do it, that his mistrust and anger might be proved out.

Either way, it was time for something to be done. If the trust wasn't there anymore, then business couldn't go on as usual. It was time to stop the merry-go-round and get off. He hoped the stuff with Cameron blew over and turned out to be nothing. He hoped that he found some arbitrary guy who knew a little too much and was giving it up. He hoped that he would be able to end it without having to 'end it'. But if the NCIS was already talking to Cameron, he doubted that would be possible. Business was business and personal was personal; this was both.

It was time to protect himself. Time to protect what was his.

It was time to be proactive, attack the problem before it blew up in his face. Better safe than sorry, as the saying went.

chapter 51

Lunch hour traffic was light and Cameron navigated it easily, rolling quietly across the Coronado Bay Bridge in his dark blue five series BMW. The stereo pumped out some mindless top forty tunes, tinny voices singing senseless lyrics. It was all background noise. Lost in thought he watched the water travel on into the distance, melding finally with the sky along the horizon. Brightly colored sails dotted the deep blue water, puffed proudly and fat with wind. He was never much of a sailor, didn't really know much about boats at all. He'd only been sailing once or twice and that was years ago with his best friend at the time, Terrence, manning the helm and telling him what to do and how to do it.

The bridge gave way to the tollbooth, which yielded ground to the smaller houses at the front of the island. Downtown Coronado slid past his window. It was quaint, palm-lined streets sporting small coffee shops and bookshops, a couple of diners and a handful of surf shops. People milled around, walking from store to store, sharing a cup of coffee at the local Starbuck's. No one was in a hurry.

He turned right before reaching the Hotel del Coronado. It was a magnificent reminder of an age long since passed for this part of California, an age of grace and elegance, where a stay at the world famous hotel was a sign of wealth and status. But the hotel had aged and it now competed with the shinier, newer structures that lined the harbor walk, towering buildings of steel and glass. People still traveled from around the world to enjoy its five star service, but much of the reasoning now had to do with nostalgia vice status.

Looking down at the digital clock in the dash, he knew that things were blowing up all over San Diego at that very second. Somewhere, probably sitting in his car, Noah was swearing at the top of his lungs and promising death to whoever had sold him out. His chance to deliver would come soon enough. Storenn and his team were only now realizing that they had a live one. The heat would really be on them now to deliver, the publicity of the seizure would show forward progress and the higher ups would be demanding that Storenn close the book on the case.

It was all coming together.

A few more nudges, and everything would be in place.

chapter 52

Kalina was out in the yard, stretching as Cameron pulled up into the long driveway. She smiled past the sweat that soaked her baggy shirt and plastered her hair to her head. He looked distracted as he stepped out of the car, but his face lit up as he approached her.

"Long run?" he asked, walking up and kissing her salty lips.

"About five miles," she replied between breaths. "Just got back."

"You wanna grab some lunch?"

She smiled. "You buying?"

"Yeah. Go catch a shower and I'll throw something on the grill."

"Since when do you have the time for that?"

He grinned stupidly. "Time's relative. I figured with everything we've got going on, why not weasel out of the office for a couple of hours to have some lunch with you? Not like it's gonna make things any worse. Now get your pretty little self up into the shower and I'll get lunch going."

Kalina's stomach growled in anticipation. She wasn't really aware of just how hungry she was. Cameron was a decent enough cook. He was patient enough to at least make the attempt. Kalina was far too busy to dedicate any real time to meal preparation. Without him, she would probably subsist on delivery, canned goods and fruit. She'd seen some chicken marinating in the refrigerator when she made herself breakfast. She wasn't planning on it for lunch but was happy none-the-less. It was that or the old reliable - macaroni and cheese.

She peeled off her clothing as she ran up the stairs and threw it in the hamper in the bathroom. In seconds she was standing under the steaming water, letting it soak into her taught muscles. She stretched again in the shower, letting the hot water work its magic on her. A long run and a good lunch, she might have to take a nap after Cameron headed back to work.

"You never bend over like that when I'm in the shower with you."

She looked up surprised and a little embarrassed, she hadn't heard him come in or noticed him peeking through the shower curtain.

"Since when?" she retorted.

"I don't know, just wanted to break the ice."

"I thought you were making me lunch, grill boy."

"That's grill master to you, woman," he said with a laugh. "Besides it's already started. I just wanted to know if you set up that meeting for me."

"It's set for four o'clock, at least that's what the message I left for him said. You sure this is the way you want to handle this, Cam?" Her voice was nervous.

He shrugged. "Got to, baby. I have to make sure that things are on track for this. That involves really pissing Noah off. If he doesn't come after me, nothing else is going to work out the way it's supposed to. Don't worry about it, it'll all be over by the end of the week."

It made her a little uncomfortable to hear him describe it like he would a high school basketball game. She scowled, wrinkling her brow.

"Hey," he said, getting her attention. "Seriously. Don't worry about it. It will work itself out. Now, what do you want to drink?"

"Diet Coke, no ice," she said flicking water at him. "You'd better get back down there before you burn my lunch, grill master."

He shut the door behind him and she leaned back into the water. It might only take the rest of the week for things to work themselves out, but there were parts of this plan that Kalina wasn't so excited about seeing happen. It was dangerous. And the danger was coming from all sides. She lathered her body; the soap filled scrunchy scraping softly along her smooth skin. It was going to be a long week.

chapter 53

Noah listened to the phone message, scribbling the directions onto the scrap of paper on his desk. He swore under his breath. He'd heard more from Cameron in the past three days than he had in the past three months. Now it was another meeting. This time down town in his lawyer's swanky offices. It was a smart place to get together; none of the cops following him would dare to walk into those offices.

It didn't take a rocket scientist to guess what Cameron wanted. Noah wanted the same thing. Trouble was that neither of them was going to get what they wanted out of this. Cameron had to know that. Why the hell was he pushing so hard? If Cameron would just give him the room to figure it out he would get to the bottom of it. But no, they were going to meet and it was going to get ugly.

Four o'clock would come soon enough. This was turning out to be an absolutely worthless week at work. All of this external activity was starting to affect the job and was drawing the Chief's attention. Attention at this point wasn't good news. Attracting Chief De Jesus' negative attention could only serve to complicate things, make it harder for him to get around. There was no getting away from the khaki collective.

He would have to deal with it as best he could. It was just going to be the week for bad news.

chapter 54

James sat across from Cameron in the small Mexican restaurant. It was an out of the way place, a real hole in the wall. The outside was made up like some turn of the century Mexican villa, white stucco walls and red brick. But age and lack of care had allowed the stucco to gray and the brick to darken. The interior maintained that old world charm with plastic plants in the corners and blue and white Spanish tiles lining the lower half of the walls. The lighting in the place, lights turned down low with candles lit at every table, lent a very Tarantino-esque quality to the meeting. Any second now he expected Mexican gangsters or Chinese Triad to burst into the room and mow everyone down in a hail of bullets. It was almost enough to bring a smile to his lips, but the events of the morning and early afternoon had him in a serious mood to get some questions answered.

Cameron beat him to the punch. "So, I hear y'all stopped by the house yesterday."

James swallowed hard. He'd heard about the fiasco at the Morris woman's house several times over the past twenty-four hours, and not just from Sarah. He'd gotten an ear full of it from Vince with a second helping from Kalina Morris's high priced lawyer. Apparently, she didn't like being insulted in her own home and was very seriously considering, at Mr. Howeth's suggestion, filing a formal grievance about it. James was absolutely furious. Of all the stupid things to do and of all the stupid times to do them. He had no idea how Rollins had prevented herself from simply slapping Keleman silly on the spot.

"Look, I'm sorry about all of that. It never should have happened. Agent Keleman knows he messed up." James was more than sure about that point.

"Pissed me off when I heard about it, but I guess Kali handled it all right. I wouldn't suggest rooting around the house for a while though."

James grinned through gritted teeth. It was damn near impossible to hold the weak smile, but he managed.

Cameron downed a couple of chips, crunching away as if he hadn't a care in the world. Finally, he stopped chewing. "So what did you call me here for? You could have apologized on the phone. It's a pain in the ass to get out of work to meet you at odd times of the day and I'm just not that good at coming up with lame excuses."

"You didn't seem to have any trouble getting out for your two hour lunch this afternoon. It'd have been a hell of a lot easier for me to just stop by your office, but since we're playing all this cloak and dagger nonsense, I figured what the heck. If you'd prefer, I could start doing it that way."

The grimace on Cameron's face was answer enough.

"So, anyhow," James continued, "I wanted to answer your question. Yes, we are working together. And yes, we did find the stash you sent us after. Ten keys of uncut heroin. Someone's gonna be pissed."

Cameron shrugged his shoulders, non-committal.

"So you made your point, Leasig. You've got information. And now I need answers. So how are they doing it? How are they keeping it all straight? Stuffing it in the bottom of paint cans, seems like there'd be lots of confusion, possible lost product and a good chance that the wrong guy gets his hands on the wrong paint can."

Cameron crunched a tortilla chip smothered in salsa. "Not really, if you think about it."

James had thought about it and had come to the conclusion that it would be confusing and that there was a good chance that the wrong guy would get a hold of the wrong paint can. Otherwise he wouldn't have said it.

"They use the Navy's supply system to move product all over the world. All it takes is a few people in the right places to make sure that it runs smoothly, you know, keep track of things."

James eyed him squarely. He doubted he'd get his answer, but what the hell. "And those people would be?" He left it hanging there.

Cameron laughed around another chip, shaking his head. "I don't think so. I'll break down how they move stuff around, how they keep it safe, how they get it off the boats, but you get no names or infrastructure until Friday morning. It's my only safety valve. Saves me from you, saves me from them. You're just gonna have to be patient, Special Agent Storenn."

"You could call me James, you know. I do have a first name."

"I know your name, Special Agent Storenn. I just want to make sure that I remember the nature of our association. We aren't friends now and we aren't gonna be friends in the future. We're adversaries, Special Agent Storenn, using one another to meet our own ends. You aren't a person to me, with a name and a life. You're an NCIS Special Agent. I don't want to be lulled into thinking anything different."

James listened quietly. Leasig wasn't wrong; they were never going to be buddies. That was fine with James; he wasn't looking for another friend. "So we were talking infrastructure..."

"All right. Let's say you want to get ten keys of coke up from South America, get them stateside. Let's say you want to get it out to Virginia. So you pick a country where you have a known distributor, like Costa Rica, and wait for a ship to pull in. The various Battle Group supply systems know where all of the ships are going and when they'll be there. They've gotta be able to send stuff out. So the ship pulls in and all of this stuff is waiting on the pier for them.

"A lot of foreign ports use native help. So somewhere in the mass of supplies that gets loaded up are five extra buckets of paint. They didn't request them, they don't really need them, but there they are. Once they go onto the boat, the serial numbers are recorded by supply and the cans get tossed into the paint locker."

"Which is when someone could grab one by mistake." James interrupted.

Cameron shook his head. "They'd have to go digging to do it. When they throw new paint into the locker, they rotate the old stuff up to the front and slide the new stuff into the back. Out of sight, out of mind. The Navy plays mule and doesn't even know it. Hell, the guys who are logging it and loading it and moving it around don't know about it. They're doing it for free. And it only gets easier if someone on the boat is on the take to baby-sit the cans until they hit stateside. You'd be amazed how many guys will turn their heads or check up on stuff for you for just a couple hundred extra bucks and never ask questions. Use the same guys over and over and they treat it like it's a part-time job."

James couldn't believe that it could be that easy. With the literal billions of dollars being spent on the drug war every year, these guys were walking in right under everyone's noses. They logged it and tracked it and used the military to transport it. It was enough to turn his stomach.

"So now your product is stateside. You have all of the appropriate paperwork so customs is no problem. They walk the dogs through, but there's no way they can smell anything over the paint. After customs, it's all a matter of requisition forms. The guy at squadron or division sends out the appropriate form with the appropriate serial numbers on it and those cans disappear from the paint locker. The navy will ship it anywhere you want it to go, no questions asked. Even Virginia."

James whistled low. It was that simple after all. "So really, the whole operation is run by just a few key individuals."

"No. A few guys handle moving product around. Money is where a majority of the players get involved. Sure you might pay someone to escort the cans, make sure they get where they're supposed to. But that's the exception, not the rule. Somewhere along the line you have to deliver the product and collect the cash. That takes more than a guy with a pencil. That takes guys willing to put a round in someone. It requires muscle and a lack of compassion, not an inexpensive combination to come by. And that same muscle collects debts, loans, losses, etc. All pay positions and none of them cheap."

James was flabbergasted by the numbers running around in his head. It was almost incomprehensible. "So, no couriers?"

Cameron shrugged. "I'd say ten out of eleven runs just gets shipped around with nothing but serial numbers for tracking. Only larger shipments or stuff going on boats with guys already on the dole get escorted. Like I said before, it's the exception not the rule."

He cut off suddenly as the old Latina waitress waddled over to them, steaming plates in hand. Cameron smiled as she set his plate of burritos smothered in sauce down in front of him. James had to admit; it smelled delicious. The table remained quiet for several minutes as each man dug into the food in front of him. James had shredded beef enchiladas. They were as delicious as they smelled. He knew that his stomach would make him pay later for the spicy fare, but right now he didn't really care.

James tried to collect his thoughts as he chewed his meal. Hundreds of millions of dollars just floating around, traveling around in duty vans and criss-crossing the country in government transports. The paperwork would be a nightmare. How could a handful of sailors, in conjunction with their normal duties, manage it? Another thought struck him.

"If what you're saying is accurate, this organization could feasibly be moving hundreds of millions of dollars in drugs every year. Maybe as much as a billion."

"It's not like every ship that hits a port comes back filled to the waterline with smack. Hell, if they come back with anything at all on board, it's generally less than the weight you found today. It has to be small amounts in arbitrary shipments, otherwise it draws attention. People start asking questions, and that's just not good for business. It would be stupid to try to force it or make shipments too large or too frequent. No shipment is ever over twenty keys. Besides, think of how many ships there are out there. Definitely no need to push things."

"So how large is the planning group for this? Ten, fifteen guys?" he asked around a mouthful of beans.

Cameron shook his head. "One guy runs the whole operation. It's tracked and watched and delivered by a handful of guys, but one guy coordinates it all. The buys, the sells, money distribution. Other people might actually handle the cash or deliver the product, but one guy makes sure it gets done."

James quit chewing, incredulity marking his face. "One guy does it all." The disbelief in his voice was unmistakable.

"Pretty much keeps a finger on all of it. Don't get me wrong; he's one smart, busy bastard. He gets a lot of help with execution. I mean, it's not like he's out there taking the risks or anything. He does his thing and he does it well. Keeps everything broken up so that no one knows what anyone else is doing. Everyone feels like they're on their own, just fulfilling their small role. All the guys sending those cans around, they each think that they're the only ones doing it. They don't know each other. And nobody really knows who's in charge. It's not like he sits down and does face to face meetings with people. He's invisible, hiding in plain view and nothing like you're expecting. You meet him and you're thinking he's nice, personable. Yeah, maybe a little rough, maybe he could kick your ass. But you're not sitting there thinking he could have you whacked just by snapping his fingers."

It was a lot to chew on. None of it presented any real answers, just a lot more questions – ones he'd have to sit down and organize in order to make sure he had it all right and wasn't confusing anything. There was, of course, the one question that had been bothering him since the night before. It had him feeling used. It had burned in the back of his brain all day long and now, with all of this new information lying on the table before him, it begged to be asked.

"It all kinda makes sense, everything you've said. But you're still holding out on the real questions. That aside, there is one thing that bothers me in all of this. You said 'this guy' keeps everything separated, no one knows everything that's going on, no one knows who all of the players are or the positions they hold. That no one but him has the big picture."

Cameron nodded, chewing his rice thoughtfully.

"Then how are you so well informed?" James hoped that this would foul up his game plan a little, maybe shake his confidence and his story.

There was no response to the question, just continued chewing, like he was trying to find the right words to express it. He swallowed his rice and took a sip of water, leveling a withering gaze.

"I never claimed to be a virgin, Special Agent Storenn. I never told you I wasn't involved, only that I'd help you shut it down. I've danced my dance for more than three years now, closer than I ever wanted to be to shit I never wanted to get involved with in the first place. My only way out is to ensure that it goes down permanently and that the guy behind it all never sees it coming. I'm not going to put my head in the noose for you. If you're really jonesin' to figure out where I fit in to all of this, you're gonna have to do it on your own, 'cause I'm sure as hell not gonna to help you. In the meantime, I've got work to do."

"Let me bring the two of you in, Cameron. We'll protect you; both of you."

Cameron shook his head adamantly. "While I can't say that I don't appreciate the gesture on your part, I'm gonna stick with Friday morning. I need the time to handle a few more issues. The timetable remains the same."

"You're playing with fire here, Cameron. That seizure this morning is going to raise a lot of eyebrows on the street. If anyone figures out you were the one that leaked the info, there will be hell to pay. There will be very little we can do to help you at that point."

Cameron's expression went blank, a professional poker player sitting at a high stakes table trying not to tip his hand. As controlled as he was, there was no hiding the ferocity in his eyes. The anger was a palpable thing.

"That a threat, Special Agent Storenn? Let me put your mind at ease. They're not snatching my ass up off the street like they did Monk. Not gonna happen that way, I assure you. I won't place myself in a situation that would allow it. Just don't send some booger-eating simpleton to cover me and it will all work out, despite your assertions. And on Friday, you get the rest of your answers."

James sighed with frustration, suddenly not hungry for the meal cooling on the table in front of him. A deal with the devil, holes big enough to drive a Mack truck through, and only one direction to head – forward. For better or worse, there was far too much was riding on this to not see it through to completion.

Chewing a mouthful of beans and the remains of a tortilla, only a third of his plate clean, Cameron stood up. "I hate to eat and run, but my work day is through and I've still got places to go and people to see." He reached into his wallet and threw a twenty-dollar bill on the table. "That should cover the both of us. Don't worry, I'll be in touch."

James sat there for several long minutes after Cameron left, pushing the food around his plate. He was struggling with how he was going to convince the man to give himself over to police custody. He believed that Cameron's confidence was probably well founded; he knew he wouldn't want to tangle with him. But these guys were playing for keeps, and no matter how tough Leasig might be, James knew for a fact he wasn't bullet proof. There had to be a way. Finally giving up on the remains of the meal, James stood up and headed for the door.

chapter 55

Corporal John Cappellano gave his partner a sympathetic look. Sergeant Ken Hackley was making the afternoon report and instead of talking to Storenn's answering machine, as had been the practice over the past few report periods, he had gotten a hold of the man himself. Ever since the horrendous misstep Sunday evening by their brothers in blue, the both of them remained exceedingly cautious around Supervisory Special Agent Storenn. He'd made his position on Petty Officer Monk's murder and the teams culpability in the events leading up to that low point graphically clear during the re-grouping effort Monday morning.

Cappellano had no desire to be on the receiving end of whatever ass-chewing would ensue should anything untoward happen to their charge, especially considering the suspensions that had been handed down by the department.

"No, sir. There were no stops along the way. He went straight from the meeting with you." There was a pause as a muffled burst of speech came out of the receiver. Sergeant Hackley rolled his eyes as he listened. "Yes, sir. I'm positive that it is his lawyer's office. Cappellano trailed him in and checked the sign next to the door. They are definitely the offices of Edmund Howeth."

He paused again to listen to the stream of verbiage coming from the small phone. "No, sir. He didn't appear to be in any kind of hurry. He was alone though. There is no sign of Ms. Morris' car in the parking lot."

Paul could feel his frustration building as the questioning went on. He understood everyone's apprehension with this, but come on already. Just let them do the job.

"Yes, sir, we'll report when he goes on the move again."

Sergeant Hackley clicked off the phone and laid it on the console between the seats. "Holy crap!" he exclaimed. "Nothing like getting the third degree."

"So what'd he want?"

"Nothing I couldn't have said in a single sentence. Just follow him out to where ever he goes from here and we'll turn over when it looks like he's settled for a good stretch."

"Hurry up and wait," Cappellano muttered, taking a long pull from the bottle of soda he was holding. "Hurry up and wait."

chapter 56

"Why the hell am I here?"

A blank look was his answer. "Meaning?"

"With everything that's going on, with all the heat coming down, why the hell would you bring me out here to talk with you? We could have done this over the phone."

"I didn't want to do it over the phone. I wanted to look you in the face and make sure that there were no misunderstandings between us on this. The MILIUS got snaked this morning. I want to know how and who."

Noah looked around the sparse room, a conference room Cameron borrowed for the afternoon. The surroundings were high end; mahogany table, dark leather chairs, and expensive artwork. Rather than comforting, the room only added to Noah's disquiet. Noah didn't like being out of his element. He disliked the accusing tone in Cameron's voice even more.

"I don't know."

Cameron squared off, taking a step forward. "I'm looking for a better answer than 'I don't know'."

Noah's ire was up already; he was furious over the loss of their shipment and less than happy about being in this meeting. "Why don't you ask Pinfield about it?"

"What the hell does he have to do with this?"

"I don't know, Cameron. You're the one playing all the games. You're the one getting questioned by the NCIS; the one with the cops following him everywhere. You've got cops at the club, cops sitting outside your house, cops out in the parking lot right now watching the door. All that and you're asking me why shit's falling apart?"

Cameron's eyes darkened dangerously; a villainous stare that consumed with fire and promised violence. "I warned you on Monday that something was going on. Apparently, I wasted my breath. Let me try again. I'll speak slowly so you can keep up. We just lost about a million and a quarter in product, better than a million in profit. Not acceptable. Someone turned and my name now rests with the NCIS. Also, not acceptable. I'm not going to jail, Noah. I won't be caged. Feel free to interpret that any way you want, I don't really give a fuck!"

There would be no middle ground on this. Neither of them was going to jail and only one would live to see the end of their enterprise. There was no question of that in Noah's mind now. No question at all. The air vibrated, the tension a roiling mass that crushed the air out of Noah's lungs as the room shrank around him. Cameron stood there, a coiled spring. Noah could see the muscles on his forearms clenching and unclenching and he took a step backwards, opening the distance between them.

"That's an unfortunate point of view, Cameron. I'd hate for things to end badly."

Cameron launched himself, closing the distance in a blur of motion, his strong hand smacking tightly around Noah's throat and slamming him soundly into the wall. Noah grabbed at Cameron's wrist, struggling against the iron grip. He could feel the pulse pounding in his temples and black pinpoints began to fray the edges of his vision as his oxygen disappeared. Cameron ignored his efforts and leaned in so that his lips were near to brushing the other mans ear.

"Don't walk that path, Noah. You've got to stay focused. You've got one chance on this. Screw it up and I'll have your guts for garters."

He let go and Noah slumped against the wall, the stale air of the room filling his lungs. His ears rang as the blood rushed back. Lifting his hand, he touched the raw welts around his neck. His vision cleared quickly and murder filled his eyes.

Cameron judged him from a few steps back, a disappointed parent observing a belligerent child. He shook his head. "I want answers, Noah. I want them yesterday."

Noah shook his head, rage coloring his vision red. His hand unconsciously slid back towards the nine-millimeter pistol in his belt.

Cameron stepped back in, menacing in his approach. "Don't make that mistake."

Noah forced his empty hand back to his side, barely able to control himself but at least cognizant of all the witnesses in the surrounding rooms. Now was not the time.

The door opened and closed and Noah was, once again, left alone with his anger and embarrassment. He wanted to scream. He wanted to break something. Anything would do; a table, a chair, someone's face. His breathing back to normal, he tore open the door and headed out into the offices praying for someone to get in his way.

chapter 57

The music was angry and fast, vulgar words of violence and depravity set to an electronic beat and backed up by a mixing board. Kalina heard it echoing through the house as soon as she stepped through the door and she knew that things couldn't be good. She set the bag of groceries on the kitchen counter and walked through the living room towards the den at the back of the house they'd converted to a weight room two years earlier.

She heard the heavy smacks before she got to the door and looked in. Cameron was soaked to the bone, dripping sweat as he attacked the heavy bag hanging from the ceiling. He punched and kicked, attacking ferociously. His hands, wrapped in heavy cloth and red leather bag gloves, struck the swaying black bag with a rapid fire burst; an explosive staccato of speed and sound. He moved smoothly, adjusting his body position and punches to the sway of the bag. It was an angry dance. She watched from the door as he decimated his mental adversary. Nearly a minute passed without let up. His chest was heaving. The music ended and he stopped suddenly, grasping the bag about its middle and leaning in to it for support.

"I'm glad that's not me," Kalina said from the doorway.

He whipped about, startled, his hands in front of him, defending.

"Expecting trouble?" she asked.

He smiled half-heartedly, his hands going down to hang at his sides. He reached over and clicked off the stereo just as another bass pounding tune began to vibrate the speakers. "No, just getting a little work out in before dinner."

His eyes were dark circles. Kalina knew that he hadn't been sleeping the past several nights. He tossed and turned, fitful. She knew he was nervous about things working out and that he would never burden her with that knowledge no matter how much it ate him up inside. Cameron would rather chew glass than burden her with his worries. It was always 'gonna be all right' with him. But even his bright smile seemed forced now, dimmed by the effort required to muster it forward. He was carrying too much and the melancholy mood was obvious.

"You all right, Cam?" she asked stepping in to the room. She knew he'd never let on to anything, but she had to hope. He took on the world for her; she wanted to ease his pain.

"I'm fine, baby. Just got a little bit of a headache. I didn't sleep so well last night."

"You sure that's it?"

He shrugged and changed the subject. "So what're we doing for dinner tonight? I had a late snack, but could probably eat something about six thirty, seven o'clock."

An exasperated sigh escaped her. He was the rock that others crushed themselves against. There was no budging or forcing him. She tried not to let her worry show, but it wasn't an overly successful venture. "I don't know, maybe we could stop on the way to the club and pick something up."

"You really want to go to the club tonight? I thought maybe we could get a movie and relax." His voice was heavy and drawn.

"You're a bad influence. We'll pick up a movie on the way too. I want to stop by and check in, make sure everything is going well. We'll be home by eight. I can do the books and check the receipts tomorrow. There's a lot to be done before Saturday morning."

He sidled over to her, the half-hearted smile looking much more sincere. "You're a good woman, Kalina Morris. You are a very good woman to me."

She felt her heart jump; she loved when he said that.

He held out his arms as he approached, intending to wrap them around her, give her a hug. She made a face, wrinkling her little nose and scrunching her eyes in exaggerated disgust. She held her hands in front of her and backed away.

"I don't think so. If you want any of this, you'll be taking a shower and washing your sweaty self. Don't get near me, I mean it!"

Cameron laughed her. "You're gonna hurt my feelings, playing like that."

She turned and started back towards the kitchen to put away the groceries. "Bathe and we'll negotiate," she called back over her shoulder. She didn't need to be in the room to know that as soon as she walked out, his smile had faded to be replaced with a look of concentration. It was the look he wore constantly now whenever he thought no one was paying attention. It was the look that worried her.

chapter 58

Jessica looked through the candlelight, enjoying how the yellow flames reflected in James' eyes as he told his story. She tried to concentrate on what he was saying, but those eyes of his were just so dang distracting.

"I mean, c'mon, that's ridiculous! Using the Navy supply system? That only narrows our suspect pool down to every Sailor on every ship in the entire Navy with a few landlocked supply side guys thrown in to boot. What the hell is that?"

"I don't know, James. It doesn't really surprise me. All it takes is a little knowledge and some creativity and people will figure out a way to twist the system to fit their needs. If you think about it, this one is really pretty straight forward, brilliant in its simplicity."

He shook his head with a lost look on his face. "I know; but the brass on these guys…"

She studied his face. "The brass on these guys? Don't you mean the brass on this guy?"

James shrugged noncommittally. "I don't know, Jess. Everything about this guy screams that he's the one we're after. But nothing shows. There's nothing at all connecting him to any of this besides what he's given us. He's not tipping his hand – he's helpful, but not too helpful. This is so unbelievably frustrating. It's right there, right at the tip of my fingers, but I just can't get a hold of it."

"Too convenient," she agreed.

And it was.

Pure providence that Leasig would walk into the picture at that exact time with all of the answers to all of the questions; Jessica wasn't buying it either. She was about as big a fan of coincidence as James was and just about as sure that he was running a game on them. Problem was that she was just as frustrated with trying to prove it all, especially within their very limited time frame.

"Maybe we should just bring him in."

James shook his head emphatically. "I told you before, grabbing this guy will do nothing other than ensure that whatever info we are getting from him will stop altogether; one way or another. It's not a risk I'm willing to take at this point."

"I thought you said he was a survivor."

"Survivor, yes; bulletproof, no. I don't think there's any way to take him in quietly if he doesn't want to go, which he doesn't. Since we have nothing of substance to charge him with, his girl's lawyer would punish us with all kinds of claims of harassment and prejudicial prosecution. I don't even want to think of the public relations nightmare that would go on if he got killed as a result, we'd end up doing time. No. He's got to come in on his own."

James stopped to saw off a piece of steak and stuff it in his mouth. He chewed thoughtfully, staring off into the dimly lit space of the restaurant. Jessica wondered what was running through his head. Was it just business and he was here grazing with a fellow cop or was he here having dinner with her? It was a basic question; maybe one that the feminists around the precinct wouldn't like but one that meant something to her. He washed the steak down with a swallow of beer.

"How's the steak?"

He blinked and his face flushed pink. "Sorry, Jess. The steak's good. How's yours treating you?"

"Can't complain."

He studied his plate for several moments.

"You waiting for it to move?" Jessica asked with a wry grin.

He looked up again, his eyes locking with hers. "No, just a lot on my mind. So much has happened over the last several days, you know, the world's kinda moving at warp speed right now."

"I know how you feel." Her heart fluttered in her chest and her lungs seized for a second. She felt like she was holding her breath. It was not what he said, but the tone of voice when he said it. He had that look on his face again, like there was more that he wanted to say. She paused to give him a chance to say it, but he stuffed another piece of meat in his mouth and started chewing. She swore silently in the back of her head, wanting him to break the stalemate. Frustrated by his silence, she decided to force the issue. "Do you want to get the rest of this to go? Maybe finish up out on the boat?"

Jessica had to forcibly hold back her smile as he choked down the half chewed meat, nearly gagging as he struggled to get it down his throat. He coughed and took a swig of beer.

"With you?" he asked stupidly.

"If you'd like," she replied coyly, a skilled angler setting the hook.

His face colored. The distance and distracted concentration melted as relief and anticipation rushed in to replace them. How odd that a man of his age, with his confident demeanor could be so harried at the thought of asking a woman out.

"I wouldn't think you'd have to ask."

"One of us had to," was her sly response. She stood and picked up her handbag. "Now if you'll excuse me, I'm going to go powder my nose."

She turned without looking back. A smug grin played across her lips as she weaved her way through the room. She knew without doubt that he was scrambling for boxes and the check behind her. Even with the craziness of the day, it was definitely shaping up to be a good night.

chapter 59

The traffic outside the window passed by, a blur of red and white lights glowing brightly in the half-light of sunset. Out over the beach, the sky was enflamed with brilliant oranges and reds, the bloody sun only a sliver on the horizon. The night was beginning to come alive. Joggers made their way along the broad walks of the Harbor Walk and families and friends ambled along in small knots, sharing the sights of the tourist section of the city. The Glass Lamp district glowed, it's restaurants packed with happy people dining and drinking and sharing conversations about the day.

It was all lost on Noah. He mulled over the events of the day, trying to separate himself emotionally from what had gone on. The ending was going to be bad. No matter how he looked at it, no matter how he ran the scenario through his head, he came to the same conclusion. Cameron was selling him down the river. One way or another, he was in bed with that cop, Storenn, and sooner or later they would be knocking on his door. The only problem was how to react. No one had been arrested today. The drugs and the money they would have brought with them were nothing but wasted energy and bad dreams now. What was the reaction they were looking for?

Cameron knew Noah had a temper and that the violent streak in him ran deep and wide. Maybe that was the key. Maybe Cameron was hoping that he would put it together and come after him. Basically, let Noah screw himself over by jumping in too quickly. If Storenn and the cops were watching his back, Noah would get snatched up the second he tried to take Cameron out.

He pursed his lips angrily and scowled at the thought. Was that stuck-up bastard so certain he was stupid enough to just throw himself to the wolves? Not a chance in hell.

But the question remained, how should he respond? He couldn't lose a million dollars in uncut heroin and not react in some fashion. Perhaps he would just follow Cameron's lead, see where the cold-blooded bastard took him. Let him set the pace of the conversation and the tone of the blame, play it like he didn't suspect a thing. Let them all just go on thinking he was stupid.

And when the opening presented itself, he'd be ready to take advantage of it. There would be an opening; everyone made mistakes. Even Cameron Leasig.

chapter 60

Cameron sat at his laptop, scanning through a series of text. Kalina, unable to concentrate on reading, put down her book and walked over to where he sat. She nudged his arm to get his attention.

"So what you working on?" she asked.

He smiled up at her. "Had a little meeting with Noah this afternoon."

"I guessed that from your dance with the heavy bag."

He chuckled at her and wrapped an arm around her slim waist. "He's pretty pissed."

"You do seem to have that effect on people."

"Oh, come on now. You don't seem to mind so much."

"I'm the exception. No one else can stand you. Really."

"Anyway. I don't think that he's quite pissed enough, so I thought that I'd encourage him a little."

Kalina grimaced, afraid of the answer to the question she was about to ask. "What are you going to do?"

"Well," he started, pulling his arm from around her and squaring on the laptop, "a couple of weeks ago I hired a guy I know to get into Noah's computer and add a tracking program." He gestured to the text on the screen. "It tracks every keystroke that he makes on his computer and periodically e-mails me a file with all of the text."

Kalina shrugged. "So."

He was quiet for a second as he continued to scan, obviously looking for something. When he found it he looked up at her and smiled. "So…it gives us access to this."

Turning back, he struck a series of keys and he was suddenly at the Banque Nationale de Paris website. Another series of keystrokes and they were looking at the balances of Noah's bank accounts.

"Oh my," Cameron chuckled under his breath. "Noah's a saver. I'll bet when he wakes up tomorrow and finds his millions missing he'll be pissed enough to play."

Kalina watched him type and her stomach tightened. If Noah hadn't wanted Cameron's blood before, there would be no quenching his thirst for it when he discovered this.

"Cameron…"

"He's gotta want it, baby. If he's not going to do it on his own, I've gotta help him. Besides, he's not going to need all that money where he's going. I figure that between this little act here and the visitor I'm sending out to visit our friend Storenn, everyone is gonna be more than happy to get this over with."

"I guess," she sighed, wishing that she had just kept to her book. She had no idea what visitor Cameron was talking about and was fairly certain that she was better off for it. She would rather be lost in the cheesy romance novel she was forcing herself through than adding to the already sizable catalogue of ulcer inducing craziness she was dealing with.

He pressed the enter key and the numbers all changed to zeros. It was done. The money was flying through cyberspace to a destination only Cameron knew. She could tell him to put it back, but he wouldn't. For the thousandth time in the past three days she prayed that he knew what he was doing. All she could do was trust that he did. It would have to be enough.

With his task done, he powered down the computer pulled her down onto his lap. "You ready for that movie?"

Her mind begged for distraction. She leaned into him and let him kiss her on the neck. "I guess so."

thursday, june 10

chapter 61

The creak of the cabin door woke James from his thin slumber. The slight rocking of the boat in its berth tried to put him back under, but it was time to get up anyway. His body ached in a good way, the result of using muscles he wasn't even aware he had to pull off the pair of marathon sessions he and Jessica had managed in the tight quarters of the cabin.

His mind drifted momentarily. Every fantasy he'd had of Jessica paled in comparison to the reality of that was her; the skin – softer, the kisses – hotter, the body – tighter, the sex – more athletic. He couldn't help but smile a goofy schoolboy's smile as he reflected on the evening and the hours leading up to the pale light of sunrise. He felt sorry for anyone who had been trying to get some peace and quiet in any of the adjoining slips.

A scuff of movement by the door focused his attention like a laser beam. He lay there motionless for a moment, listening and giving his eyes a chance to adjust to the half-light of the room, painfully aware of his nakedness. His pistol was in the nightstand behind him. There was no way to get to it without rolling over. Another scuff of movement, foot of the bed, port side. James tried to maintain his breathing – an impossible task since he couldn't possibly know how he was breathing while asleep. But it was a thought that seemed reasonable at the time.

"Morning, James. I know you're awake, so why don't you roll over nice and easy so we can talk?"

The room was a mix of familiar shadows. The nightstand that held his nine-millimeter pistol was attached to the bulkhead some three feet away. It might as well have been a mile. James rolled over slowly. A figure wearing a silky black stocking mask stood at the foot of the bed by the wooden cabinet doors. The dark sweater and pants he was wearing blurred the lines of his body against the darkened wall, a black on black retrospective. The pistol in his hand was easy to pick out as it was pointed directly at James' head.

"That's better," the voice said soothingly.

The lapping of the water against the hull of the boat filled the silent space in the room as James worked to hold his opponents eyes. They were bone-chilling chips of dark, unforgiving granite. James would have preferred wild eyes, wide and twitchy, vice the calculated murder that he was staring into now.

"You've got the gun. What would you like to talk about?" James asked, trying to sound cool and collected.

James shifted his weight on the bed, the anger welling like a hot balloon in his stomach. His eyes flicked over to the nightstand. A quick move could cover the distance to his weapon and he could put this prick down. The cocking of a pistol cut through the space between the two men.

"I was sent as a warning. Seek your fortune elsewhere. You interfere with another shipment and I'll return to paint that bulkhead behind you with whatever happens to be floating around in that skull of yours." The voice was dispassionate, matter-of-fact. Creepy.

James decided that this wasn't the time or place to inform this chucklehead that going after a federal agent was about as stupid a thing as he could possibly do. Law enforcement tended to take care of their own. Attacking any officer, federal or not, was an affront to the entire community and ensured a quick and nasty response.

"You come back here talking tough and I'll shove that gun up your ass," James stated acerbically, trying to get a rise from his visitor.

"And your girl Jessica will die in a manner that'll make Monk's passing look like a day at the spa."

The man in black didn't miss a beat.

Blood rushed into James' ears as he struggled to keep his anger in check. He bit his lip to silence the explosion of vulgarity and vitriol he wanted to spew. The hot, coppery taste of blood filled his mouth as his teeth went through the skin.

From his perch by the desk the dark visitor grinned behind his mask; James could hear it in his voice. "I see we understand each other. Stay the fuck out of my way, James. It's not just your life you're playing with."

James readied himself for a lunge at the nightstand.

"We're not done."

"Yes, we are, James. If you see me again, it will be the image you take to the grave. Tell Jessica I said hello."

James watched him walk out of the room, a dark clothed wraith that may never have even been there.

chapter 62

In less than an hour James, Jessica, and Vincent sat behind closed doors as James relayed the disturbing events of the morning. All of them took the threat seriously; it was an ever-present factor of the job.

"So what do you want to do?" Vincent asked plainly, eyeing the both of them. "Your asses on the line here, I'll let you make the call."

James regarded his boss evenly. He knew that this wasn't a game they were playing, but they were barking up the wrong tree if they thought they were going to intimidate him with a few threats. Though his protective hackles bristled at the thought of anyone coming after Jessica, he was confident she felt the same way about it.

"Nothing to be done, far as I can tell. I'm not gonna cut and run because some jerk off in a mask breaks into my boat and waves a gun at me. Besides, if whoever it was really wanted me dead, that guy could've smoked me in my sleep."

"I'm not saying back off. I'm saying that you may want to step carefully until you have Leasig in custody. No wandering off the reservation. That interdiction yesterday pissed some people off. You can't afford to connect Leasig to that by being seen with him."

Jessica shrugged. "Business as usual. I know what you're saying, Vince. And I feel you on this, I really do. But It'd be a mistake to let some unsub make us 'step carefully'. We change anything at all even one iota and we're just sending a message of weakness. We can't afford that. We can't let anyone think that we're gonna back down simply because they threaten us. We do that, we might as well hang it up."

James stood up from the table, adjusting his tie and sport coat. "It's a one day float. I'll give the team a heads up. Other than that, we'll do what we can to prepare for tomorrow."

Jessica followed James' lead, scooting back from the table. There was nothing else to say. There was no way either of them was going to back down or back off. They would carry on; do their respective jobs. They were cops. Carrying on was what they did best.

chapter 63

Evan Pinsone shuffled through the papers and, finding the appropriate list of notes, cleared his voice and looked at James.

"So, what have you got for me, Evan?" asked James, his attention fully centered on the tired looking young agent standing before his desk.

He cleared his throat again. "I'll start with the girl. The specifics are in the reports," he started, nodding towards the two thick envelopes lying on the corner of the desk. "Kalina Morris was born on Maui. She is what we consider a classic broken vessel case. Abused as a kid, both physically and mentally, she ran away at sixteen and ended up stripping on Oahu. That's where she met Randall Godfrey – a thirty-four year old Second Class Machinist Mate. By nineteen she was married and stripping in San Diego. Godfrey was, of course, a carbon copy of her father, an abusive alcoholic with a strong backhand. "

James knew the scenario – it was far from a unique story, especially among strippers. But no matter how many times he heard it, it never ceased in pissing him off. And yet at the same time the woman he met just two days earlier seemed a far cry from the typical home made victim. She was actually a far cry from that stereotype; there was certain air of confidence and success about her – she was master of her domain.

"Apparently, that's when she and Cameron Leasig crossed paths. He was bouncing at the club she was dancing at. The cycle of abuse went on with Godfrey; the police and hospital reports listing the particulars are in the folders. And then, three days after her twenty-second birthday, Godfrey was listed lost at sea, his body never recovered. After Godfrey's disappearance, her life seemed to take a serious turn for the better. By twenty-six, she'd earned her bachelor's degree in business management from SDSU and owned one of the most prosperous clubs in San Diego. Pretty dramatic change."

Definitely was, James thought to himself. He could guess at the cause.

"Now, at thirty-one, she's doing very well for herself. She's a millionaire, couple of times over. Owns the note on the club and on the Mediterranean style mansion she and Cameron call home in Coronado. She drives a newer BMW five series, as does Cameron. She paid cash for both."

He looked up from his notes and chuckled. "Guess we're just in the wrong business."

James shared his smile. "Guess so."

"The only other info I have on her," he said, turning back to his notes, "is that she donates a large amount of time and money working with three different charities here in town. One works with victims of child abuse; gives free counseling to kids and adults who have been on the wrong side of it. The other two are halfway houses for abused women trying to leave their spouses. They offer skills training, counseling services and legal services."

James nodded, listening intently. He understood the charities, trying to help others with shared experiences. Helping those who couldn't help themselves. He respected the gesture.

"So what's the story on Mr. Cameron Leasig?"

"Not much there really. He was born and raised in Yuma, Arizona. Father was Alexander Leasig, a retired Petty Officer First Class with twenty years of service including two tours in Nam. He was a drunk. His wife, Lauren, left when Cameron was seven. Nothing out of the ordinary with the childhood. Average student throughout high school. He wrestled, played football and boxed, never a standout, though. Joined the navy at eighteen and, as far as we can tell, never went back. The last thirteen years have been lackluster. A copy of his service jacket is in his envelope. Decent enough evaluations, competent at the job, never been in trouble for anything we could find. He pretty much just gets by. The only hobbies we could find were that he does Aikido twice a week and manages Kalina's club. I'd say he was pretty much a forgettable human being, except for the fact that just about everybody on base knows who he is and we couldn't find one who would say anything bad about him."

"What do you mean?"

"Well, since his record was so anorexic, we went out and tried to get some interviews. It was pretty damn ridiculous. You'll understand when you read through the stuff. Everybody has some memorable story about this guy, he's like the freakin' Pope. Everybody owes him for one thing or another. 'He got me a job, he got my kid a job, he lent me money, he got me tickets to take my wife to the ballet for our anniversary.' I mean the list goes on and on. I'd actually like to meet this guy just to see if his halo's as bright as they make it out to be."

Interesting. It didn't quite fit, like opposite sides of the same coin. On one side he's bland and easily dismissed while on the other he's the first guy people go to when they need help. The second type would be exactly the type of guy that could bring about the evident changes in a woman with a past like Kalina's – a guy who helps and heals and supports. James wondered which side was the real Cameron Leasig; bland and forgettable or outgoing and helpful. His guess was neither and both at the same time. Two sides of the same coin was a bad analogy for someone sporting more faces than Lon

Chaney. James had talked to Leasig twice now and had found him intense and confident, a far cry from the type of guy he would expect to just disappear into the background; that is, unless he wanted to. He would have some interesting reading to do later on.

"Great work, Evan. Especially on such short notice. I really appreciate it."

A smile crossed Evan's face, a little bit of pride for praise that he rarely saw. "Not a problem, James. Just a little more notice next time, OK."

James returned the smile. "I'll try." He reached out and picked up the two manila envelopes, impressed with their thickness and weight. It might take a little longer to get through these than he originally thought. "I'll read through these this afternoon and get back to you if I have any questions."

Evan took it for the polite dismissal it was. "I'll be around till about four, four-thirty."

chapter 64

They stood in the cleaning closet at the back of the building, surrounded by graying, over-used mops and rusty buckets. A single bare bulb dangled from the middle of the watermarked ceiling casting a harsh light; shadows, dark and forbidding, filled the corners and the gaps under the shelving that were overloaded with oddly shaped bottles of cleaning supplies. It was as strange a place as any for the two to meet.

Noah was tired of the sneaking around. Secrecy was par for the course, given the lifestyle he'd chosen, but this skulking around in broom closets was beyond the pale. He wanted no further contact with Cameron. Every meeting was an added and, by his estimation, unnecessary risk. He'd already decided on his course of action. This meeting only reinforced those thoughts.

"So you're sure about this?"

"As sure as I can be about anything now," Cameron replied heatedly. "They'll be waiting for me tomorrow morning when I come in to work."

"Where the hell are you getting this? I've talked to everyone I know and nobody seems to know anything about this. No one's saying anything about you."

"What do you want me to say? I know what I know. They're playing it close to the vest – makes sense considering their track record."

Noah fixed him with a hard look. He tried to read Cameron's thoughts, tried to get past tight set of the jaw and the stare that meant bore through him. Cameron didn't seem nervous, a little tired, maybe even a little on edge, but not the slightest bit nervous. That in and of itself had an unnerving affect on Noah. Cameron was a smart bastard who people constantly underestimated. They were blinded by the easy going smile and the cool façade. But Noah wasn't one of those Kool-Aid drinking fools.

Cameron Leasig had a plan and Noah had to figure out what that plan entailed, what Cameron was going to pull to get himself out of this.

"So what's the plan? They take you into custody and then what? You talk like a bitch, turn me and everyone else in? Or have you already pleaded your way out of that?"

The accusation filled the space between them, bristling electricity.

"No to all of it. You're going to make me righteous."

Noah's jaw dropped. "I'm gonna what?"

"You're going to get me out of this, going to come up with something dramatic and bold that'll give them nothing to look for. I don't care what it is, but you're going to make it work."

"You've got to be kidding me. You want me to risk my neck so that you can walk away? What happens to me – jail forever? Bullshit! I might have been born at night, but it wasn't last night. I'm not going to be the one who throws it all away so you can walk scot-free." Noah shook his head in disbelief. How could Cameron even think that he was stupid enough to walk into such a weak-assed trap?

"There's no choice in the matter, Noah. I'm not going to mark myself by running. You do your part on this, you do what you do best and we both walk out unscathed. You'll be rid of me forever; I'll disappear."

"If you're ready to bolt anyway, why not jump a plane tonight? Why do I gotta put myself out there?"

"It's not run, it's disappear. I take a walk now and I'll have to run forever. Not the life I have planned. There has to be an event to raise doubts, lend some credibility to a disappearance. Something that makes them look for a body vice a person. That's all you. Besides, you've got no choice in this, Noah. If you don't get me out of this, I'll deal you away without so much as batting an eye."

"What's to stop me from just punching a new asshole in your forehead and ending this forever? Don't you fucking threaten me, Cameron! You won't live to see the morning!"

"And what's to stop me from snapping your neck where you stand? You wouldn't make it to the door, Noah. No screams, no one to help you or do your dirty work. Look around you. There's just me and you and the wash buckets. So what's to stop me from ending it right here and now?"

Noah looked around nervously. There wasn't anywhere to go, Cameron was between him and the door and he knew that although he was slightly larger than his opponent, he was over matched by a considerable stretch in both skill and strength. Any move towards the door would be an exercise in futility and he knew it. He replied with a shrug of his thick shoulders.

"What's stopping me is the fact that I need you to get me out of this. What's stopping you is the fact you need me out of this. It's also the fact that you know me well enough to know that if anything happens, anything at all, the cops'll get every stitch of information I have on you and you will go away forever."

Cameron had him over a barrel and Noah couldn't tell if he was bluffing. But it didn't matter; he was looking at a dead man. Time hadn't caught up to that fact yet, but it would soon. The muscles in his jaw flexed, standing out like cables, so tightly they began to hurt.

"When was the last time you checked your balances at the Banque Nationale de Paris, Noah?"

The question caught Noah completely off guard. He felt like he'd been punched squarely in the chest, robbing his lungs of air. Spots swam in front of his eyes as he tried to comprehend it. He took a sharp breath and his eyes narrowed.

"You've got to be careful with that kind of money, my friend. Fifteen million is more than many people will see in a lifetime, much less just have lying around in some dusty old offshore bank account. Don't worry, though. It's safe. And when you get me out of all this, it will grow by another two and a half million. We'll call it an exit fee."

Noah didn't know how to respond. How had Cameron found out about his accounts and how much money was there? Had he accessed them? Or was it all another mind game? But to what end?

"So I can count on you?"

"I'll be there," Noah said through clenched teeth. He meant it; he would figure something out and he would be there. Cameron might not be celebrating that fact tomorrow evening, but Noah wouldn't miss it for the world. It was beyond the question of business or pleasure now. His response had become a necessity. He could only assume the worst about his accounts for now. He would find out the truth about it all soon enough.

Cameron eyed him evenly. "Think on how you want this to end, Noah. It's all up to you. We can both walk. Don't make a bad decision."

Noah just stood there, a granite statue of hate and anger. There was no reply, no movement, no agreement on any level.

Cameron may have started the whole enterprise, but he relied heavily on Noah to get things done. For years now they had worked as partners. Cameron danced behind the scenes, using his many contacts to keep the product and money flowing while Noah pounded it out on the front lines, ensuring that the lines of distribution remained open and free. The partnership was profitable for them both, yielding up uncounted millions. It galled Noah that he could be replaced on Cameron's whim, while the same could not be said in reverse. While Noah ran the front end of the business, dealing with the customers, there was a great deal he didn't know about the supply side. Cameron was good at keeping his secrets; called it insulation. Noah knew that it was nothing if not a means for maintaining control.

Noah made his decision. Cameron could think he was still in control of the situation, that things were going to go as planned. He wouldn't live to see a jail cell. Cameron walked from the cramped room, closing the door behind him and leaving Noah alone to stew in his fury.

chapter 65

The calm before the storm. James hated that period, the one where you sat around waiting for the other shoe to drop. There was really nothing left for him to do. He'd reserved a van for the next morning to pick up Cameron. He'd made arrangements for Agents Rollins and Keleman to ride shotgun on the pickup, a little insurance just in case anything unexpected happened. He'd even reserved an interrogation room so that he and Cameron could sit down and talk in private.

The research was pretty much done, he would of course read through the files again tonight just to get facts straight and formulate solid questions for his interrogation. That would take some time, putting together that list of questions in some kind of order that made sense. He'd also go through the backgrounds tonight and see if anything struck him for inclusion to the interview. There really wasn't time or resources available to do much more than had already been done.

Images from his confrontation on the boat earlier in the day filled his mind darkly. The CSU had swept the boat for prints, coming up empty handed. Not a surprise. The man who faced him this morning was a professional hitter; he wouldn't have left anything to mark his passing. James played the whole event over in his mind, listening to the gruff voice. He was lucky that someone was just trying to warn him off. He figured that whoever had it in for him was probably going to be royally pissed off by this time tomorrow; he wouldn't be getting the simple courtesy of a warning next time around.

Cameron Leasig and the information he brought with him was quite the prize. He chuckled to himself as he looked around his empty office. There was no way that anything Leasig turned over as evidence would have anything to do with him. Had Vince been in the room, James would have put an entire paycheck against it. There would be no evidence against Cameron Leasig. That was something that struck James as odd about this whole deal too. Leasig had never requested immunity from prosecution. James kept waiting for Kalina's high priced attorney to step in and negotiate on his behalf, but that hadn't happened yet. Of course that didn't mean that it wouldn't happen tomorrow.

He looked down at the hands slowly ticking by on his watch. He was going to be late picking Jessica up at her apartment.

chapter 66

James and Jessica sat in the silver Accord, looking at the massive house. Neither seemed to be in that much of a hurry to hop out and go ring the doorbell. It had to happen, the warning had to be given and the plea had to be made. James did not like the idea of threatening a woman and Jessica did not care for the idea of pleading with a suspect. None of it made for a good time.

James finally moved, opening the car door and heading up the walk. Jessica had to trot to catch up to him. They had discussed their tactics and goals ad nauseam lying in the bunk of the boat the previous night. It was strange after-sex talk, not romantic or loving in the slightest, but it was the two of them; each obsessed with thoughts of the case. To Jessica it was a breath of fresh air not to have to worry about the man in her life not understanding or getting pissed about other things being on her mind. James understood completely. They bounced ideas off each other. Visiting Kalina Morris and trying to talk some sense into her was Jess's idea.

The door opened before the two of them made it to the broad porch. Kalina stood there with a scowl on her face. She was dressed in tight black stretch shorts and a baggy old surf t-shirt. She wore no make-up and her long midnight hair was pulled up into a ponytail, and she still looked like a model running out to a photo shoot. Jessica noted the appraising look from James and made a mental note to torture him about it later. Jess was already less than sympathetic towards Kalina Morris, having a hard time feeling sorry for the multi-millionaire girlfriend of a drug lord. The unconscious look from James just made her want to roast the ex-stripper that much more.

"Unless you two are planning on going for a run around the block with me, I don't know why you're here," she said sarcastically, looking down her nose at both of them.

"We'd like a few moments of your time, Ms. Morris, that's all."

"Really, Mr. Storenn? Just a few moments of my time? Sorry, but I've got a very busy day ahead of me. Perhaps you could send other agents out to insult me on Monday next week. Does that work for you? Monday?" Her remarks were acid as she stepped to go by them.

Jessica stepped into her path, not letting her by. "Really, Ms. Morris, we'd just like to talk to you for a moment."

"Having already spoken to my lawyer once, I wouldn't think you'd be so quick to come back here. You can rest assured though that you will be hearing from him again, with a formal complaint this time."

James told Jessica to expect a chill reception, considering the remarks and threats her lawyer had delivered last time the Service had come calling. They were definitely getting one. But Jessica could see the strain in Kalina's face and knew she was just playing tough. There was an uneasiness in her eyes when she looked at them, the jaw line held a little too taut. The back a little too straight. The dark circles under Kalina's almond eyes that spoke of restless slumber and long nights up worrying. The skin around the nails on her left hand had been chewed away, leaving pink slivers of raw, worried skin behind. The pressure was mounting and whatever else was going on, Kalina's nerves were starting to fray. Jessica recognized the signs; she had seen them grow on James over the last several months. Now they were just another piece of his outfit. A small part of Jessica suddenly felt sorry for her, but she pushed it back down and listened the cop in her saying that it was karma in action.

Jessica stood her ground. "We can play this either way, Ms. Morris; here on your turf or down at the station house where every perp in the city can see you escorted in."

Kalina paused, eyeing the both of them distrustfully.

"Cameron came to us on this, Ms. Morris," James threw in hopefully. "Now we have concerns and we're coming back to you. Please, just a moment of your time."

Kalina looked around, eyeing the neighborhood. She looked down and checked her the silver face of her watch. "You have three minutes," she said flatly.

There would be no argument or discussion about it. She turned and headed back into the house, the cop and the Agent following closely behind her.

chapter 67

Kalina led the pair into the neatly appointed living room and let them settle into the large cushions of the couch. She was less than comfortable having these two in her house. The other two Agents had been easy to figure out, Cameron fed her every question they had asked days before they ever darkened the doorway. Their ignorance and her temper had done the rest. She and Cameron both took it as a good sign that junior Agents had been sent initially, time was not their friend on this little adventure. But now, here in her living room, sat the Supervisory Agent and the lead Detective for the task force. She tried to maintain the show of indignation she'd felt before, tried to remain offended by the rudeness and pompous behavior of previous visitors; but her discomfort was evident in the adrenaline rush she felt as her heart picked up a few beats. The tightness in her belly wouldn't go away and she was fighting to keep her breathing even. She hated that feeling; it was the same weakness that had allowed her to be a punching bag for some twenty-two years of her life and she hated being reminded of that.

Instead of dwelling on it, she tried to fight back, looking over the two of them, studying them as they did the same to her. She recognized Special Agent Storenn from the Club. He looked to be in much better shape than he had been on Monday night, better rested at the very least. His suit was clean and pressed and his strong jaw was smoothly shaven. He was still ever alert, his eyes focused and penetrating, trying to dig out whatever secrets she had buried. He reminded her of Cameron in that respect. In contrast, his face was a mix of emotion, as though he really didn't want to be sitting in her living room any more than she wanted him there. That thought intrigued Kalina. Why would he be uncomfortable about coming here? Was it the threat of legal action against the task force? No, not that. Something else she couldn't put her finger on.

The female was, Kalina could only guess, Detective Muir. Cameron described her as bright and driven. He left out the fact she was attractive. So many of the female cops she'd seen in her years looked like guys with tits; it was ridiculous. They all possessed the same androgynous cookie cutter body type with the broad shoulders and thick waists. Detective Muir didn't fit that stereotype. She was small, almost petite; muscular in the way of athleticism while still retaining the gentle shapes of her gender. She didn't carry much in the way of size but she definitely carried a great deal of confidence and a serious demeanor. Her eyes were quick and the tightness around her mouth said that she wasn't happy they were here either, but for a different reason.

Detective Muir didn't look uncomfortable; she looked mildly pissed. Kalina measured her as a woman not to be crossed.

With her guests settled, Kalina looked down at her watch. "The clock is ticking," she stated flatly.

Agent Storenn looked over to the Detective and started in. "Things are getting out of control, Ms. Morris. That little tidbit Cameron coughed up the other evening as a show of good faith really rocked the boat; no pun intended. There are some very angry people out and about in the city today because of that seizure and I," he paused, correcting himself, "we have serious concerns about Cameron's safety at this point."

Kalina didn't blink at the news. She knew there were issues; that the street wasn't exactly the safest place right now, but Cameron knew what he was doing.

"You don't seem so concerned, though," Detective Jessica observed. "Why is that?"

The room was thick with silent tension. They were obviously waiting for an answer. Kalina decided to let them mull it over for a bit. She tried to look bored with the line of questioning, despite her misgivings about its pointed direction.

"You know what I think, Ms. Morris?" the blonde continued. "I think that you're not worried about your boyfriend because you know that he's the one pulling the strings. Cameron Leasig is the man behind it all. And all of this," she gestured widely with her arms, "all of this is a front. A brick and mortar illusion you're in all the way up to your pretty little neck. And you know that when the house of cards comes tumbling down, you're going to be caught inside. You're his money front, Ms. Morris. You've both been lucky up until now, but Cameron has played one game to many and your luck has run out – you have two choices, get nailed by his associates or get nailed by us. With us, at least the both of you will live."

Kali took a deep breath and let it out slowly; seriously uncomfortable with the direction this discussion was taking. She locked eyes with her female adversary. "One, if you think that I'm not worried about Cameron's safety, well, you're just not paying attention. I worry about him, but Cameron is a big boy. He's more than capable of handling himself. If you discovered anything about him in the last several days, I'd think it would be that. Two, the only thing I know he's 'behind' is the desk he rides every day. Three, the illusion you're describing doesn't exist. My books are clean, as is my club; you can subpoena every record I have at any point in time or just ask the cops you've had parked in there since Tuesday evening. I'm not a front for anything and I resent the accusation.

"I hope that's not all you had for me; some loose accusations and a little bit of intimidation? You're wasting my time instead of upholding your end of the deal. You made a promise, Agent Storenn. You swore you'd have Cameron's back until tomorrow. Instead you're running around trying to put a knife in it. If you were really worried, you would be on him like a blanket. But you're not. You're here. And why is that, Detective? You know what I think? I think you're looking your gift horse in the mouth, praying to God that it's Trojan so that you can prove how smart you are."

Jessica's eyes blazed at the sarcasm. She looked like she was going to come off the couch swinging.

James held his hand up, dragging Kalina's eyes away from the Detective's and forcing her focus on him. His voice was calm when he spoke and the discomfort was gone from his face. This was the serious, confident James Storenn she remembered. "That's not exactly it, Kalina. We know Cameron's in over his head, no matter your assertions. We know he's got some weight behind him, that he's not some low level player. He knows too much for it to be otherwise. We know that you're selling the club and that this house is under contract. We know that you've been pooling assets for months and converting them into cash for the last several weeks, all of it long before anything happened to Anderson Monk. You knew that events would be leading you here and now you're setting yourselves up for a run and you're trying to use us a smoke screen for your great escape."

Kalina didn't even blink. The information wasn't exactly a revelation to her. She made up her mind that Cameron was right; it really didn't matter if the authorities knew about their plans to get out of town. Really, it made the Fed's job all that much easier; all of the paperwork would be done when moving day came.

"And? What does it matter to you what the motivations are as long as you get your information and shut the bad guys down? I would think it would be a win-win for your office having people who were ready to move. And what would you prefer we do? Sit around after you have all of the information and let these goons take us apart? Let them destroy our house, the club while we struggle trying to unload it all? I don't think so."

"If we can find out all of this information, Ms. Morris, so can the guys you're running from. They will figure out what is going on and they will come after you. Talk to Cameron and get him to come in – now, before anything happens to either one of you."

Kalina shook her head at him and stood up. "No. I don't trust you to protect us, Agent Storenn. Yes, we are working on our own agenda, but so are you. Tomorrow morning will have to be soon enough for the lot of you.

Do your jobs and it will all work out; keep wasting your time harassing me and you'll have a whole different set of problems on your hands."

James arched an eyebrow at that last comment and started to ask about it, but Kalina wasn't paying attention to him any more. She glanced at her watch and then looked up expectantly at the both of them.

"Times up."

chapter 68

The blank inventory forms lay on the desk, a reminder of the work that needed to be done before Noah called it a day. Chief DeJesus walked through the door, scowling to see him staring off into nothing. "Petty Officer Lawson? That inventory needs to be on my desk before the end of the day."

He blinked slowly and looked over at her. It took a second for her words to sink in. "Roger that, Chief."

She shook her head as she continued on to her larger office in the back of the broad room. He watched her go, imagining the sweetness of snapping her neck. Not that he'd do it, he actually liked her, but the thought crossed his mind anyway. It brought him back to his earlier conversation with Cameron.

What the hell did Cameron know about his accounts? Noah had fought the urge all day long to access the web and log onto his accounts just to be sure that everything was all right. It would set off some serious alarms with the guys that monitored the internet traffic for the Navy; bring up questions he didn't want asked. The statement was barbed, meant to get under his skin; Noah just couldn't figure out if it was a threat or an observation and the uncertainty was eating away at his insides.

The rest of the conversation bothered him as well. He was pissed at himself for not calling Cameron's bluff. There was no way that he would have tried anything at work. No way. He couldn't convince himself of it though. Cameron was one tough son of a bitch who could fight like nobody's business. Noah had only seen it twice in all of the time they'd known each other; and each time it had been a sight to behold. The first time was at the club when some guy backhanded Kalina. Cameron was bouncing at the time. He came over a table, diving into the guy, giving up a good six inches of height and a solid forty pounds. Before any of the other bouncers could get over there to help out, Cameron had him on the ground screaming with a broken arm and a broken jaw. It had taken a matter of seconds.

The second time, Cameron was out numbered two on one. Noah was pulling up to the restaurant to meet him when the guys grabbed him and tried to drag him into an alley alongside it. He figured Cameron could use a little humbling, so he stayed in his car to watch the show, figuring that if things got too rough he'd jump out and help. No saving gesture was necessary, though. Both of Cameron's assailants realized they'd grabbed the tiger by the tail the second they got into the alley. Cameron wasn't scared, he didn't beg or hand over his wallet. He fought back, thrashing against their holds and trying to do damage. The would-be muggers were terrified to let go. And then one of them made that very mistake. As soon as his grip came loose, Cameron reversed it on him, grabbing him in a painful hold and slamming him face first into the brick wall. The guy fell to the ground only semi-conscious. The second man, seeing what had befallen his partner, tried to turn and run. It was his turn to be dragged into the alley. Cameron proceeded to beat the living shit out of the both of them, kicking and punching until the both of them were lying on the ground curled up protectively. It was a bloody mess. At dinner, he never even mentioned the fact he'd been jumped.

Noah shuddered involuntarily. He hated the fact that he was afraid of Cameron, that without a weapon and the aspect of surprise, there was no real likelihood that he would come out on top in a physical confrontation. He simply couldn't match Cameron's skill and fearlessness, and knowing that ensured he would lose. It was what had held his hand and his tongue earlier in the day and what would spend the rest of the day sticking like needles in the back of his brain.

Things would be different tomorrow though. He would be ready and he would have backup. Noah looked down at the list of names in the little green notebook in front of him. Of the three of them, the only one he knew for sure didn't owe Cameron in one form or another was Silas. He circled the name and made a note to call and talk to him.

He heard the Chief's door open behind him and he bent over the inventory paperwork, checking it against the numbers on his screen. He hated the quarterly supply inventory; comparing beginning inventories to shipping logs to receipts to standing inventories. It was a never-ending task.

"Petty Officer Lawson."

He turned to look at her. "Yes, Chief?"

"I'm going to take off for lunch, you've got the shop."

He nodded.

"And when May gets back from his appointment, have him help you with the numbers. Have him get last month's receipts together. That should keep him busy."

Noah smiled. DeJesus wasn't that bad for a Chief, Noah actually got on with her fairly well. Her problem was that she was a workaholic and a perfectionist and had a hard time with anyone who worked for her that wasn't. And that pretty much described everyone who worked for her. At least she wasn't going to be too much of a bitch about this. She might nag a bit but all she really wanted was to get the job done. It would be, and she'd be pleased as punch about it until the next deadline came in. Then they'd start it all again.

Sighing, he started to look at the inventory sheets in earnest. If he wanted to get out of there any time soon, he was going to have to get the work done. Putting it off wasn't going to cut it and would just cause a fuss that he didn't need right now. He slid the notebook into his dungaree shirt pocket and picked up the calculator. He could probably get the preliminary numbers together before May got back from dental and then they could blaze through the receipts.

chapter 69

"**H**ey there, handsome. What are you doing for lunch?"

Cameron didn't answer for a second, concentrating on the letter of recommendation he was rewriting for his division officer.

"Don't really have plans."

Kalina frowned into the phone. He sounded tired and unhappy, more of the melancholy mood that had hung over his head for the last few days. The stress of the situation was getting to him. The fact that the whole event would be played out in less than twenty-four hours only added to the pressure she was sure he was feeling. She couldn't remember seeing him this distraught since his father had passed away some three years earlier.

They had never been close and Cam rarely spoke of him. When he did, it was always in vague references to a childhood he seemed to be viewing through frosted glass, blurring the details and covering the unwanted memories. Somewhere in the past the shared road of their lives parted and Cameron had no desire to revisit the days when it was joined. It was sad that he maintained the separation; it removed them from any family at all and left them alone in the world.

The forced distance hadn't been enough to prevent him from grieving upon hearing of the man's passing. Kalina thought he'd be stoic about the whole thing, his normally calm self. But it had been a dark day. Cameron sulked throughout the day, and later that evening surprised her even more by drinking himself into a blind stupor. It was the only time she'd ever seen him drunk, before or since. As the alcohol hit his system, he spoke to her of the embarrassment he grew up with, having a drunk for a dad. They were always broke; the old man couldn't hold a job after retiring from the Navy. He recounted a painful anecdote of how his father had showed up to his school to pick him up once so drunk he could hardly walk and how the principal had called the police to take him away. The story made him weep – another first for her that evening. Cameron was aghast at his father's lack of self-control; both with money and with drink. The elder Leasig had beaten discipline into Cameron the boy, but couldn't find a way to practice it himself. He was a slovenly disgrace.

After the funeral, Cameron stopped by the house to go through some of his father's things. Up in the bedroom closet he found a shoebox full of papers. They were letters to Cameron, letters begging forgiveness, letters talking about how proud he was of the man he was sure his son had grown up to be. They were letters never sent to a son he doubted would ever read them.

Mixed among the letters were pages of poetry and small sketches of landscapes remembered by the old man from his travels. The shoebox was the only thing Cameron had taken with him when he left the dingy house.

He wore the tired sadness on his face for weeks with Kalina chasing him about, trying to cheer him up. And then one day it was gone. He made his peace and was fine, back in control. He never spoke of his father again, though Kalina did notice that a small picture of the man appeared amongst the forest of framed photos on the mantle in the living room.

He wore that same tired, heavy look now his voice had that same strained sound, like a guitar string stretched too tightly. It worried her. He wasn't in mourning. The losses they faced were many, but he was determined to carry that load on his own. She wished he would ask for help. She wished he would at least admit that he was worried. The fact was written all over his tired face.

"Why don't you come on home and I'll whip something up for us?"

"I've got a lot of work to do here. I don't know if I'm gonna get any lunch today at all, let alone one that would take me all the way back out to the house."

"I'll tell you what, I'll bring it to you. Take about a half hour and eat with me." Her voice was almost pleading. She wanted to talk to him about her run-in with Storenn and the lady detective. Had she handled it correctly, said the appropriate things? Kalina felt she had, but doubt was creeping in, wrapping its powerful tentacles around her chest, squeezing 'til she couldn't breath. She couldn't talk to Cameron about it over the phone; there was no telling who might be listening in.

Cameron sighed. He sounded so tired.

"Please. I'll stop by Judo's on the way, pick up some sushi."

"That sounds great, baby. I'll be out front waiting for you in about forty five minutes."

Relief washed through her. Was she really this dependant on him? Did she really care? "I'll be there with bells on."

He chuckled into the phone. "Wear more than that. We're not trying to start a riot up in this joint."

"Hey, that anal office is your albatross. I'll show up wearing whatever it is I show up wearing and they're just gonna have to deal with it," she said playfully.

"Momma always said I'd end up with a wild one."

She could hear the smile in his voice.

"Well, I guess since we're eating at your office dessert will have to keep until later. I'll see you in about forty five."

"Thanks, babe," he said, his voice strong and deep. "Love you."

She smiled, hanging up the phone. There was hope yet. Just one more day of this crap hanging over their heads and it would all be over. The Navy, Noah, the police - everything would be done with and they could move on with their lives. Only one more day to go.

chapter 70

It was another glorious San Diego day out on the harbor. The sky was baby blue and cloudless, the breeze was cool and light, barely enough to wrinkle the glassy surface of the water. The boat swayed gently. James drank in the sun while he drank down his beer. If he had to do detail work, it might as well be in surroundings that he found comfortable. The deck of the small cabin behind him was lined with papers, records of the three dead sailors he knew about and Cameron's, which he got from Evan earlier in the morning.

His eyes felt like they were going to fall out. He rubbed them with the back of his hand and looked over to where Jessica sat hunched over the file she was reviewing. They had both been through each of the records, constructing a timeline of when and where each man served. They listed superiors, Leading Petty Officers, Commanding Officers, any and every name he could get off of documentation. James was looking for some kind of connection, anything that would link Leasig to those dead informants.

After three hours, he'd come up with pretty much nothing. The only connection he had was the one he walked in with, Monk working as a bouncer at 'Club Kittie'. He knew that it might be tough; all of the men were different rates from Cameron. Anwar Belk was a Boatswain's Mate, Kevin Johnson was a Boatswain's Mate and Anderson Monk had been a Machinist Mate. They all could have feasibly worked on the same ship at the same time. As a Yeoman, Leasig could go pretty much anywhere in the fleet. Every ship and every command had several. But there was nothing in any of the records that showed where the men might have crossed paths.

In the paperwork he came across a sheet with the name Thomas Pinfield scribbled on it. At least that was one thing he had answers for, something he could rule out. The blood on the bag tied him in quite neatly to a murder that took place outside a diner on Coronado earlier in the week. It sucked that he happened to be in the Navy, but it definitely looked like a city problem now.

He took another long pull on his beer, still watching Jessica as she hovered over the file. She was a Godsend, really. She made him feel like a person again and not just some workaholic machine. He thought back to the passion of the previous night and found himself smiling. Jessica's head came up and she smiled broadly at him. He toasted her with his beer bottle and he could swear that she blushed as her smile broadened and she looked back down to her folder. God, she was a beautiful woman. Shaking his head to clear it of the lustful thoughts that were creeping in. There was still a lot of ground to cover and he wanted to be sure they were ready for what the next few days would bring. At the very least they would be fresh on these ancillary aspects of the case when they brought Cameron in for questioning the next day.

chapter 71

The receipts were checking exactly against the inventory requests. Noah stood up and stretched his back and shoulders. "I'm gonna take a break. I'll be back in about ten."

May was lost in the paperwork. He nodded without looking up. "Take a piss for me while you're out." It was one of his favorite sayings, apparently something his older brother used to say when they'd play video games when he was younger.

He got a half smile for his efforts. "Sure."

Noah headed for the lounge. He dug the notebook out of his pocket and flipped through finding the page he was writing on earlier. He read through the short list again as he walked into the room. Picking up the black phone with one hand, he dialed the number from memory with the other.

He got an answering service. "Silas, it's Noah. I've got a last minute job for you. Call my cell after seven tonight and we'll talk. Later." He hung up the receiver and headed for the soda machine.

chapter 72

Kali sat in the club box and looked down on the packed room beneath her. The four stages were whirlwinds of activity as beautiful, naked women danced on each one. She remembered when she danced, how nervous she was the first time she ever stepped on stage. The club was nothing like this back then, she thought. Nope, back in the day it was a right old dive with two rickety stages and bad lighting. The sound system sucked. The bar sucked. Hell, the club sucked.

She sighed. Now there were four stages, each newly refinished and solid as a rock. The sound system was booming and the lighting was exquisite. The bar was one of the best stocked in the entire city. Kali put a lot of money into this club; a lot of sweat and hard work. And she was the queen of all she surveyed.

It was going to be a shame to give it all up.

Not that she was overly infatuated with this life style; there were aspects of it that she completely despised - the constant flow of seedy characters, the never ending string of used up women, the constant fight to keep the drugs and prostitution out of her club. The job was enormous, and often times depressing, watching people that you knew and cared about self-destruct. But it had allowed her and Cameron so much freedom to do the things they wanted and needed to do. And it was a reminder of where she had come from, what she once was and never would be again. This building housed a lot of memories.

Back by the emergency exit was where she first met Cameron. They talked for about two hours that night – he almost got fired and Randy had beaten her unconscious when they got home. Down by where the bar stood now was where she signed the contracts to get a piece of the club. Eleven months later she signed for sole ownership in the same spot.

She smiled to herself.

Cameron made her enroll in college the very next day, insisting that she had to learn about business if she was going to be successful in it. As if Cameron would ever let her fail. He was so smart - intuitive about things - that at times he was a little spooky. His support made her feel that anything was possible.

Still smiling, she looked back over her shoulder to the diploma hanging on the wall behind the desk. Four and a half years of brutal scheduling and work to get that piece of paper. It had been one of the proudest days of her life. Cameron was there for that, too.

He was always there; pushing her, helping her, telling her that things would be all right. His supreme confidence in her had propelled her past so many obstacles and to such heights as she could never have imagined on her own. And he was always there.

The lights and people below blurred in a wash of color as her eyes teared up. "Shit!" she swore, dabbing at her eyes.

It was going be a shame to give it up, especially to a slime ball like Tony La Paola.

A blast of bass and electronic music filled the room as the door opened. She looked around and smiled as Cameron came walking towards her, a thick bouquet of different pastel colored tulips clutched tightly in his hand. They were her favorite flower and just about impossible to get in the summer time. She loved the simple beauty of the flower, its delicate smell.

"Evening, beautiful," he said handing her the flowers and kissing her full on the mouth. He looked at her, his humor turning to concern. "You been crying?"

She nodded. "Just been thinking about walking away from this place. After so many years here and all of the work we've done. It's going to be a sad day when La Paola takes her away."

Cameron wrapped an arm around her waist and pulled her close, their hips pressing against each other. "What do you say about you and me getting outta here, let Wanda take over for the evening?"

"I don't know, Cam. There's a lot of work to get done in the next day and a half."

"Baby, there's nothing but paperwork to be done and you hired the best in the business to make sure it's done correctly. You don't have to hold their hands."

"You sure you're all right, Cameron? Talk of cutting corners from the human planner is cause for worry."

He smiled widely in response. "I'm fine, woman. Just thought it might be nice to get out of the club for the night."

"What do you have in mind?" Kalina asked coyly, her tears wiped away.

"I don't know, maybe start with a hot shower and see where it leads. I'll wash your hair for you," he tempted.

She looked around the office and out the window into the club. "I don't know," she teased.

He glanced over his shoulder at the door and leaned into her so he could whisper in her ear. "I'm not wearing any underwear," he said softly, a mischievous grim on his face.

Laughing, she pushed him away. "Well, I can't pass up an offer like that. Let me get Wanda on the phone and get her up here."

"She's standing right outside the door."

Kalina shook her head. "Cad!" she said sarcastically, smacking him lightly on the shoulder. "What are we waiting for?"

chapter 73

James sat in the middle of his bed, the background reports stacked in piles all around him. It was a loose system, trying to separate out the various time periods and major events.

Kalina's file read like a nightmare. She'd been in and out of more hospitals by the age of ten with suspect 'accidents' than he cared to count and through more in the three years she was with Godfrey than he even knew were in the San Diego area. Broken bones, bruised bones, lacerations, deep tissue bruises, and the list ran on, often repeating itself. The pictures from the police files were appalling.

He didn't understand how the magnificent woman he'd met at the club could have ever been subject to such abuse or how any man could look into that beautiful face and want to destroy it. It was a crime he could never fathom or stomach. It was cowardice, a sickness requiring the pain and suffering of the weak to take the edge off of one's own painful feelings of inadequacy.

Flipping through the more current files, he was amazed by the turn around in her life since Godfrey didn't come back with his ship.

The whole man overboard thing was interesting in and of itself. Cameron Leasig was stationed on the same ship at the same time. He was on watch when the alarm went off and the search began. It was noted in both the police and the insurance reports on the crime. He must have been a suspect at one point in the investigation. James didn't think they were too far off the mark. He might have done the same thing had he seen such beauty being destroyed.

In the end, though, being that there was absolutely no proof that it was otherwise, the authorities had ruled it an accident. Nobody complained too loudly. By all accounts, Randall Godfrey was a flaming asshole that rubbed just about everyone he came into contact with the wrong way. He was a problem at work; he was a problem at home. James figured everybody probably let out a big sigh of relief that he was gone.

He knew that Kalina must have. No more beatings, no more hospital visits at three o'clock in the morning. No more fear.

That must have been where Cameron stepped in. She bought into the club with the insurance money from Godfrey's death. According to the tax records, Cameron continued bouncing there until a year later when Kalina bought out her partner and took over the club entirely. He leafed through more of the tax records. As far as he could tell it all seemed to be on the level, steadily improving profits coupled with repairs and rebuilding. She survived an audit three years ago without a single major discrepancy. James was impressed by her meticulousness in record keeping.

Her college transcripts were fair, she graduated with a two point eight four grade point average. Impressive for a girl who finished high school through the mail. She had a lot of fight in her.

The information on the charities was interesting to him. She dumped a lot of money into all three of them, but it was interesting to note that she had personally set up one of the halfway houses as a not-for-profit business. It was the same year she was audited. He noted that it was set up blind, so that the board of directors and those she was helping would never know who it was helping to keep them afloat. The other two charities were done the same way, large anonymous donations made each year.

Dealing with so much bad and then using it to do so much good. James thought that it might be something to know Ms. Morris outside of this case, to know her as a person. He was sure it would be something indeed.

Other than the inconvenient fact she was Cameron Leasig's girlfriend, James couldn't see where she was connected. 'Club Kittie' was successful, but not so successful someone could use it to launder hundreds of millions of dollars in only a few short years. Nowhere near that much money had even passed through those doors in the entire time the club had been standing. He wondered how much she knew about Cameron and his connection to the drug trafficking that was going on. Maybe she was just unlucky in her choice again, got involved with the wrong guy. Or did she? She was obviously happy. He obviously cared for her a great deal, at least enough to continue with something this perilous just to ensure she stayed safe.

He sighed and rubbed his tired eyes. It was getting late and he needed some sleep. Tomorrow was the big day. He stretched his back, feeling the cramped muscles pull and give.

chapter 74

The nine-millimeter pistol was a powerful looking weapon lying there on the table. It was well oiled and maintained, shining dully in the lamplight. The black brown grip showed little wear, this was a gun that was only used on special occasions. Five full clips lay on the table next to it, a half empty box of bullets open beside them. The brass jackets were shiny, giving off a pleasant golden glow. The riches of an empire lined up in neat rows, fifteen million dollars worth of lead-filled death.

The money was gone. Noah checked and rechecked the accounts. He called the bank, screaming at the manager. There was nothing that could be done, he was told. The accounts were accessed with his personally selected passwords. The security protocols had been met.

Noah wanted to break something; he wanted to lash out. He wanted to kill. But as explosively as his temper swelled, he caught hold of it and forced it back down. Instead of destroying his apartment or heading out to find a surrogate upon whom to unleash his rage, Noah swallowed his anger. The disappearance of the money was a setback; a crippling, mind-numbing setback. Some of his fortune could be made up with monies garnered from shipments already in motion. That didn't change the fact that a trust had been breached. It also didn't change tomorrow's end result; it only changed the path.

Noah pressed another gleaming shell into the clip he was loading. There would be hell to pay; the account was well past due. There could be no other possible reaction to Cameron's blatant disrespect and the ruination it caused.

He looked at the pistol on the table and smiled wickedly. He picked it up, appreciating its weight in his hand, the natural feel of the grip in his grasp. The clip slammed home and a golden round chambered with the mechanical rasp of oiled metal on metal. It was a thing of beauty and power. Art really. And in the morning he was going to take it to the show. Noah had his plan. He had his wingman, he had his timetable and he had his weapon. All that was left was the execution.

chapter 75

Steam filled the bathroom. Hot water poured out of the gold toned showerhead, sluicing down over Kalina's naked body. Shampoo ran down her torso, sliding down around the curves of her breasts and over her taut belly. The smell of coconut and lime mixed with the steam, lending a tropical sense to the thick air. Cameron stood behind her, massaging her scalp, washing her hair. Her almond eyes were closed, comfort easing into tense muscles and relaxation washing over her.

Finished, Cameron reached down and smacked her on her firm backside. "Rinse," he ordered, stepping around her.

She leaned her head back, letting the hot water wash the soap away. God, it felt great. The water followed the same path down her torso the soap had, rinsing it all away and leaving her skin smelling fresh and clean.

She knew Cameron was in front of her, watching her rinse. He loved to look at her body and she never felt self conscious about it. It felt natural to her that he should like her body. And then she felt his lips on her stomach. Taking a half step forward to keep the water behind her, she looked down on him. He was on his knees, his hands around her waist, his mouth kissing down past her belly button. He paused for a second and looked adoringly up at her, a mischievous smile on his face.

"You're bad," she said wistfully.

The smile broadening, he returned his attentions to her waiting body, his hands firmly gripping her backside and pulling her in to him. In seconds her head was back again, eyes closed. She gasped, her breathing suddenly ragged as he devoured her. Her hands tangled in his hair, gripping the back of his head tightly to maintain her balance as the pleasure ebbed and flowed through her quivering body.

chapter 76

Cameron's file was more of a problem for James than Kalina's had been, not nearly as grotesque, but just as disturbing in its own right. There wasn't much of anything there. Closer examination revealed little more than what Pinsone had told him earlier that day. And that bothered James, especially considering the conversation they'd had yesterday afternoon.

He could pretty much disappear without anyone ever knowing about it. There was absolutely nothing memorable about the guy in any of his records; he was just an ordinary guy. The guy who stood in the shadows and slipped around unnoticed because he didn't cause waves and wasn't being groomed.

And yet everyone had something to say about him. Of the fifteen interviews Pinsone had conducted, every single one of them ended up being about how Leasig had helped or befriended them in some way or another. He had to agree with Evan on this one, the guy looked ready for sainthood.

But there was that comment Cameron had made the day before at lunch. 'You meet this guy and you're thinking he's nice, personable. Yeah, maybe a little rough; maybe he could kick your ass. But you're not sitting there thinking he could have you whacked just by snapping his fingers.' James wondered what would happen if Cameron decided to snap his fingers.

He had too much fire and direction to be a behind the scenes player. He was too confident. Everything James saw in the man was in direct contrast to the picture that was painted in his file.

And there were the sports. He was obviously in shape. Combine that with a guy who grew up wrestling and boxing and was now committed to Aikido and you had a person who could most likely handle himself very well. That could go a long way in explaining his confidence. But even if it could, so what? What insights did it give about the man?

There were too many conflicts between paper and reality. This guy might just be the man behind it all. He knew too much, was far too confident and pushy. Or he was just a guy who got involved with something that he didn't understand and was afraid for both his and his woman's lives and was looking for a way out. Maybe he didn't know whom to trust. That was plausible, given all of the murder and mayhem that had surrounded the case.

And what the hell did Cameron need all of this time for? He wasn't doing anything. According to the reports James had received every few hours over the last couple of days; nothing was going on. No unusual activity he could see, at least. There was lunch with Kalina and a couple of trips to the club and the gym, but that was pretty much it outside of work and home. The only item of question was a stop off at his lawyer's office the day before, but he hadn't been there but for about fifteen minutes. While James knew that all sorts of shady activity could happen in a lawyer's office in the short span of a quarter hour, he suspected that the brief meeting, whatever its topic, wasn't the reason behind the time demand.

    Again, he was left with more questions than answers.

    James hated this case. He hated it with everything he had in him.

chapter 77

They lay there in the cool comfort of the room, the night air evaporating the slick sweat that covered their bodies. Sheets and blankets lay piled on the floor, pushed off the bed in the heat of their lovemaking, which had been desperate and athletic. They lay naked and tired, nestled as spoons and relaxed beyond worry for what the next day would bring. Kalina felt his lips on her neck, a light kiss that sent shivers through her. She smiled, content in those arms, at peace in their bed.

She rolled over into his body so that she could face him. He moved to accommodate her, rolling onto his back and allowing her to lay half on him; one leg over his, pelvis on his hip, breast on his chest, head on his shoulder, arm laying across him. She felt lazy and comfortable and when she looked up at his face, she fell in love with him all over again.

"You look like the cat that caught the mouse," he said quietly, noticing her contented grin.

"I'd hardly call you a mouse."

He held her, his arm around the back of her shoulders. It was enough, his strong embrace, the warmth of his skin seeping uninhibited into hers. It was enough to see her through anything.

"We've come a long way, beautiful."

She nodded, suddenly sleepy. She didn't want to think about tomorrow. He started to speak again, but she smothered his words with a heated kiss. She wanted the night to end as it was - perfect, sublime. She kissed him until there were no more protestations, no attempts to utter the words that would shatter the fragility of the moment. He gave in quickly, allowing her the silence she craved. She buried her face into his shoulder and closed her eyes, the steady lullaby of his breathing and the unwavering rhythm of his heartbeat lulling her into slumber.

He kissed her hair, caressing her back lightly with his free hand. "I love you, Kalina Morris," he whispered. "Sleep sweet."

She drifted off with a smile on her face.

friday, june 11

chapter 78

Kali watched Cameron shave and dress for work, a knot of fear filling her belly. It started just like every other day - up early, hot shower, shaving in the steam-covered mirror. But it wasn't every other day. Today was the day that everything in both their lives would be changed forever and the enormity of it all weighed heavily on her. He smiled at her, as she lay there sleepily, bundled in the warmth of the soft sheets.

He came over and kissed her head. She closed her eyes and breathed his clean scent deeply. His skin was warm and smooth and smelt like soap. He tousled her tangled hair and turned to get dressed. She thought right then of begging him back into bed, enticing him to hold her again. To make love to her once more. But he was late already and traffic would only make him later. So she lay there watching him ready himself for the day, sliding into a pair of jeans and a white t-shirt.

She looked at him questioningly.

"I'll change later."

She nodded, understanding.

He walked over to the bed again, sitting down next to her. She snuggled in close, wrapping her arms around his waist and pulling herself even closer. He slid his hand down her back; short nails scratching gently across soft skin. She purred and arched her back.

"I gotta go now, beautiful," he said softly.

She was suddenly choked up. On the edge of tears, she buried her face into his hip. He stroked her hair gently.

"It's gonna be all right, Kali."

She chided herself for a child and looked up at his handsome face. He was smiling down at her. She loved his smile. She loved him and all of the amazing things he meant to her. But the dread that was solidifying in her chest, constricting her breathing and strangling her heart, stole her ability to smile back. Her eyes were wet.

"I'm gonna be fine. Everything will work out…"

"Don't you say it," she interrupted. "Just be careful today. Stay safe. For me." She was pleading with him, knowing the penalties for failure.

He smiled again, warm and comforting. "I'll be careful, baby. You watch yourself too. And make sure you're ready to go when it's time."

"I will."

He bent down again and kissed her on the mouth, his tongue sweet and minty. She savored it along with the warmth from his powerful hug. They lingered there for a while, arms wrapped around one another, locked in a passionate kiss. She didn't want to let him go. She wanted to hold him there in her arms and keep him safe and warm, tell the world he'd gone and changed his mind. But she knew that couldn't happen.

Today was inevitable. Whether it happened now or ten years from now, she knew it had to happen. He'd explained it all. How they'd never truly be free, they'd always be looking over their shoulders. It was the only way.

Grudgingly, she allowed the embrace to part. He looked down into her eyes, her face. She didn't know what she'd do if she lost him. Life without Cameron wouldn't be living; it'd be surviving. He caressed her face and stood up.

"I'll se you later, beautiful. Don't worry."

But she did. She worried about what he had to do; worried about what she had to do. She worried about how everything would play out. And watching him walk out the door and into god-only-knew-what did nothing to ease those pangs. She listened for the front door, hoping that instead of hearing it close she would hears his footsteps mounting the stairs as he came back to her. But the door opened and shut with a hollow bang that echoed in her chest.

"Be careful," she said softly to the empty room. There was no response to sooth her and she curled up in the cool linens of the bed and wept.

chapter 79

James sat bolt upright in his bed, mental alarms blaring in his suddenly wide-awake brain. Something was definitely very wrong. Looking around the room, he caught the electronic leer of the alarm clock mocking him from the safety of the nightstand.

"Shit!" he swore as he jumped from the bed and rushed towards the ivy colored bathroom.

Of all the days to oversleep, James couldn't believe that he'd picked today. It was damn near poetic – he was going to be late for his own bust.

Rushing into the bathroom, he turned on the sink so that the water could heat up. He watched little droplets splash up onto the base of the mirror. They joined a host of other residue and water spots that lined the bottom of the glass. James grimaced, trying to remember the last time he had taken the time to clean the bathroom. "Gotta do something about that," he said to no one at all.

He smiled suddenly as he realized the whole inanity of his train of thought. Less than two hours away from one of the most important actions of his career and he was standing here contemplating his failings as a housekeeper.

Steam rose appealingly from the sink and James wet his face and reached across the counter for his shaving gel. "I really outta grow a goatee," he murmured under his breath as he lathered up. Simple thoughts flowed as he ran the razor under the hot stream and looked at his worn reflection in the mirror. The bags were still there, accented now by the foamy white cream all over the lower half of his face. He lifted the razor and ran it down his cheek. With a satisfyingly sandpapery scrape, he carved a broad path of smooth skin from the thick soap. He wondered absently how Jessica felt about facial hair. As he lowered the razor to rinse it, a knock sounded loudly at the front door.

"Crap!" he swore, looking around for something to cover himself. "I'll be right there!" he called out to who ever it was waiting.

Grabbing a towel from the rack, he wrapped up and headed for the front door. As automatically as he headed to answer the door, he stopped, the alarms in his head suddenly tripping like a jackhammer. Another knock at the door, quick and insistent. James slid his nine-millimeter service pistol from the shoulder holster hanging over the back of his dining room chair, pulling the slide back to ensure that a round was chambered.

"Who is it?" he asked, cautious as he approached the door.

"Martin Torrissi."

James didn't recognize the name. He depressed the safety, sliding his index finger along the trigger.

"Who?"

"Officer Martin Torrissi. Detective Muir sent me to check in with you and provide an escort to the pick up."

James pulled his finger off the trigger with a wry grin on his face. She must have spotted the car he had ordered parked outside her apartment and felt that turnabout was fair play. He slid the bolt back and reached for the knob.

"I should have expected…"

The door exploded inwards, smashing into his neck and shoulder. James flew back into the room, landing in a confused heap on his back. His service pistol bounced from his grip, sliding across the carpet and coming to rest next to the couch. James, painfully aware of his nakedness, grabbed for the towel that was now lying in loose pile on the floor near his knees. His head screamed and his vision grayed for a second. As it cleared, two large men rushed into the room, each wearing dark blue coveralls and a black ski mask.

Before James could move to defend himself, the men swarmed, punching and kicking and stomping. He tried to curl up into a ball, anything to protect his head and face. But the kicks rained down – each one blasting through his defenses and slamming into his body. He couldn't breath. The grunting and puffing of his assailants mixed bizarrely with the ringing in his ears and the thuds and smacks of their attack, grinding out a macabre soundtrack to the worst beating of his life. His vision was a blind mess of brilliant light swirled into randomly looming and fading patches of midnight.

A heavy black work boot connected with the back of his head and James went out like someone flipped a switch.

chapter 80

Jessica sat in her car, waiting for James to show up. Where the hell was he? How could he be late for this? She looked down at her cell phone and thought about dialing his apartment, but she didn't want to be one of "those" women; keeping tabs on her man and telling him what to do. Not that he didn't deserve a talking to after posting a guard on her door last night. That conversation would have to wait until they were alone. For the time being, she hoped that he showed up before his witness did.

"Multiple shots fired at the Anchor Watch Condominiums, 22000 block of Sea Bird Avenue." The statement broke through the quiet static of the police band radio in the dash. "Cars in the area, please respond."

James lived in the Anchor Watch Condos.

A chill raced up Jessica's spine, turning her stomach to mush and locking around her heart. James' tardiness now had an ominous overtone to it. James wasn't one to be late. Something was wrong.

Ice slid into her veins as she dialed James' cell phone. After five electronic rings, the answering machine picked up. Swearing, she clicked the phone off without leaving a message and dialed his home number. Once again, an answering machine picked up, cheerfully requesting her to leave a name and a number. As she clicked off the phone, an unfamiliar sense of helplessness crept into her consciousness. James was in trouble, she was suddenly sure of it. She paused to consider her options.

Leasig was coming in – that was a done deal. There were two fully capable Special Agents here to collect him and get him safely to the headquarters building on Welles Street. James had no such coverage. She looked at her watch. She could be there in fewer than fifteen minutes. Twelve minutes with her siren and lights. The decision made, she pushed open her car door and stepped out onto the gravel.

"Sarah," she called out to the two agents sitting in the white cargo van next to her. Special Agent Rollins looked over from the driver's side of the van. "There's something going down at James' condo. Shots fired. I can't raise him on either of his phones and there's no contact on the radio. I'm heading out there. If he shows up here, kick him in the head and tell him to get a hold of me. If not, the two of you get Leasig to headquarters straight away. Keep your eyes open and call for backup if you feel you need it."

"Roger that."

Jessica slipped back into the driver's seat of her car, cranking the engine and speeding across the gravel lot, her police lights already on.

chapter 81

Kali stood there, flexing every muscle in her body. Her jaw was clenched so tightly that it hurt. Her ribs and stomach throbbed from the blows, bruises already showing on her tanned skin. The room around her was all a shambles, the coffee table and end tables overturned, books scattered all over the floor.

"You scared?" The silky malevolence of the voice slid into her brain and touched those primal centers that controlled fear. He smiled to see her shudder.

Kali nodded between controlled gasps, tears streaming down her face. As scared as she was, as much as it hurt, she refused to cry out and let him take pleasure from her pain.

The balled fist crashed into her jaw, snapping her head up and back. Her vision swam along black currents. Before her head came back, the fist slammed in again. Her head swam and sparks flew. Her balance disappeared and she began to fall. Another crack rocked her as she collapsed to the floor, unconscious of the blood flowing from her mouth and nose and onto the light carpet.

chapter 82

Cameron pulled into the lot in front of the low tan building that housed his office, gravel crunching under his tires. He was almost an hour late for work. He'd called in to cover the tardiness, explaining it away with car trouble. It didn't really matter; it wasn't like he was going to make it in to the office anyway. No, he was going to be met by the NCIS and he was going to allow himself to be taken in to protective custody.

He'd stopped along the way and grabbed breakfast at the local Denny's, some ham and eggs and toast. Might as well die on a full stomach. The cops would just have to wait for him. He spotted the white government van as soon as he entered the lot. They'd waited, how thoughtful.

He took a deep breath and shut off the engine. The doors to the white van opened and a pair of agents stepped out. One was a young looking male, short with light brown hair. The other was a tall, lean female with dark hair pulled tightly back against her head. They spoke briefly, the neatly dressed woman referring to a notebook she was carrying in her left hand. A decision apparently made, they turned and walked towards his car.

Cameron let them come, waiting until they were standing near the shiny front bumper before stepping out to greet them. He'd changed into his coveralls at the restaurant, a uniform that he wasn't authorized to wear in his office. But the NCIS didn't know that. "Where's Storenn?" His voice was hard, demanding.

"Mr. Leasig, I'm Special Agent Rollins and this is Special Agent Keleman. We were sent down by Special Agent Storenn to meet you and bring you in." She was trying to sound reassuring.

"Bullshit. My deal was with Storenn. Where the hell is he?"

She shook her head. "He's been detained elsewhere, Mr. Leasig, but will meet us at the NCIS headquarters building shortly. If you'd like, you can call the Division Leading Agent, Vincent Tameric, and verify our credentials."

Cameron looked around, checking the lot. The young Keleman looked around, too, inspecting the broad lot full of cars.

"Let me see your badges and ID," Cameron said finally. As they fished the identical black wallets out, Cameron looked at Keleman. "Rollins and Keleman. I know those names. Where do I know your names from?"

Neither of the agents answered his question. They looked anxious to get him into the back of their van and out of the area.

"How long the two of you been partners?" he pressed.

"A couple of weeks," he answered back.

Nodding, Cameron took the offered credentials and looked them over. "What's your badge number?" he asked the Agent Rollins.

"A317-219." She rattled it off like a mantra.

Cameron nodded. "What's his?" he asked tipping his head in Keleman's direction.

A completely befuddled look came over her face. She looked at her younger partner, shrugging, and then looked back at Cameron. "I don't know," she said simply.

He handed the thin leather wallets back to the both of them. "Good enough for me. Let's get this show on the road."

Surprised, the agents looked at one another again. Apparently, without Storenn there to back them up, they'd expected much more of a fight than they'd got. Agent Rollins waved a hand in front of her, inviting Cameron to follow Agent Keleman towards the van. And so they walked in a line, loading Cameron into the windowless back of the van when they got there.

chapter 83

Slipping unnoticed into traffic, James Storenn's stolen Accord paced the large white van. Noah watched silently, savoring the activities of his busy morning. Beating that bitch Kalina had been more than a pleasure. It was something he had dreamed about for years and now, having done it, he was happily surprised that it'd felt as good as he'd imagined. God, how many times had he wanted to bash her pretty little face in! He felt the anger and excitement building in him again.

  The only thing better than that had been stomping the living hell out of that cop, Storenn. They'd taken him by complete surprise, literally catching him in his birthday suit. He relived the scene again, kicking and stomping the prone agent until there was no movement. The meaty blows played themselves out in his mind and a cruel grin played across his lips.

  And now came the proverbial cherry on top, the act to top them all. He watched as the van rolled on, staring at the white metal as though he could see right through it, could actually see his prey sitting comfortably in the back, relaxing as though he had not a care in the world. The tension rose in his gut, crawling through his chest and up through his throat. The mile markers whipped by, counting down to his victim's ultimate demise. The marker for mile forty passed his window. It was time for Cameron Leasig to die.

chapter 84

"What's with the backpack?" Special Agent Keleman asked gamely from the front seat.

Cameron eyed him evenly. "I'm guessing that I'm going to be in your company for a few days at the very least. A couple of pairs of drawers and some personal items might be nice. I also brought a book – figure I've got to pass the time somehow."

Keleman shrugged in response and Cameron looked at his watch, a slight grin slipping across his face.

"I have been racking my brain trying to figure it out, but now I remember where I've heard your names before. Weren't you the agents that stopped by the house and asked Kali all of those questions?"

Rollins watched him in the mirror, her jaw suddenly tightening. She hadn't wanted him to know that. "Yes, Mr. Leasig. That was us," she replied calmly. The color was already rising in her cheeks; the embarrassment over how that interview was handled still made her angry.

Cameron looked towards the back of Keleman's head. "So you'd be the guy that decided to come over to my house and insult my girlfriend?"

The shoulder and neck muscles tensed and the head swung part way around so that Cameron could see half of the man's face. "That's not how it was intended. I didn't mean for her to hear…"

"You decided to insult me then, by saying those nasty things behind her back?"

The neck was turning red, color creeping up from his collar and crawling up into his hairline. "No. I never should have said what I did. I did it without thinking and I am truly sorry if I hurt her feelings."

The grin slid back onto Cameron's face. The young agent was flustered and nervous.

"What's so funny?" Rollins asked, trying to change the subject.

"Nothing really. I just find this strangely ironic. Here I am with the two of you on what is probably going to be one of the longest days of my life. The two agents my girlfriend just filed a harassment complaint about. Ah, sweet irony."

Keleman huffed, his red cheeks ballooning for a second. "She filed a complaint? I would have apologized." he started, but Cameron cut him off.

"But you didn't."

"That's because she said that if I came around again she'd file the complaint."

Cameron just shrugged his shoulders. "Like I said – ironic."

"Just leave it alone, Bob," Rollins said, seeing Cameron smile in the mirror. "He's just trying to get a rise outta you. We'll have him down to headquarters in about half an hour and then we'll be rid of him."

Keleman shot Cameron a dirty look over his shoulder and then focused his attention out the front window. As soon as his eyes were elsewhere, Cameron looked down at his watch again. Time was getting away from him.

The soft chatter from the front seat, a senior agent trying to distract a more junior agent from the aggravations of their passenger, washed over Cameron, doing little to ease his inner sense of immediacy. If things didn't start happening soon, he was going to have to get them started on his own and that could end up being messy. Cameron reached down and lifted his backpack from the floor between his feet, thinking only of the nine-millimeter semi automatic pistol lying at the bottom. He couldn't afford to end up at NCIS headquarters.

chapter 85

Engaged in conversation, neither of the agents noticed the silver Honda Accord slide by, pausing briefly alongside the van before moving several car lengths ahead and then over into their lane. Rollins laughed and glanced over as Keleman imitated Vincent Tameric addressing the troops. When she turned her attention back on the road, it was already too late. The Accord's tires were already screeching their banshee wail of doom, taillights burning angry red.

A million possibilities ran through Special Agent Rollins' head, but her limbs, frozen by shock, were abominably slow to react. 'Like molasses in January,' her father would have said. Her right foot slammed down onto the brake pedals. Smoke poured off the tires as rubber slid across the asphalt, melting and screaming in protest. She jerked on the wheel, trying to maintain control of the vehicle. Keleman screamed and braced for impact in his seat.

The collision happened in real time, the van slamming into the Accord's trunk with enough force to crumple it like foil. The airbags exploded out, smashing viciously into the two agents. Rollins felt the femur in her right thigh snap, fireworks of exquisite pain clouding her vision. Her left arm slipped off of the steering wheel as the bones in her wrist splintered, sending her head first into the driver-side window, propelled by the force of the airbag. Blackness consumed her as her head shattered the glass.

chapter 86

Vince couldn't believe how the morning was proceeding. The phone was ringing off the hook with different agencies and links in the chain of command looking for answers. The house of his informant was in flames with the informant's girlfriend now on her way to shock trauma. A report of shots fired at the residence of his Supervisory Agent was all over the airways with support on the way. Storenn, of course, was missing in action. Vince was beginning to fear the worst. Detective Muir was nowhere to be found either. Vince could only surmise that she was en route to James' place.

The whole world was going to hell, sliding quickly down that slippery slope.

The only good news was that Leasig was safe in the custody of Rollins and Keleman and speeding his way to headquarters. If that had to be his silver lining, so be it. At least one thing was going right.

chapter 87

Noah was slammed forward by the impact of the van. He felt his neck and back snap as they tried to push past the restraints that held him into his seat. He looked over at Silas. He had a dazed look on his face.

"Take the driver, I'll get the passenger side and take care of Cameron."

Silas shook his head as if clearing it and unbuckled his seatbelt. The black ski mask he was wearing on his head like a beanie slid down easily over his face, hiding his identity as he stepped from the car, nine-millimeter pistol in one of his black-gloved hands.

Already out of the car and on his way, Noah nodded his approval. Silas was working out just fine. He strode past the crumpled trunk, barely even registering the damage, and walked straight to the passenger side of the car where a young looking agent was wresting with a blood covered airbag, trying to get it out of his smashed face. Noah tapped the metal trim of the door with the muzzle of his pistol, getting the agents attention.

He looked pathetic, blood smeared all over his face, mixing with the tears the trickled from his eyes to effectively blind him. He'd obviously wiped at them, bloody fingerprints marked his eyebrows and cheeks. Blinking, he tried to see who was there.

Noah decided to put him out of his misery, loudly firing two slugs into the agents head, blood arcing back into the van, across the front seat and onto Silas who was standing at the driver's side window.

"Shit, man. Now I got to get this cleaned," he complained.

"Just finish her and be ready to roll," Noah snapped back as he turned and headed towards the side door of the van. It was time for him to do what he'd come for, time to do something he'd thought about a lot recently, something he found he wanted to do very much. It was time to end Cameron Leasig's life. He smiled a predatory smile, a wolf looking at a trussed-up sheep and longing for the coppery taste of its blood.

chapter 88

The siren wailed in Kalina's ears. Her eyes fluttered briefly, blinded by the too bright white light directly over her. Shadows played across her limited sight, speaking loudly and quickly to one another. She was lost, no idea where the hell she was. And her head felt like someone used it for a soccer ball. She tried to move, but a hand caught her shoulder and pushed her back down to the hard mattress. She tried to speak, but her jaw wasn't cooperating. Her mouth tasted like an ashtray.

"Ms. Morris."

The voice seemed to come from all around her; an unnerving fact but the bass-filled voice was calm and reassuring.

"Relax, Ms. Morris. You're in an ambulance heading to Balboa Hospital. You've been through a serious trauma."

Her eyes were blurry. She squinted and blinked trying to clear them.

"What happened?" she managed, her lips barely moving. She winced at what little movement there was. She struggled against the pain in her lungs and throat and head.

"There was a fire at your house."

She didn't remember a fire.

She remembered there was something important she wasn't supposed to forget. She remembered dinner; salmon and rice with a glass of white wine. She remembered curling up in bed with Cameron; they made love into the early morning hours, laughing and kissing and sweating with one another. She remembered breakfast; cereal with berries in it and a cup of juice. She didn't remember a fire.

She had to remember.

"You inhaled a lot of smoke. There is also a lot of bruising on your ribs and your face. Your hands were bound."

She remembered working out; a long run right after Cameron left for work. She remembered taking a shower. She remembered turning on the TV to watch the news. And she remembered a knock at the door.

Beeping filled the inside of the ambulance as her breathing grew rapid and harsh. Her lungs and throat burned with the effort.

"Relax, Ms. Morris. Relax. You're safe."

She barely heard the deep voice.

She remembered a fist crashing into her head, lights exploding with the connection. She remembered a face, smiling at her as she went down. She remembered a name.

"Noah," she forced past her swollen lips. It came out a scratchy whisper. The blurry white light was graying.

"What was that Ms. Morris?" the voice questioned, thick with concern.

"Noah Lawson," she managed once more. And the gray faded to black, the siren faded to silence, and the pain faded to nothing.

chapter 89

The windowless side door of the van was locked, stymieing his attempt to get at Cameron. He punched the white metal with a gloved hand, curses flowing liquidly under his breath, and walked towards the back of the vehicle. Traffic whizzed by, no one even slowing to see if they were all right. Noah grasped the silver handle of the door and yanked it hard. The door flew open in his hand.

Peeking inside, he looked past the hodge-podge mess of scattered tools and cleaning supplies trying to catch sight of his intended victim. He spied a black work boot hanging over the edge of the blue naugahyde seat. He smiled to himself, exultant in the face of victory, and stepped into the van, closing the door behind him. There was no responsive movement from the seat in front of him. Stumbling through the clutter on the floor, he waded up to the seat with his nine millimeter at the ready.

Noah was suddenly very aware of the closeness of his surroundings. The only exit was the way he came in. There were no windows and the spider-webbed windshield was black with a mixture of oil and smoke. The stench of hot oil and steam filled the interior of the van, coating his nostrils.

He was almost disappointed to see Cameron lying across the broad seat, seemingly unconscious. The driver's blood surrounded Cameron's head like a grisly halo, fine crimson droplets shining black against the dark blue of the seat cover. Noah pulled up his mask, revealing his face. Cameron had to know that it was Noah who ended his life, know that it was Noah who won out in the end. That knowledge was massively important. Cameron had to die with that recognition burning in his eyes.

Why was Cameron in coveralls?

The thought burst into his churning mind, that out of place detail. Tires crunched and squeaked to a halt behind the smoking van, pulling Noah's eyes and attention away from his prostrate victim. The vehicle's powerful engine shut idled, a steady threatening growl. Help had arrived in timely fashion, much quicker than Noah had planned.

Shit - he thought. *Running out of time.*

Noah glanced down at his watch impatiently. The seconds were getting away from him. A car door opened and slammed shut. It had to be a Highway Patrol officer. Noah cursed vehemently under his breath, hoping against hope that Silas handled the cop. They had to get the hell out of Dodge. Now.

Noah held his breath, following the crunching footfalls along the length of the van. A radio squawked near the driver's side window and frenetic voice abruptly called out. "Dispatch, car three-three! Eleven-ninety-nine, repeat …"

Shots erupted, five blasts in rapid succession, cutting off the anxious call for help. Noah smiled evilly. He had chosen well; Silas was working out just fine.

The smile died on his face as he turned his attentions back to his intended victim. Cameron lay in the same spot on the van seat, his eyes black with violence, an even blacker nine-millimeter pistol gripped tightly in his hand.

"Hey there, Noah."

chapter 90

Silas' hands were shaking. Ninety-nine percent excitement, one percent fear. Or maybe it was one percent excitement, ninety-nine percent fear. There was no way of telling; the unpredictable nature of working with a psychopath wore on people, screwed with their heads. Excited or scared didn't matter in the larger scheme, that cop was dead, killed by the gun in Silas' hand; another casualty of Noah's vengeance fueled spree of death and destruction. Five people dead and they only just reached their target.

Silas hoped that whoever was in the back of that van with Noah was worth the amazing amount of crap they'd churned up, because, despite California's staunchly liberal bent, the death penalty would definitely be on the table should the two of them get caught. Assuming the cops didn't kill them first. And that whole 'going out in a blaze of glory' garbage was exactly that – garbage. Silas had been shot before and had absolutely no intentions of letting it happen again. Bullet wounds hurt like a mother.

He raised a hand, unconsciously running his fingers diagonally down his chest, tracing the deep bruise made by his seatbelt in the crash. The bones in his chest hurt. Maybe a cracked rib or two, not an unreasonable side effect of being rear-ended at highway speed. They made out better than the Feds in the van, whatever the pain.

Cars whipped by, shiny blurs of sound; traffic barely slowing to rubberneck the accident. Perhaps the black stocking mask had something to do with that. People didn't want to get involved with obvious bad news. That wouldn't stop them from dialing nine-one-one and reporting it though. He expected helicopters anytime now. That would suck. There was no outrunning air support.

He checked his watch. It was past time to go. They agreed before the collision that they only had sixty seconds to make the kill and be gone. Sixty-three seconds had already ticked by. Silas took a step towards the driver's side of the banged up car. Shots rang out from inside the van, muffled cannon fire.

Sighing with relief, he swung himself back towards the passenger's side. With so many things that could have gone wrong - the job was done. He was so money.

chapter 91

Jessica screeched to a halt in the parking lot. The chatter on her police band radio served to drive her into near hysterics as she weaved through traffic. There was no real good news breaking through the static as she shut off the engine and leapt from the vehicle. An ambulance, two fire trucks and a like number of black and whites sat pell-mell in front of the building, their multi-colored lights spinning silently. A small crowd stood behind the yellow taped cordon. She pushed her way through the crush of bodies wondering what the hell all of these people were doing just standing around like this on a Friday morning. Didn't these people have jobs to be at?

Making her way to the barricade, she flashed her Detective shield and started up the stairs. The door to James' apartment was burst inward on its hinges. A black scuff marked where the door had been kicked open. Jessica half smiled. That scuff was evidence.

A cadre of dark uniforms milled about the living room. The CSU would be pissed when they got there. There were too many feet in the crime scene. Her thoughts of preserving evidence were summarily dismissed as she gained sight of James lying pathetically there on the carpet. There was blood. So much blood. His face was hidden behind rapidly darkening bruises and a mask of speckled crimson. Red flecks marked his shoulder and chest, gathering to stain the heavy bandages the paramedics taped over the two bullet wounds. His skin was pale and slicked with sweat and welts and bruises showed all over his torso. His right arm was bent at an impossible angle. Jessica fought back her stomach's need to empty itself.

The paramedics spoke reassuringly and low, trying to assess the situation without overly panicking their patient. They hooked up blood and administered much needed pain relief. The moments passed as intolerable hours.

"Is he going to be all right?" Jessica finally asked when she could take no more.

The paramedic regarded her quickly. "He'll make it. He's gonna feel like hell for a while, but I think he'll pull through."

Jessica felt the relief wash over her as she watched them load James up onto the gurney and start him down towards the ambulance.

saturday, june 12

chapter 92

The next twenty-four hours were a blur of pain and blankness for James Storenn. Conversations melded with memories mixed with dreams all stirred together with pain and medication. When he woke up in the sterile white room, he had no idea where he was or why. One move brought blinding pain to his ribs, arms and head all at once. He winced and looked down. The cast on his arm and the multitude of tubes sticking out of him told him he was in the hospital.

He couldn't remember how he got there.

The heavy wood door swung silently open. Jessica walked in reading a piece of paper.

"Hey, Jess," James croaked out, his voice thin and gravelly.

Jessica looked up, surprise painting her face. "You're awake!"

James nodded, barely able to move his head.

The paper forgotten, Jessica ran over and wrapped her arms around his neck. The move brought blinding pain and James squealed out in protest. Regaining herself and blushing slightly, Jessica sat down in the red faux-leather and wood chair next to his bed, dabbing at her wet eyes. Relief and concern filled her angel's face.

"I was beginning to think you weren't going to come out of it. How are you feeling?"

"Like a used piñata."

Jessica lent him a half smile. "Well, you definitely look the part. They really did a number on you."

"Thanks," James said wryly. "Think I could get some water?"

Jessica reached over to the table and picked up a pitcher of water, pouring a small plastic cup full. She turned and handed it to James. "Here you go. You want some help with that?"

James shook his head no and lifted the pale blue cup to his lips. The water was cool, soothing the dryness of his mouth and throat. He sighed as it sluiced down, feeling it form into a cold pool at the bottom of his empty stomach. "Thanks."

"Not a problem."

They sat there in silence for a few minutes, James working his way through the cup of water.

"What the hell happened?" James asked finally.

Jessica smiled at him, a strange look on her face. "Do you mean besides somebody, we can only assume at this point that it was Lawson or one of his goons, beating the holy hell out of you? It wasn't a pretty sight. Aside from that, the whole world ended, pretty much. You want the long or short version of it?"

"I don't think I'm going anywhere anytime soon. Give me the long."

Jessica took a deep breath, sheathed his good hand in her two small ones and began to fill him in on the previous day's happenings. She told him everything. She told him about Kalina Morris being beaten to a pulp by Noah Lawson and being left to die when her house was set on fire. She reported Cameron Leasig's death and about how Kalina had to be sedated after flying into hysterics upon hearing of it. Jessica spoke of the deaths of the two accompanying agents and the murder of Officer Edward Hicks; throwing in the tidbit about finding his Accord burnt to a cinder under an overpass, an unidentified body in the driver's seat.

James couldn't believe his ears. He sat there stunned, listening in awe as the story unfolded. As it finally drew to a close his head was spinning.

"You sure about Leasig?"

Jessica looked at him evenly. "Yes, James. I got them to make me a copy of the squad car video that pretty much shows the entire thing; brought it here just for you."

Standing, she walked over to the TV and turned it on. She pushed play on the VCR and walked back to the chair.

The screen flickered black and white and gray. The picture snapped up showing the hood of a police cruiser pulling up behind a collision. The date and time and car identifier were posted in white in the upper right hand corner of the screen.

"Dispatch, this is car three-three. I've got a nine-oh-one on the eastbound Five, just past exit thirty-seven. Large white van with government plates rear-ended a late model silver Honda Accord. Requesting back up and an ambulance. Will investigate and advise."

"Car three-three this is car three-niner. I'm two minutes out and en route."

"Roger that, car three-niner. Two minutes out and rolling, over."

The unit stopped a full car length behind the van, Officer Hicks climbing out and walking up past the front of the cruiser. He was tall and stocky and walked with confidence and ease. His uniform was sharply pressed, immaculate. His light hair was short, newly trimmed. Officer Hicks was an impressive representative of the law whose presence would make someone think twice before trying anything on his beat. From the camera angle, he appeared young; maybe in his early thirties.

The camera followed him as he walked alongside the van. Coming up to the driver's side door, he suddenly jerked his head, looking around frantically and grabbing at his shoulder radio. A gloved hand appeared from the space in front of the van, a nine-millimeter, judging by the size of the gun, grasped in it.

"Dispatch, car three-three! Eleven-ninety-nine, repeat ..." The voice was frantic on the radio.

The slug that slammed through his skull and into his brain silenced that voice forever. Officer Hicks flew back hard against the concrete divider, painting it with blood. The person in front of the van took a half step forward, showing an arm covered with dark material and part of a black ski mask. The gun flashed three more times, Hicks' body jumping as it took each round to the chest.

The right half of the back door to the van suddenly flew open and a large man jumped out. He was muscular big and moved lightly. He was dressed in dark coveralls, gloves, black boots and a black ski mask, just as his partner probably was. There was no telling of race or hair or eye color. All that was available was gender and build.

He paused at the back of the van, looking into it. He picked up a flare from a box in front of him, uncapped it and lit it off. Flames shot out of the tip. He tossed it in and walked around the back of the van, disappearing to the passenger side. The insides of the van began to glow brighter and brighter until flames and dark smoke poured out the back. The shadow that marked the presence of the Accord disappeared from the picture as is sped away.

Only forty-eight seconds had ticked off of the clock in the corner. The tape kept running. Flames engulfed the entire van and blood pooled wider and wider around Officer Hicks' bullet-riddled body. More than a hundred seconds more passed before car three-nine arrived for back up.

By then it was well over.

James sat there, defeated. He couldn't believe what he had just witnessed. Jessica sat in silence trying to give her partner time to chew on the new information, digest it.

"So," James started glumly, "Cameron's dead. We didn't get his evidence, so we are pretty much shit outta luck here."

"One door closes, another opens up."

"Meaning?" He tried not to sound harsh, to keep the anger out of his voice. It wasn't Jessica's fault that things had gone so badly. He felt like crap as he saw the hurt pass over her face. But she didn't pull away from him.

Instead, she pulled the chair even closer to the bed so that around so that she was only a few inches away from him. "Look, Noah Lawson is the man who Kalina says beat the crap out of her. He's been UA since yesterday morning. Leasig might have succeeded in bringing our man out for us anyway. We have a name now. We find Lawson, we find our man. And then we prosecute the living hell out of him and throw him away for the rest of his natural life, maybe a little longer"

James nodded, taking it in and analyzing it.

"We put out an APB with the local police, we're watching the airports here and in Los Angeles, as well as the exits to Mexico. Also got somebody sitting outside his house. So far there's nothing, but if he sticks his head up, we'll be there and we'll have him."

James nodded again. He wanted to be happy about the roses that were apparently blooming in this pile of manure, but so much had happened that he couldn't sort it all in his head.

"What's wrong?" Jessica asked.

"You're probably right. We know for a fact that was Leasig's body in that van?" He asked, already knowing the answer.

"Yeah, James. It all checked out. Dental records, medical records; it all matched up perfectly. Cameron Leasig is no longer among the living."

"How's Kalina doing?" James asked.

"Lawson did a number on her - lots of bruises on the ribs and around the face. He damn near broke her jaw. Other than being stiff, sore and recovering from the mother of all headaches, she's a hell of a lot better off than you are. She'll be out of here later this afternoon."

James looked sullen. He studied his blanket for a few moments, a basic herringbone stitch of green and blue cotton and polyester fibers. "I should check on her," he said, his voice low.

Jessica shook her head disapprovingly. "I wouldn't if I were you. She's got a lot on her mind right now. She's angry and hurt and I doubt that she'd take too kindly to you right now."

"You don't sound like you're guessing on this."

"No, she pretty much said exactly that. Not those exact words, but you get the drift. She has to have someone to blame right now, you're a convenient target."

"I'm the one that promised him that we could take care of him, keep the both of them safe."

"Don't do that, James. Don't you start on the blame game, too. There's more than enough to go around right now. But we've got to concentrate on the fact that the bad guy's still out there. We have a face now; it's time to hunt the bastard down and bring him in."

James didn't say anything for a bit. He just lay there thinking about how the last ninety-six hours had wreaked complete havoc with his life. And suddenly he was very tired. He yawned. Crap, it even hurt to yawn.

Jessica took the cue. "Hey, I'm gonna get out of here so you can get some rest. Doc's already gonna have my head for bugging you as much as I have. Vince said that he and Miranda will stop by later to check in on you. He said for me to tell you to try to stay out of trouble and get some rest."

"Thanks, Jess." James squeezed her fingers lightly. They were warm and soft. She squeezed back and he smiled sleepily. "Can you stay for a while?" His voice was thick and slow.

Jessica smiled around the tears that were blossoming at the corners of her eyes and nodded. "Sure, I can do that."

He smiled through the pain, comforted by her presence. He couldn't find the strength to talk with her, despite his strong desire to do so; and she seemed contented to just sit there and hold his hand and watch him drift in and out of slumber. After a while his head began to hurt and the facts and faces and times and events all began to blur and swim around in his head, colliding with one another.

He heard his nurse come in and chat with Jessica briefly. The words swirled thick and slow on his tired ears. He didn't try to make out the details; he just let the soft hum wash over him. It might have been the medication hitting his veins, but James was suddenly sure that he could hear Jessica's smile. That smile could stop time. And James let it do just that as he focused on that happy image and slipped into the warmth of a drug-induced slumber.

monday, june 14

chapter 93

Monday morning dawned gloomy and dark. A cold front settled over the area and brought with it a series of nasty thunderstorms that poured chill rain throughout Sunday night and into the early morning hours. Sunrise marked a period between downpours and the morning air was thick and silent with heavy gray clouds mottling the sky.

The dismal weather matched James' black mood as he sat in silence, watching Cameron Leasig's funeral from a pew near the back of the church. His sense of responsibility and guilt for what had happened clung to him, unwanted houseguests that had overstayed their welcome and refused to leave. The small golden urn holding Cameron Leasig's ashes sat lonely on the alter next to a picture of the man in younger, happier days. Guilt washed over James every time he glanced up and looked at the urn or the beautiful woman draped in black mourning sitting to the side.

Kalina tried to speak, tried to deliver a eulogy honoring the man she loved, but emotion stole her voice and left her sobbing before the congregation. Tearfully, she simply announced her love and thanks and opened the floor to the audience and reclaimed her seat.

"James, this isn't healthy. We should get out of here."

He looked over at Jessica, sheathed in a dark blue dress and simple make-up. She had warned him against coming to the funeral and had insisted on accompanying him when he decided against her advice. He knew she was uncomfortable, but he felt a debt that had to be answered. He took her hand in his good one and gave it a squeeze.

Person after person stood to profess how kind and caring and giving Cameron had been. With each anecdote, James felt worse. He wasn't sure how much longer he would be able to take this outpouring of remembrance and praise. He couldn't help but think back to Evan Pinsone's crack about investigating the Pope and Mother Theresa. Judging by the massive turnout and ocean of sorrow and fond memories, the comparison seemed to be right on the mark.

After a half an hour, the priest stood and walked over to the podium. "Thank you all for your kind words."

James sighed with deep relief, starting to feel that if it continued he would have to go home and swallow a bullet to put himself out of his misery.

"Please stand."

The congregation stood en masse, James struggling against the fire coursing through his limbs to join them. Standing proved more painful than the sitting had been. He knew that he should still be in the hospital; Jessica made that point more than once. She railed at him to take his pain medication, but he was hesitant to take anything that would dull his senses. He was regretting that decision now. The wooden pews were brutal.

"Bow your heads. Our Father who art in heaven..."

James recited the Lord's Prayer quietly, losing his voice as he stood there looking at his feet. Silence greeted the end of the prayer and the funeral party stood and began walking down the aisle. He felt his throat catch as Kalina stopped at the first pew and spoke briefly with the people standing there. She moved with such strength and dignity. With each pew the muscles in his stomach tightened.

She had only briefly spoken to him since the hit three days ago. Her bruises had lightened imperceptibly and the make-up could not hide them completely. She was badly shaken by everything that had happened and had used him as an outlet for her anger and frustration. He had taken that abuse from her, taking it for what it was. It was almost soothing to have her justify his guilty feelings for him. She concluded by telling him that she wanted no further contact with him or his office unless it was to tell her that they had found the man responsible for Cameron's death.

She was two pews away, greeting her fellow mourners. Comforting them as they tried to console her.

He stood frozen in his tracks. He could feel Jessica's eyes boring into his back. She hadn't wanted to come in the first place; she was only there to support him.

One pew away.

James wasn't sure what he was going to say. He hadn't planned on this meeting. He hadn't even wanted her to know that he was there. There was no avoiding that now. She was standing right in front of him. Her almond shaped eyes were dark and puffy from crying, lines marked her make-up. She met him steely-eyed.

"I told you I didn't want to see you, Agent Storenn. Was I unclear on that?" Her voice was calm and controlled.

He swallowed hard. "No, ma'am. Just wanted to pay my respects."

Her eyes never left his face. "He was a good man, Agent Storenn. You might not believe that, but it's true. He wasn't perfect and he didn't always do the right thing, but he helped a lot of people." She paused. "He saved my life, in more ways than one." The last was barely audible, lost as she struggled to maintain control of her voice, control of her composure. Her black-gloved hands reached out, grasping his good left hand, something hard and pointy pressing into his palm. He made no attempt to pull back. "Cameron told me to give this to you if anything went wrong. Just like him, really, to be ready for anything." Her voice broke at the last and her eyes softened for a second, welling up at some memory. Fresh tears ran down bruised cheeks. She didn't raise a hand to wipe them away, but wore them bravely instead.

James just wanted to die that she was doing this here and now. His face grew hot and flushed red with shame and embarrassment.

"It's what Noah was looking for at the house. Cameron said you would find the answers at your bank." Her voice was husky with emotion.

James could only nod.

Satisfied that she had fulfilled her obligation to Cameron, Kalina turned to leave. James reached out, stopping her by her shoulder.

"I am sorry, Kalina," he stated simply.

Her eyes hardened to daggers, razor sharp and cold. His fingers recoiled from her arm and any further apologies froze in his throat.

"Don't," she said, her voice every bit as hard and cold as her eyes. "He trusted you and he died for it."

And she was gone, a flurry of black silk and lace and a cordon of close friends and well wishers. James just stood there and watched her go, the key clutched tightly in his hand and a silent promise burning in the back of his brain.

chapter 94

Jessica watched James' rented dark blue Impala pull out of the parking lot of her building. He was hurting and wanted to be alone. Jessica knew that alone meant sitting on his boat, drinking to dull the pain. It was a stupid path to tread and it pissed her off to see him heading down it. He was better than this martyred mourner he was playing and she knew it. She had half a mind to follow him out to the boat and jerk his chain until the fire came back in his eyes. But she didn't move from the lobby. She watched the taillights grow smaller and blend with the steady traffic of the street.

This was something he would have to figure out on his own. She would be there for him, be there when he pulled his head out of the mire but she wasn't his mother and she wasn't going to baby him. She just hoped that it was sooner than later that he decided to get back into the game.

chapter 95

James sat at the kitchen table, a bottle of beer sat on the table near his enfeebled right arm, condensation running down the sides to mark the tabletop with a wet circle. He watched the beads of water race each other down the brown glass, watched them meld with other beads, gaining weight and speed as they slid down to pool at the bottles base. He was still wearing the black suit he'd worn to the funeral. He was still in mourning.

Reaching across his body, he picked up the beer and took a long pull on it, nearly draining it. This case blew. It was the most personally expensive undertaking he'd ever attempted. The nightmares and frustration and loss of sleep, they were nothing when compared to the sense of failure he now felt. The professional ridicule and abandonment were nothing compared to the face of the widow he saw today. The accusation and the hatred of Kalina Morris's stare, they battered him more effectively than Noah Lawson ever could have.

And she had taken the time out of her mourning to deliver him that key. It sat across the table from him, the brass shiny in under the single light of the dining room. He stared at it angrily, blaming it for the guilt he felt over the day's events. She delivered it at the funeral, fulfilling the final wishes of the man she loved. She swallowed her hatred and anger and hurt and handed him that key and all he could manage was a simple 'I'm sorry'.

He finished the last of the beer in the bottle and got up, slinging the empty into the trashcan and stalking over to the refrigerator. He pulled out another ice-cold bottle and wandered back into the dining room. The key on the edge of the table gleamed at him, shiny and happy in the face of his funk.

The fact that Cameron had even created such an insurance policy burned at James, it showed what low regard he held for the agent. That he expected failure. That the flippant remark he'd made about ending up a charred and battered corpse during their first fateful meeting had ended up being prophetic and accurate. James had met those low expectations. He looked at the key again, grumbling under his breath. The beers had begun to take their toll on him, deepening the bleakness of his mood and sense of guilt. His eyes began to water and he had a hard time focusing them.

He was tired, drained of all energy. He hurt all over. His heart was gone and his body craved sleep, even if it were alcohol induced. Turning, he headed back for the bedroom, beer in hand. Tomorrow would be another day, a day where just maybe he would get some answers. Or not. His gloom was complete, 'or not' was the answer he settled on. He settled onto the bed fully clothed and in moments drifted off into fitful slumber, the full beer resting on the nightstand.

tuesday, june 15

chapter 96

James fidgeted with the small bronze key in his jacket pocket. His sat in front of the downtown offices of the First National Credit Union, his rented Impala illegally parked, waiting most impatiently for the manager to open the doors for business. He was still pretty banged up; the bruises on his face still dark, though the swelling had gone down noticeably. They melded with the dark bags under his eyes that plainly showed his lack of restful sleep. There was no help for his broken ribs or his right arm except for the time required for the bones to knit. The tenderness in his shoulder and chest, both places where bullets had passed through his body, could not be avoided; the stitches made every movement an experiment in pain. He was a mess.

"You doing all right there, James?" Jessica asked. "I figured you'd be hopping around like a wee school girl to get this done. You look like you just drank sour milk."

She got a shrug for her efforts.

"Just wanna end this. I'm tired of building things up and getting all excited about them only to have the rug yanked out at the last minute."

He sounded tired and frustrated, two perfectly normal emotions, all things considered equally. James simply couldn't get past the funeral and his brief encounter with Kalina. The physical beating he'd taken, coupled with the mental one he was currently giving himself had ensured that he'd hardly slept over the last several days. The guilt over not being there, of giving his word and failing to live up to it ate at him. He promised Cameron that he would protect them; he promised them that they would be safe in his care. And he had failed.

Lying there at night, insomnia denying him rest, he read through the case files that mounted up during his stay in the hospital. There was a lot of information there. He read through Lawson's record, seeing the two Captain's masts for assault and the multitude of counselings for disrespect. Both fit the profile for a violent criminal, which no one at this point doubted Noah Lawson was. His disappearance coincided with the assaults and murders of Friday morning and Kalina's eyewitness account named him as her assailant. Everything pointed towards Noah Lawson as the most probable culprit in this bloody scheme. James wanted him under lock and key.

He wanted justice for the dead and revenge for himself. And he was determined to get it, determined to get him – dead or alive, Noah Lawson would be brought to justice.

But lack of sleep and a drive to close the case weren't the only things on James' mind. He also wanted to know what was in the safety deposit box. The key had burned a hole in his pocket throughout the afternoon and all night long, toying with him, messing with his imagination. He was almost afraid to open the damn thing now. Every grim scenario imaginable, every movie plot twist, every nightmarish discovery in every horror flick he'd ever seen had passed through his head at one time or another over the last eighteen hours. And now that he was sitting here, he was more nervous than not about running into that bank and pinning all of his hopes on what was in that box. He was terrified of opening the hardened metal container and finding nothing but a cloth-lined box of wasted time and expectation. He didn't know if he could take another major set back.

A long period of silence filled the small area of the car until James looked up at Jessica. "What are you worried about, James? That we'll open up that safe deposit box and find some note saying 'Ha, Ha!! Screw you for getting me killed'? You didn't kill him, Lawson did."

James shrugged and smiled. "No. I don't think that Leasig was a 'go quietly into that good night' type of guy. I think he was pissed and had something to say and nothing, not even death, was gonna keep him from saying it. I just don't want to put too much importance on this key. But I can't help it, can't stop it from growing. I want every answer to every question I've had about this case to be in that box and I'm worried that it won't be there. The answers just won't be there."

Jessica wished James would quit beating himself up over the events of the previous week, quit trying so hard to make it all right. It was a senseless situation and nothing was going to change that, nothing could make what had happened right. There was no way to make sense of it. James was just going to have to come to grips with that. She knew that it was all still too fresh to forget, but there was no blame to be dealt out. Leasig chose to get involved with what was going on, just as he chose to come forward. James had done everything within his power to keep Leasig safe, but the bad guys got one over on them. Unfortunately, Leasig paid the ultimate price for his participation. It was unfortunate. But it happened. Hell, if there was anyone to be blamed for what had happened, it was Noah Lawson.

She knew that James couldn't see it that way right now. She knew that he was going to have to take some time off and figure out how to deal with that. But any proposed vacation or down time would have to wait until the case was broken, until James had his answers and was able to make some arrests. Maybe if he could deal out some sort of justice, bring the case towards resolution, maybe then he would be able to move on. Maybe that would be enough to make it right for him.

The seconds ticked away with impossible slowness. Jessica sipped her coffee and just let the atmosphere hang, morning mist awaiting banishment by the sun. The clock finally rolled around to nine and the manager appeared behind the double glass doors, inserted his key and unlocked the branch office. They watched it in silence, James just sitting there fingering the key, his stomach turning in knots.

"Jess?"

"Yeah?"

"Thanks."

She smiled into her cup and breathed in the smooth aroma. It was going to be all right with them. He would be good and they would be good. "Wouldn't have missed it for the world."

"Easy for you to say."

She nodded and took another sip. "You ready for this?"

He shrugged. "Ready as I'm gonna be."

Jessica grabbed the warrant and they climbed out of the car and walked into the bank together.

epilogue
wednesday, august 25

James Storenn sat in his large office reading the report. It was hard to believe that only a month and a half had passed since Cameron Leasig's funeral. So much had happened in that time. The massive amount of evidence in the resulting four safety deposit boxes was so much more wide spread than even he dared to imagine. The stockpile contained absolutely everything: pictures, photocopies, tapes, bank records and videodisks. It broke down the entire organization, top to bottom.

All evidence pointed to Noah Lawson as the man pulling the strings. He was a ghost though. Tracking the various account numbers listed, it appeared that Noah started moving money via wire transfer through a maze of off shore accounts only days before Leasig was murdered. More than fifteen million dollars disappeared into the ether, the bulk of which was transferred the day before the hit. A plane ticket to San Francisco, Lawson's hometown, yielded nothing. No hotel rooms or rental cars, no credit cards, nothing. Noah Lawson was gone.

The NCIS and DEA and local police tore the town apart looking for him, making it more than evident that anyone harboring or helping him would share his fate. Nothing had come of it though. James was positive that he'd made it out of the country and was probably basking on some tropical beach, drinking boat drinks and getting a tan. But with the technology available and the cooperation of various local and national agencies, James was just as confident that it was only a matter of time before Noah Lawson reappeared on the radar screen. He would make a mistake and the entire world would come rushing in.

The evidence in the boxes wasn't just against Lawson, though. There was an entire laundry list of persons implicated and indicted for their roles in the organization – foreign officials, civilians, police, NCIS agents, government officials, and Sailors of every pay grade from E-3 through O-7. The list went on and on and it appeared that no one was safe. In all one hundred thirty seven people were indicted with a mountain of damning evidence against each one. Interrogations yielded more names and accusations as the ripples of the mounting scandal set to rock the Navy to its core. The name Noah Lawson came up infrequently and always with a hushed breath of fear; he was a scary man who wouldn't hesitate to take care of business. Cameron was never mentioned once.

James, of course, won the bet he'd made with himself weeks before concerning the contents of the evidence; there wasn't a stitch of information regarding Cameron Leasig and his connection to the organization. Nothing at all that even hinted as to how deeply he was involved or what his precise roll had been. It was unfortunate that they would never learn the whole truth about Cameron. His story hung heavy on James' mind, a book with an exciting first chapter and an explosive finish with nothing but blank pages in between. He was an enigma that wouldn't allow itself to be solved, and that bothered James a great deal. The overwhelming lack of evidence begged for further investigation and explanation. The answers would have to wait until Lawson was brought in to provide them; there appeared no other way.

With the case making national headlines, James and Jessica both got more than their fair share of recognition. Both received medals for valor. James was promoted and there were rumors thick in the air about Jessica becoming the first female Captain in the San Diego City Department. Jessica wasn't exactly excited about the prospect of giving up the street for a desk job; she was about as far from being a desk-jockey as a person could get. It was nice – all of the recognition for their roles in bringing down what turned out to be one of the largest drug smuggling operations on the West Coast. But what James really wanted, they didn't have. That was Noah Lawson in a jail cell with multiple life sentences. It would keep. Patience was the key.

James looked down at the report again and shook his head. This was truly unfortunate. He followed the movements of Ms. Kalina Morris after the funeral, hoping that she would not fall prey to a vengeful Noah Lawson and meet an untimely demise. There was also the fact in the back of James' mind that Cameron had found a way out, that he had somehow outsmarted them all and was sitting around somewhere laughing his ass off as they stumbled around in the dark looking for answers. If that proved to be the case, James had no doubts at all that he would contact Kalina, that he would find a way to be with her. But it hadn't happened. Cameron was dead and he wasn't coming back.

Following the funeral, Kalina stayed in San Diego for a couple of weeks getting her things in order. She sold 'Club Kittie' for an undisclosed amount of money, an amount that James was sure probably sat very comfortably in the millions. She also sold the lot where the blackened remains of her house stood, explaining to friends that she simply couldn't rebuild without Cameron by her side. She didn't want to live there without him, looking every day at the views they once shared. All of that, combined with Cameron's insurance monies, another million dollars in the bank that Kalina apparently wanted no part of.

James thought about bringing her in for questioning, just to see if she could shed any more light on the case. She had made out pretty well from the whole ordeal, after all. That made her somewhat suspect. But he hadn't done it. All he could think about was her draped in black, tears running down her face as she stared at him accusingly. He was pretty sure he couldn't face her again unless he had Lawson in custody.

So he tracked her quietly, turning over the surveillance to the Hawaii office when she went home to stay with a cousin on Maui. The reports were mundane, a fact which made him more than happy. She spent time on the beach, reading and sunbathing, spending lots of time alone. Apparently, she was sorting things out. After nearly a month of identical reports, he pretty much stopped reading them. And now this.

At the age of thirty-one, Ms. Kalina Morris was dead. Her car was driven off the highway three days ago. It plummeted some seventy-five feet down onto the rocks and into the water. The car was completely destroyed and the body was only found this morning. Some tourist walking along the beach in Kaanapali saw it wash up on the shore. It was bloated and half eaten, but there was enough there for her cousin to recognize the destroyed remains. The death was ruled an accident, but James couldn't get past the shattered look on her face the day of the funeral. Somewhere inside, he wasn't so sure that it hadn't been suicide. The guilt still ate at him.

He laid the report on his desk and sighed unhappily. *So much for a happy ending to this case* – he thought.

Noah Lawson had another stolen life to answer for.

He looked at the picture on his desk and glowered; Jessica on the boat out off the coast of Baja. She was glorious. Tanned skin, wind blown hair and an impish grin. She was the only good thing to come out of this case. Whatever else, she had proved to be his happy ending and he wondered not for the first time how he would react if she were taken from him.

Noah had much to answer for and James was determined to see that he did.

Mrs. Marcel Daras stepped off the plane in Bergen, Norway. She was tall and tan, a sleek feline figure that slinked along the gangway as she made her way to the terminal. Long black hair framed a smooth Polynesian face with almond shaped eyes so deeply brown they appeared black. Her long, dark gray dress clung seductively to her lithe shape, accentuating her legs and hips as she strolled. She could have been a model stepping out of a fashion shoot instead of off an airplane after nine hours in flight.

Despite her confident air and inviting smile, Marcel Daras was a bundle of nerves. Her stomach was nothing but knots as she looked around for the driver who was supposed to be meeting her.

A chubby man with salt and pepper hair covering his large head stood there with her name on a hand printed sign in his thick hands. He looked to be in his mid-forties, rumpled in his dark blue suit. He smiled as she approached, greeting her warmly and asking about her flight.

They chatted politely as they gathered her bags and headed out to the large black Mercedes waiting for them in front of the airport. Her excitement hadn't let her doze off even momentarily on the long plane ride and now she was absolutely exhausted. The gentle ride of the car and the plush comfort of the overstuffed leather seats combined to dull her senses and try to force her into sleep. She fought the urge throughout the hour long drive, keeping her eyes on the magnificent views as the lush green landscape slid liquidly past her window. The mountains and the lakes and the houses, she wished that she had kept her camera with her.

It was mid-afternoon when they pulled into the gravel lot in front of a quaint little mountain retreat. The hand burned sign over the green painted double doors said *Bjornefjorden Gjestetunet*. Marcel looked down at the itinerary in her hands. This was the place. Not exactly what she expected, but it would do nicely. Olaf, her driver, hopped out and began unloading her luggage. She climbed out of the comfortable seat and walked into the lobby.

It was all done in stone and exposed beam construction, reminding her of an ancient hunting lodge with its massive stone fireplace and fur covered couches. The floor was planked and darkly stained with hand woven decorative rugs lending color to the cavernous room. A beautiful young lady with her long brown hair pulled back from her smiling face greeted her from behind the large, natural wood reception desk.

"*Velkommen til Bjornefjorden Gjestetunet.*"

Marcel just shook her head, slightly embarrassed that she had no idea what was just said to her. "English?" she requested.

The girl smiled broader, nodding. "Welcome to the Bjornefjorden Guesthouse. May I help you?" Her voice was heavily accented, but her English was clear and smooth. Her blue eyes shone brightly as she looked at Marcel.

Marcel sighed with relief. She hated not being able to communicate with those around her. In her limited travels she had always tried to stick to English speaking countries for that exact reason. She hated looking ignorant. "Yes. I have a reservation. The name is Daras. Marcel Daras." She smiled back at the girl.

"Daras?" she said to herself, looking down at the thick reservation book lying on the counter. She turned a page and then her face brightened. "Daras. Oh, yes, you are in room one eleven – *Honsehuset*. I will take you to you right there." She bent down fumbled around under the counter with a tray full of keys on thick wooden key chains. She came up with a red face and a beautiful smile. "We go?"

"*Honsehuset?*" Marcel asked, nodding and trying to copy the girl's pronunciation and inflection.

The girl smiled over her shoulder as she walked out the double doors. "Yes. It means, how do you say? Chicken house? Henhouse?"

"Henhouse?" Marcel said with a half smile. It figured. "Great."

They walked across the gravel lot, past a large stone planter with a family of cats rolling around in it and into a broad wooden building. The walls, the floors, the ceilings were all the same blonde colored wood. Doors lined the small hallway. The whole cabin feeling came back to her as they stepped to the right and the woman opened the door to her room.

"*Honsehuset*," she said, raising her arm and swinging it out in front of her like a girl on a game show showing her what she'd won.

It was a cute room with the same blonde hardwood decorating all four corners. To the right there was a white overstuffed couch and matching chair with a light colored coffee table sitting between them. Along the left wall just inside the door was a small kitchen with a tiny silver sink and stove. A small dinette set stood right next to it, freshly cut mountain flowers in a vase centered on it. A wooden door stood beyond the couch on the right. The entire back of the room was sheathed in blue and green pastel curtains.

The girl pointed to the door. "Your bedroom is down those stairs. The deck is beyond the curtains. Please make yourself at home. If you have questions or needs, please dial zero - zero." She nodded her head in the direction of the low bookcase standing next to the chair; the phone lay unobtrusively on the second shelf. They obviously didn't expect a lot of calls to come from this room.

Marcel smiled and nodded. "Thanks. I think I'll be all right."

The girl smiled and excused herself, leaving Marcel standing alone in the middle of the room. She looked around. The room was quaint and light and not cluttered. She noted the complete lack of a television or radio in the room. She smiled. It was just like him to pick some completely remote place for them to get away to.

Sighing, she looked around the room again. "Let's get some air in here," she said to no one in particular, walking over to the curtains. She pulled them apart and gasped at the view in front of her. She opened the longer curtain and opened the door, walking out onto the deck. It was like she'd just walked into a post card.

The clear blue water of the Fjords stretched out in all directions, bordered by mountains that burst from the depths to race skyward. Four small, tree covered islands interrupted the glassy surface of the azure waters.

The sky was clear and blue and perfectly cloudless. She couldn't tear her eyes from the scenery; it was simply breathtaking.

She sighed heavily and sat down on one of the white plastic chairs standing arbitrarily on the deck, determined to lose herself in the sweet smelling breeze and warm sunshine. She watched a small bird fly loops over the green trees, calling out to a group of birds playing in a stone bird bath down in the back yard.

The door to the room jiggled with a metallic rasp and opened, waking Marcel from her brief reverie. She looked around and there he was.

His brown hair was a little longer than she remembered, hanging over his ears and shaggy in the back. He was a little leaner, his polo shirt and khaki shorts baggy on him. But it was definitely him, hauling three sacks of groceries into the room.

She jumped up from her chair, a huge smile painted on her beautiful face, and ran through the door and into the room, diving into him as he dropped the bags to the floor. He wrapped his strong arms around her and she melted into him, laughing and crying at the same time. She buried her face in his neck. "I was so scared," she mumbled. "I was so scared."

He kissed her neck then her cheek and then her pretty mouth. Her tongue tingled from the passion and intensity.

After several long minutes he pulled back slightly, looking into her face without easing his hold about her small waist. "It's all right," he said, his voice soothing, almost as though he were trying to calm a frightened child. "It's gonna be all right, baby. I'm here now. I'm right here." He touched her face, trying to wipe away her tears.

But the tears of relief flowed freely down her face, foiling his attempts. Her heart was light, as though a massive weight had been lifted from her chest giving her room to breath. He held her tighter, caressing her back comfortingly. "I know, baby, I know. But I'm here. It all turned out all right." The heat of his breath slid along her neck, sending chills down her spine.

"God, it's good to see you," he said with an impish grin on his face.

She kissed him again, deep and hard, pressing her body on him and feeling him respond. Still kissing they maneuvered towards the door next to the couch, the door that lead down into their bedroom. His hand traveled down her back and settled on the round firmness of her backside. He gave her butt a light swat as she fiddled with the door handle.

"So you missed me?" he asked with mock innocence.

She responded by pushing him through the door ahead of her and closing tightly behind them.

They sat at the white plastic table out on the deck, watching the sun slide down over the mountains on the other side of the Fjords. The sky was awash with purples and lavenders and pinks, the colors reflecting darkly on the clean water. The food in front of them cooled with the night air. As beautiful as the view was, they couldn't take their eyes off one another.

"God, I missed you," he said, stroking her smooth cheek with the back of his hand. His smile was content and easy, adding to the completeness that was filling her spirit. She hadn't seen this smile in a long time.

A pained look crossed her visage. "You have no idea what it was like. I watched that tape from the police car and there was the funeral and scattering those ashes. I didn't know where you were and I couldn't talk to you. It was too real."

"I told you it would be all right, baby; that you'd know it went wrong if the bodies didn't match the medical and dental records. I went through a lot of trouble to get those things switched around."

"I know," she said softly. "Just that so many things could have gone wrong: Noah and the NCIS and the police and the fire department and the insurance people. All of them asking questions. And it all happened so quickly and then you were gone. I was miserable not knowing, having to wait for them to come back and tell me you were dead. And then sitting through that funeral was absolutely horrible; all of those people getting up and talking about you. It was like I had lost you. You'd died and I couldn't say good-bye. It wasn't acting anymore. I was a complete wreck."

He stroked her cheek again and then leaned in and kissed her. "I'm sorry, baby. I didn't want you to have to go through all of that, but it was the only way."

She fixed him with a curious look, as if studying him. "I suppose you pretty much know what went on with everything. What I want to know is how you got out of that van. Noah was going there to kill you. He told me that straight forward."

"I worked all week to push him that direction. It was the only way to guarantee that he would cooperate. I have to admit; I didn't think that he was gonna go through with it. I thought I was going to have to do it on my own there for a minute. But he surprised me. Instead of coming at me when I was on my own, which, by the way, would have made things much easier for me, he hit the van. Surprised the hell outta me. He would've killed me if that cop hadn't shown up when he did. I was lying there on the seat when he got into the van. If he'd have come in shooting, I'd have been toast. But his partner, Silas, taking out the cop gave me an opening, made him look away. The rest you know. Two bullets to the head, two to the chest and I set the van on fire using the flares and lighter fluid I had stashed in my backpack."

She shuddered to think of how close it had been to being real.

"Basically did the same thing to that jackass Silas. He blew that cop away, shot him so many damn times I thought a war had started outside the van. We didn't get a quarter mile before I put him down and headed for the truck I had waiting. Then it was just burning up whatever DNA evidence there was that could connect me to anything and getting the hell outta there. I didn't think Noah would bring in anyone to help him. I got lucky."

He looked at her longingly, a sad light in his eyes. "I wanted to make sure you were all right, stop by the hospital. But I knew I couldn't. Storenn would be looking for me. They'd expect Noah and they'd catch me. As soon as I heard you were stable, I took off for the airport and jumped a shuttle for San Fran, trying to reinforce the whole Noah thing."

"And now you're here," she said quietly.

It was unnerving to hear him speak so nonchalantly about the whole affair. She'd counted on his killing Noah, but the margin for error had been so narrow. She sighed with relief that it was over. The game was ended and they could move on with their lives.

"I was saddened to hear of your untimely demise," he said, leaning in to her.

She blinked, coming back to herself. Her eyebrows knit into a sharp V as she feigned anger, comforted by his closeness. It was something she had longed for since their last parting. "At least I came to your funeral, Cameron!" she retorted, her mouth twisted in an exaggerated pout.

"Carter, baby. The name is Carter now. You go around calling me Cameron and you're gonna confuse the neighbors. Carter and Marcel Daras."

Kalina smiled at him. It was going to take some getting used to, but they had pretty much forever to do it.

"Ok then, Carter," she said pointedly, "what are we gonna do now?"

His face was thoughtful, distant. "Don't know, really. Maybe after we renew our vows, we could spend the next few years chasing the sun. I know this quiet little resort town in Delaware. Summer there and spend winters down in South Carolina or the Bahamas or something."

"Renew our vows? You mean you're finally going to make an honest woman me?" she asked, pushing away slightly.

"I don't know about all of that, but I figured we might as well make it legit." He was smiling broadly, his even white teeth shining.

She shivered and punched him. The night had snuck up on them as they spoke and the air had chilled considerably.

"You wanna go inside?"

She nodded, standing up and heading for the door. He was right behind her. "Delaware?" she asked, her voice incredulous.

"Yeah," he replied with a smirk, shutting the door behind them. "A place called Bethany Beach. You love the name Bethany."

"For a dog maybe," she said. An exasperated look crossed her face. "Delaware?"

"We could open up a book store or something."

"I don't know."

He smiled and pulled her close to him again. "We've got some time to work it out," he said. His hands found her shapely backside and rested there. She leaned into him, taking comfort in his warmth and closeness; feeling her own heat rise up.

"And besides, right now we have other business to attend to," she said pointedly, thoughts of bedroom acrobatics running rampant through her mind. She smiled as he took her hand and lead her that direction.

Tomorrow would have to take care of itself. Besides, with Cameron – no, Carter back by her side, everything would be all right.

But, Delaware?

Why not?

THE END

Acknowledgements

The list is long and dignified: Kimberly Candella, Marilyn Jones, Pamela Johnson, Ken Hackley, April Tinson, Charlene Toth, Elizabeth Nichols, Eric Cummings, Angela and Daniel Caddell, Edward Hicks, Michael Hilliard, Maria Pulitano, Lee M. Derr, and last, but definitely not least, my lovely bride, Deborah. Each of you read, critiqued, questioned, and corrected this book throughout all of the various drafts. You were forever encouraging and beyond generous with your honest feedback. This book would not be what it is without you. Thank you all for everything that you contributed.

That said, any inconsistencies or mistakes made in this book, I humbly lay at the feet of my aforementioned colleagues. Had they only read more closely, such things, if ever there are any discovered, would not be an issue.

Mom and Dad, thanks for the love of books you instilled in all of us. It is a gift I can never repay.

To all the great folks at Booklocker; thanks for your guidance in turning a printout into a manuscript and a manuscript into a book.

Printed in the United States
57187LVS00006B/307-381